Wedding Pickle

Neha Sharma

GRAPEVINE INDIA

Grapevine India Publishers Pvt. Ltd.
A-208, Second Floor,
New Moti Nagar,
New Delhi - 110015
India

grapevineindiapublishers@gmail.com

contact@grapevineindia.com

First published by M/S Grapevine India Publishers India Ltd.

Printed and bound at Thomson Press India Ltd.

Disclaimer

This is a work of fiction. All characters, organizations and situations are of author's imagination and any resemblance to any person, organization or situation is purely co-incidental.

The author respects all individuals, organizations & communities and there is no intention in this novel to hurt any individual, organization or community.

Chapter I

Avni stood by the kitchen door running through a last-minute list of things she wanted to buy for her office desk.

As she peeped into the kitchen, she saw her mother standing by the kitchen slab sorting the okras. She knew it was a bad time to go out as her relatives were coming over for a family lunch. She still asked.

"Ma, can I please step out for a while? I had some things to buy, I won't be long," she asked hoping it would be okay, but her mother, Mrs. Sharma, just looked at Avni.

She shook her head smiling to herself, she got back to chopping the okras.

"Why have you been avoiding family get-togethers recently, Avni," she said looking up at her daughter waving the knife in the air.

Avni wasn't trying to avoid them, though she hoped she could.

"Ma, you know I have to get some things for my office, I have been thinking of it for over a week. It won't take long..." she said, looking down at her list.

Her mom finally kept her knife by the kitchen slab, wiped her hands and looked at her daughter.

"We only talk about your marriage because we all want your good and for you to be happy," Avni's mom said turning to her.

"I am happy," Avni said nonplussed. She had no idea where her mother was going with this, as she looked at her mother, "I don't mind them coming. I know they are family," she said shrugging her shoulders.

Avni's mother just looked at her, with her hands on her hips, "I know why you want to go out now."

Avni shook her head and asked, "Oh really, do you?"

"You don't like them now, Avni, but they are all just concerned about your marriage," her mother said.

"Oh God, Mom," Avni said as she walked up to her mother and continued, "I know I get a little uncomfortable but that doesn't mean I will start avoiding them. I had some important work so I just needed to get out for a bit."

"So you don't mind them looking at *rishtas* for you now?" her mom asked, looking at her expectantly, as she held her hands.

"Mom, I am not ready right now and I really hope all of you understand that," Avni said looking at her mother.

Her mother left her hand, walked back to her vegetables, picked up the knife and continued chopping, "I don't know, *beta, aaj kal...*" she said looking at her daughter, "what you girls want? We gave you enough freedom, never asked you *kaun hai*? Where are you going? What are you doing? You had your time, *beta*."

She stopped cutting and sighed. Avni hated it. Everytime this topic came up; her mother would start her usual banter all over again.

Avni had heard this argument a million times but she didn't care even if it was right. She was not ready and she just wanted her mother to understand this simple fact for once. But then she knew that her mom would say, "Then you will never be ready, *beta,* even if you are 40 you will still feel like you are not ready – this is the right age."

How Avni wished she could be stuck being a teenager for her entire life, because the moment you enter your twenties, it's like the family has found some kind of a treasure! They all change, they start looking at you differently.

They all talk looking completely amazed even if you walk into the kitchen and get them a glass of water, "Oh look, *itni badi ho gayi hai,*" looking at your parents, making their eyes go all moist. All Avni thought was, "I just got a glass of water, something I have been doing for ages. What made you think I have grown up in that and what's so tragic in that for my parents to cry?" Then it just goes on, your mother hugs you goodnight every day like you are going to fly away to another planet the next morning and never come back.

Your father suddenly turns into a philosophy lecturer, being with him makes you feel like you are in an all-day life lesson class and your siblings shower you with love that makes you want to apologize a thousand times for all the fights you ever had, even if it wasn't your fault.

Last but not the least guests start turning into nightmares because every time they come over they have a biodata of the "most eligible guy for our dear Avni." Avni thought it was ridiculous the way people made biodatas, it was like a resume. One of them actually read Name, Age, the whole families' DOBs, Occupations and Salaries.

I mean seriously, Avni thought, *why I would care about how much his sister or brother-in-law are earning*? Nevertheless her family would pour over it enthusiastically, chirping for hours together and then hover around Avni for days together.

"Avni baby, *ek baar, accha* you do not want to meet at least talk on the phone no, *beta*..." her mom would say.

"Okay, if you don't want to talk, can we talk?" Avni's dad would say looking from his daughter to his wife for approval, "then if you feel like it, you can talk," he would add anxiously hoping his daughter would agree, but then stop after seeing her face which would have become small and completely red.

Then her mother would walk into her bedroom talking to herself, "What are we doing wrong? This guy is nice. She makes a face like we are going to hang her," she would say looking at her husband. He would just look down and shake his head, disappointed. It used to make Avni feel like she was committing some kind of a crime.

Avni knew this is what happened every time these "lunch parties" happened or any guest walked in, even if they did not have a guy in mind for Avni they still had to ask, "*Aur,* Uma, *kuch hua?* Have the talks started anywhere, what about the guy you were talking about the other day," they would say, looking at Avni.

How Avni wished she could just… anyway that's why she hated

talking about it, but her mother would somehow bring it up all the time.

Mr. Sharma walked into the kitchen, "They have reached downstairs and they will be here any moment. I will just go down and get..." he stopped halfway looking at his daughter.

"Avni, what happened?" her father asked.

"Mom happened," Avni rolled her eyes.

Mrs. Sharma looked at her husband for a while and then said, "Oh, don't go blaming me."

Avni looked at her father with a slight smile on her face, "As long as Mom can be normal instead of talking and worrying about when I will get married," Avni stressed pointing to both of her and her mother, "we will be fine, Dad."

"Uma, we can talk about this later," Arun, her father said.

"Yes, Mom, later," Avni stressed on the "later", "I will marry someday, but not now. Can you give it a rest?" Avni asked.

"But, *beta...*" Uma started.

"Uma, let's talk about this later, they are here," Arun said. "Now go. Kitty has come," he said as he looked at Avni.

Avni sighed a relief, she knew it was impossible for it not to be talked about but she was glad her father did understand at times.

She ran out to greet her cousin, Kitty; she was only three years younger to her. They had been the best of buddies for as long as Avni could remember.

As she walked into the hall she saw her *chachi* standing at the door. She took a deep breath and walked forward, "Hi, Aunty," she said smiling.

"Hi, Avni," she said half-hugging Avni and looking at Avni's mother as she walked in.

"Hey," Kitty walked in, hugged Avni tightly and then whispered in her ears. "Get ready for another round, we have got new prey today. How I love these gathering nowadays!" she added teasingly.

"A few more years, Kitty. Just a few more years," Avni replied patting Kitty's back.

Well the lunch, as Avni had expected and according to Kitty's "warning", did not go leaving Avni completely unnoticed. Thankfully her father didn't like the *rishta*.

"Okay, Uma. We will not go forward with this *rishta,*" Kavita Aunty said, sounding a bit disappointed.

As Avni walked in with a tray, she turned towards Avni, "You tell us, Avni, what kind of boy you would like?" Kavita Aunty asked, as she sat back on the sofa and looked at Avni.

"I don't know, I haven't given it much thought," Avni said as she served tea to everyone.

"Oh, but you must have thought of something, like should he be tall or very fair or not so fair, or should he talk well," Kavita Aunty asked, taking her cup of tea, "So we know what kind of a boy to search for you."

"I don't know, Aunty, I really don't know. It's just that I am not in a space to think about marriage right now," Avni said as she kept the tray by the dining table.

"Oh, Uma. Look at her. She is almost 24," Kavita Aunty said as she looked at Avni, "Job will keep happening but marriage should happen at the right time."

"I will know when my time will come, Aunty," Avni said smiling at Kavita Aunty as she sat down on the sofa and sipped her tea.

"You are incorrigible, Avni," Kavita Aunty said, and then looked at Uma who just shook her head.

Kitty who was sitting there listening to the conversation with a sly smile all over her face, asked, "So, whenever Avni's time will come. How do you suppose we will describe her?"

"Excuse me?" Avni said looking at Kitty.

Kitty raised her hand to shush Avni.

"Umm, she is tall for starters, quite fair. Has lovely dove-shaped eyes," Uma said looking at Avni.

Avni went completely red and hid her face in her hands.

"Yes, and she has lovely shoulder-length hair, only they curl up at the end," Kavita Aunty explained, twisting her finger as she demonstrated her curls.

Avni looked at her hair as Kavita Aunty said that.

"Oh, but of course, one can say Avni looks beautiful," Kavita Aunty said, as she caught Avni looking at her hair, "and her smile can brighten the darkest of corners," she finished, her eyes gleaming at Avni.

"Okay, enough," Avni said getting up, "Thank you, Aunty, for your kind description of me, but let's save it for another day," Avni said as she got up to collect the empty tea cups.

After a long day of sitting and gossiping about the town, daily soaps, all the faux pas, they all finally bid goodbye.

As Avni hugged Kitty goodbye, she turned to see her mom cleaning up the table.

"Mom, sit down for a while, we will do this later," Avni said walking up to her.

"Oh no, if I sit down, I won't be able to get up then," Uma said brushing the sweat off her eyebrows. Avni picked up a cloth from the kitchen to help her mom.

"The *dahi vadas* were quite nice, nah," Mrs. Sharma remarked as they were clearing the tables.

"Yes, Mom, yours are best in the town," Avni said smiling.

Mrs. Sharma smiled, "I am sure you will make better one day."

"Mom!" Avni exclaimed. Her mother shook her head laughing to herself again then she held her hands up.

"Okay, Avni. No more," she said looking at her daughter who looked like she could explode any moment.

"So, we are leaving tomorrow at six. When will you leave?" Uma asked.

"Ummm… ya, drop me on the way. Yes, I will get up at six," said Avni widening her eyes knowing how she hated getting up so early.

Avni father was a CA, who worked in greater Noida and her mother was Vice Principal at a school there hence they were staying in Greater Noida. Avni worked at a bank in Delhi and stayed with friends from her MBA college nearby, since the commute was too much otherwise.

That was as perfect as it could get, Avni thought to herself. She was earning her own money so she could do whatever she wanted to without being accountable for how much she spent.

She was living all by herself, nobody to ask her where she is going, who she is going with, no strict time lines to get back home and most of all she was staying with her friends; life could not be better.

Avni did not want any of it to change, she knew very well if she ever got married, all of this would go away in no time. Her freedom, her independence, her not being answerable to anyone for her actions, everything would be gone the moment she would give into getting married, a trap her parents wanted her to get into wholeheartedly.

"Humph," Avni frowned as she kept the kitchen towel by the side thinking of how drastically her life would change if she did give in.

"Avni, what happened? It's quite late, *beta,* go to sleep. We have to get up early also," Uma said looking at her. Avni took a deep breath.

"Okay, Ma. Goodnight," she almost snapped, hoping her mother had not caught the irritation in her voice. She plopped on to her bed and finally fell asleep after mulling for hours over how her life would change if she did get married.

Chapter II

"Mondays, Mondays, Mondays," Avni remarked as she looked at her office building.

A five-storey brick-coloured building, which branched out in four directions, it had big glass windows and stood between a sprawling garden on either sides, which Avni never had the chance to explore as she was usually so caught up with her work.

"How we all hate it!" one of her colleagues completed her thought coming up behind her.

"Yeah, sad reality of life. I am going to get some juice to energize myself a bit," Avni said walking in, as she adjusted her office badge. The one thing Avni loved about her office was the canteen. It was huge for starters, with every type of cuisine possible. She shuttled from one cuisine to another depending on her mood and taste buds everyday.

As she walked in to her office floor with the juice, she swiped her office ID to walk on to her floor. "Welcome aboard," she said sarcastically to herself. As she walked into her bay, she smiled at everyone. They all waved at her, greeted her good morning, and asked about her weekend.

Avni was never good with crowds. She was quite an introvert and liked being in her own bubble. Her home, family, a few close friends, she was happy there, Avni did not need anyone outside of that. She hated getting out of that comfort zone.

That was one of the many reasons she was reluctant towards marriage. It meant new people, new family and a whole new person to share your life with, which was like asking too much from her.

As she finally reached her desk, she kept her bag by the table and smiled at her only close friend and colleague in office, Sunaina.

"Hi, how was your weekend?" Sunaina asked.

"Hey, oh it was nice. God I hate Mondays," Avni stressed drinking her juice while looking around her floor, "How do the mails look today?"

"Not much till now but it's only 9:30 a.m. Wait till it's 10:30 a.m., work will start pouring in," replied Sunaina.

Sunaina sat right beside Avni and was Avni's age. She was the first person to have befriended Avni when she had joined her office.

They were called the "gossip queens" of their bay, not that they used to "gossip" a lot. They used to just talk a lot! And when two girls "talk a lot" it's usually termed as gossiping.

After a monotonous day at work, Avni heaved a sigh and logged herself out. All Avni could think of when she used to get back home from work was a hot cup of coffee and sleep. The latter part rarely happened as both her roomies would sit in the hall and bitch about their work, and share crazy stories of their bosses and colleagues for hours together.

Avni lived with her two MBA mates; they had shifted into an apartment while still completing their MBA and continued staying there, even when they all got into their respective jobs. The three of them decided to rent a flat near their college towards the end of their first year in MBA, as projects and studies didn't seem to end.

Their apartment was a cute two-bedroom flat. It opened into the dining area on its left and the kitchen on to its right, the hall was straight ahead, where the TV stood. Two small passages led to the bedrooms. The rooms were decently spacious and with small balconies.

Kriti, one of her roommates was a sweet nice, kind girl, someone anyone's parents would love meeting. Avni's mother was in love with Kriti; she allowed Avni to stay in an apartment knowing Kriti would be staying with her. Kriti was someone who would lend an ear to you when you needed it the most. Avni would bore Kriti all night with her banter during her college days, and she would always listen with utmost concern.

Kriti was from Gujarat and was tall, had round big eyes and lovely long hair till her waist. She was a bit plump but it suited her. She belonged to a joint business family, who were quite strict and conservative. It took Kriti a long time to convince her family to let her stay in an apartment. However, when her married sister shifted to the same city they grudgingly agreed.

Roshni, her other roommate was the opposite of Kriti. She was nice but could be quite the rebel if she wanted her way. She was full of life, but could get quite blunt if she did not like something or someone. She didn't believe in sugar-coating things and was very transparent. Roshni was Avni's best critic, and would always get Avni back on track if she ever swayed. She was a little short, with shoulder-length hair and a cute, round face.

"You won't believe what my father asked me the other day," Roshni said looking around at her friends that evening when they were all sitting by the TV. "Well, he asked me if I have someone in mind, if not then he will start looking," Roshni said.

"Welcome aboard," Avni said giving Roshni a pity smile.

"God, I hate growing up. Can you imagine getting married!" she shook all over like she was trying to shake a bad aura off her.

"Yeah, I know. The sad and hard-hitting reality of life... marriage," Avni stressed as she looked away staring into space. Her office and all the work, being in her flat had completely made her forget about this whole thing. The frustration inside her started to build up.

"Guys, I need some air," Avni said dully as she walked out. As she opened the door she asked, "Kriti, have you got a smoke?"

"Avni," Kriti looked at Avni, "I don't have any and you said you quit. It's been ages since you smoked."

Yes, it had been ages since Avni smoked, but God when she was stressed all she wanted to do was, "Ya, I know. I just felt like one... anyway..." Avni replied and went up to the terrace to get her mind of "marriage."

How could she possibly meet someone over a couple of days and decide if this is the guy she wanted to get married to, someone she could fall in love with!

Besides, being in love was just a temporary feeling; Avni felt *everyone falls in love; then they fall out of love faster than they fell in.*

She remembered talking to her father about this once, while watching TV over a weekend.

"It's not like your days, Papa, where people could commit to each other for their entire life. Nowadays life has become so fast and change has become so frequent that an equation like marriage just does not fit with the times. Besides, I have seen too much."

Her father laughed at her statement, and said jokingly, "Yes, how I keep forgetting how much you have seen and how less I have."

But Avni had seen plenty; today's guys were commitment-phobic and that was the universal truth.

"Hey, why just men? A women too can be commitment-phobic and not be true to her marriage," her cousin had argued once, when he had heard Avni's point of view.

"It's all the same, marriage still leaves you broken at the end of the day," Avni had added.

Once she had tried talking to her Kriti about this, who had said, "If you've had one bad relationship; you met one bad guy, Avni. That does not mean this world is full of jerks."

"Yeah, whatever! Can we not talk about my past?" Avni had snapped.

"Was just proving your point, see we all go through heartbreaks, Avni. I did too. So many of them but that doesn't mean I have stopped believing," Kriti had concluded.

"Yeah," Avni had sighed wondering if being that optimistic could help her too.

Actually, deep down Avni loved the idea of marriage; being with the love of your life, having your own world together, it all sounded very beautiful – only she thought it was too good to be true.

Most of time you ended up with someone you didn't love or who didn't love you. Even if you were in love, sooner or later you would fall out of it and then the only thing keeping you together would be the colourful embossed marriage certificate claiming, "Game over, you have got to be with each other till 'death does both of you apart'."

Then again, whenever Avni looked at her parents, she could still see the love, the care and the affection they have for each other. How after so many years, when her dad complimented her mother she still blushed like a new bride! Or when her sister got married five years ago, she seemed quite happy, but then she was always the mature one, somebody who could handle marriage. Avni was still just a kid, too immature to understand even the M of marriage.

Avni took a deep breath and looked up at the sky in the terrace. She could not figure out if marriage was right or wrong or if she could actually find "true love" or not. There were too many reasons for her not getting married right now in her head, a few of which her mind was making up to reaffirm her reluctance towards the institution. She knew was there were certain fears she had towards marriage and she was not ready to face them just yet. She went back down to her flat and continued watching TV to take her mind of this topic.

Chapter III

It was an early Saturday morning, Avni was fast asleep under her blanket, Roshni was surfing the net on the bed beside Avni, when suddenly, "Oh my gosh," screamed Roshni putting one hand over her mouth while the other hand fell on Avni. From under the blanket came Avni's muffled voice.

"What? It's Saturday for God's sake. What are you doing?" Avni asked.

"You will so not believe this. What a piece of news!" Roshni said.

Avni brought her head out from under the blanket and with her eyes half-closed she said, "Okay what?"

"You remember that woman Mrinal? She is engaged? Can you beat it, the bird is finally caught in a cage," Roshni exclaimed.

Avni jumped up, as if a spring were attached to her back, snatched the laptop from Roshni's lap and as she pushed her hair off her face she read Mrinal's status as 'engaged'.

Avni looked at Roshni with her mouth open with so much amusement she looked crazy for a second.

"Oh my God," Roshni finished.

"Damn, I can't believe it," Avni said.

"Well, the poor guy..." Roshni giggled, "Remember how she was in college! Woman jerk," Roshni said looking up.

"Woman jerk is not a term," Avni smiled shaking her head, going through Mrinal's profile.

"Yes, there is. I coined it and it's cool," Roshni said taking her laptop back.

"Well, well, this is interesting," Avni said getting out of bed yawning. It was a great piece of gossip and Avni could not wait to share it with the rest of her college mates for their reactions.

This was not the first time this was happening; every week she would hear of some random person she knew in school or college getting married. And everytime, Avni got excited, but it also scared her and her roommates as well, for they knew their time would come soon.

"Anyways, I am going for a shower, I have got to go shopping. I have nothing to wear," Kriti said making her pity face.

"I know how you feel, walking around in torn clothes all day," Avni replied jokingly as she got out of her bed. Avni put her hands around Kriti shoulders and continued, "My poor friend, has no place to keep another tee in her cupboard but has no clothes to wear."

"Hey, I am serious. I really don't have anything to wear and we are going to CP today," demanded Kriti.

"Yeah, okay," Avni said giving in, thinking it was time she went shopping too, her usual office heels were starting to hurt.

"How about we pick up some drinks on our way back? I have not had one for a while now," added Roshni.

Avni nodded.

After a long day of shopping, in the scorching heat of Delhi, they finally walked into McDonald's.

"Three McAloo Tikkis, no cheese," she stressed, "and three ice teas, lemon," replied Kriti as she opened her wallet to pay the lady at the counter.

Avni watched for Kriti from the table they had nabbed, "I am so hungry."

"I am here," Kriti came in with the tray, panting, making her way through the crowd. As she sat by the table, "No McVeggie, Avni, so you too get a McAloo Tikki, had no time to call, the counter lady was looking at me like she would kill me any moment."

"Well, can't blame her," Avni said looking at the counter line which just did not seem to end.

"I love that cream by the way," Kriti said as she peered into The Body Shop bag.

Roshni nodded her head in agreement; she was now impatiently opening the wrapper of her burger as though the burger would disappear from her sight if she waited any longer.

"Yes, I fell in love with it when my aunt got it for me when she came over last month," Avni replied.

"Hey," Kriti said put down her burger she was gorging on, "Your aunt reminded me of something!"

"Yeah," Avni said rolling her eyes.

"What? What fill me in," Roshni cut in.

"Ya, and I know Ria knows. She wanted to tell us the other day and you kept shushing her. I have to know now. So tell us!" demanded Kriti.

"Ohhh that, yeah," said Roshni finally getting the drift.

"Okay. It's not a big deal really, you guys will be really disappointed when I tell you," Avni said but she could not wipe the hungry looks off her roomies' faces, so she started, "Okay, well my mother was in Bangalore to see Nana."

They nodded like they could not wait to hear more.

"So, yeah she had put up my profile on the Bharat Matrimonial site," Avni mumbled looking a little embarrassed, "anyways," she continued looking up.

"They got a call from someone, their son's working in Norway and they liked my profile," Avni took a deep breath.

"Wow, Norway you lucky bi..." Roshni shushed Kriti to hear more.

Avni continued, "So my *mama*, my *mausi* and my dear mother went to their house, they also belong to Rajasthan, but settled in Bangalore long time back," Avni said rolling her eyes. "Can you imagine, they did not even speak to me about this guy? Nothing, and they go to his house meet him and his parents," Avni voice started rising.

"Okay, Avni," Kriti said putting her hands on Avni's to calm her down and looked around to see if anyone heard them.

"Well, they loved the guy and the family," Avni continued

in disbelief. Avni looked up, she was angry again. She could still remember how she fought with her mom.

"Ma, I don't care if he is good-looking, earning well, staying in Norway... Yay!" she added sarcastically, "The thing is you should have told me. You went to their house, liked the family, told them you like the guy and I don't even have a clue!"

"Then?" asked Roshni anxiously.

"Well, I said no. I didn't even look at that guy's photo. I know it was stupid, I was just being immature," Avni said, "but if I had asked for his photo after that scene, it would've become so sure from their side."

"Hmmm," Kriti said getting back to her burger.

"Told you it was not a big deal, and you'd be disappointed," Avni said.

"You are stupid. I hope you realize that," Kriti said.

"Why?" retorted Avni.

"Well, Avni, he is living in Norway. You know Norway is the best freaking country to live in according to the UN," explained Kriti.

"So I go marry some random guy just because he is living in Norway. Come on, since when did we get so shallow? I am very happy in Delhi," said Avni like she was making final closure on the situation.

"That's not our point. My point is what if he is a good guy, not like some jerks we meet in Delhi. A nice guy who loves you and takes care of you and he is doing well for himself staying in a beautiful country. Just imagine you could go stay there, get a job even better. See things like these; they will just come knock at your door, Avni. If you do not open the door, they will go away," Kriti finished.

"Opportunity came knocking at my door and I did not open it. Stop it, miss big philosopher!" Avni replied jokingly.

Roshni sighed.

"Hey, you are scared of marriage as much as I am," said Avni looking at Roshni.

"I know, Avni. But that does not mean I will go throwing away things which have even a hint of marriage in them without even having a good look," Roshni replied.

Avni had to agree she had not taken a look at any proposal with an open mind; she assumed they had something monstrous about them which would eventually turn her life upside down.

She wasn't ready just now – why was it such a big deal to understand.

"Yeah, okay," Avni, replied taking a deep breath, "Anyways it's gone, it's over. Mr. Norway must have found his Mrs. Norway by now. So why are we fighting?" Avni finished looking at both of them.

"Yeah, but we are so going to bug you. All those Europe road trips we could have had," Kriti said.

"Yeah, great! Bug me for depriving you guys. That could have been a valid point actually, you know, for saying yes," Avni said winking at them.

"Yeah. Poor Mr. Norway," Roshni and Kriti said shaking their head.

* * *

As they got home after buying their favourite red wine, they all plopped on the sofa.

The doorbell rang, they all looked at each other but no one was in the mood to get up. Soon they heard someone unlocking the door; in came Ria.

Ria was Avni's school friend; they were more like sisters. She was a lot like Kriti. Only Ria had curly hair and was way thinner than Kriti. One of the main reasons Avni was drawn towards Kriti was because she reminded her so much of Ria. Ria stayed with her brother, close to their apartment.

"Hey," all three of them said from the sofa, as they turned their heads towards Ria.

"Why do you guys look so dead?" Ria asked as she removed her shoes.

"Have you seen the temperature outside, Delhi is burning,"

Roshni said, "Why is this AC not working?" Roshni said as if talking to the remote, hitting it in her palm.

"Give it time, Rosh," Kriti said shaking her head, "We have only just come in."

"So… what did you shop?" Ria asked as she looked at the bags.

"Be my guest," Avni said looking at Ria.

"You know why I would love to get married?" Ria said rummaging through Avni's shopping bag, "to not feel guilty at all, shopping so much because then it would be with my husband's credit card," she said looking up at Avni smiling.

"Yeah, that's a pretty valid point," Avni replied smirking at Ria.

"Oh by the way, some wine guys?" Avni asked as she remembered the wine bottle by the table.

"Never say no to wine," Rosh said looking at Avni.

"Got it," Avni said getting up to open the bottle. She handed the wine to Roshni and Kriti, and then to Ria.

"Avni told us about the Norway guy," Roshni said looking at Ria.

"She did, silly women we have here. If I were you I would be sitting in Paris having my French wine," Ria said raising one shoulder.

Avni stared at her.

"What? Paris is close to Norway, right," Ria said teasing Avni.

Avni looked down shaking her head.

Chapter IV

Almost a week passed by; Avni drowned herself in her work and life seemed to go quite smoothly until she got a call from her mother during work one day.

"Hi, Mom, can I call you in a while? Okay, wait I will just go to the pantry and call you." She walked into the pantry, picked up a cookie to munch on and called her mom.

"What! Ma, so just say no, nah. I don't believe this… why… it's been months. I know I have not seen the guy but..." Avni took a deep breath.

She stopped walking up and down the pantry and sat by the coffee machine.

"I know, Avni. See it's not a big deal, he is coming to Delhi, we will meet him for breakfast at home. That's it," Avni heard her mother say.

"Mom. I am not ready, I told you. This is not the time," Avni said firmly.

"Avni, why are you doing this? He is such a nice guy. Why don't you understand?" Uma continued.

"Mom, you are not understanding, don't force me," Avni replied.

"Fine, I had already said yes to his family, now I will have to go back and tell them no. I will lose face, but it's okay. What to do, you have become so big now…" Uma started.

"Ughh, Mom, don't start again. Why did you have to say yes to them before talking to me?" Avni asked.

"He is nice boy, for my sake, Avni, please, just to keep my word, just see him once. If you don't like him then just say no; but since I have said yes already, please just meet him," Uma pleaded.

"Mom, you don't have to plead me like this," Avni said. She thought for a while. She couldn't seem to get out of this.

Just for her mother's sake, she thought.

"Okay, me, you and Papa will just meet him, and that's it," Avni said holding her head, hoping this wasn't a big mistake.

"Okay, it's just breakfast," her mom replied reassuringly.

"Cool," Avni said, she thought it was no big deal.

They would meet for breakfast and then she would say no. It would be better this way, she thought, because she could always say I at least agreed to meet the guy but something still did not feel right.

As soon as Avni got home, she called Ria.

"I don't believe this," Ria said over the phone, "you want me come over and help you decide what to wear to meet this guy you are meeting. He is the Norway one, right?"

"Yeah, all the same. I don't know," Avni said sitting down on her bed holding a bunch of clothes in one hand. "I can't seem to run away from them. I am so confused, you know. I don't even know if I want to be married. I mean I have been single for a long time. Sometimes yes, I do wish I had someone in my life. It gets lonely sometimes," Avni sighed.

"Yeah," Ria assured from the other side.

"So," Avni continued. "If I do get married, it will all change."

"It always does," Ria replied.

Avni took a deep breath. She was now frustrated for she did not know what to do and Ria wasn't even helping her much either.

"Okay, I've got to go now," Avni finally said, about to cut the call.

"Avni, I know it's tough, all of this but things do change. Sometimes they change for the better, right," Ria said.

"Ya, I really hope they do," Avni replied half-heartedly and then continued, "how do you know if this is the guy? How would I know this is it? It's crazy, you know," Avni said playing with the edge of her bedspread.

"You know, I keep thinking of the same thing and trust me I

have got no freaking clue.

How do you decide, and even if you are in love, how you do know this is it?" Ria replied.

"I did try and still failed miserably."

Yes, Avni knew Ria did fail miserably at that, she made a wrong decision. A decision that seemed so right to everyone at that point. It still went so wrong.

Avni had tried talking to her father about how she would know if this is the guy; this is what he had to say.

"Well, I met more than a dozen women before I met your mother, but I still remember when I saw your mother walking towards me, something in me just said this is it. It's like an inner call – it just comes," Avni had looked at her father like he had descended from outer space.

"Dad! Inner call?" Avni had stressed.

Her father laughed, "You will know it when you meet the person you are meant to marry."

Meant to marry – quite an interesting theory Avni used to think. If people are meant to marry each other, then how did this theory explain all the divorces?

Is that meant to happen too? Avni thought to herself.

Marrying umpteen number of times before you finally find the one or just giving up, where does the theory of "it's all written up there" come into picture here? For Avni "arranged marriages' were one of life's biggest gambles one played. You either win the lottery or lose sorely, for you never know how the other person turns out after marriage. Avni wished marriage could be left to an individual's choice; to each his own.

If she explained this logic to her parents she so knew what her mother would say, "It's all the freedom we have given you that is talking." And her father would again just be amused by her thinking and wonder when she would grow up.

"Ugghh," Avni whispered as she held her head. She did not want to think about all of this anymore. Whatever it was, like her mother had mentioned, it would just be a normal breakfast. No harm.

All this thinking was not leading Avni anywhere. It was only giving her a headache so she thought it best to drop it, say bye to Ria and sleep as she had a long day at work the next day. Avni finally fell asleep making a note in her mind to ask her mother what to wear for the "Breakfast".

When she did ask her mother the next day, her mother suggested her to wear a suit,

"Ma. Why a suit?" Avni said getting irritated. "I do not get it. I am meeting the guy. Is he that old-fashioned that he would like to see me in a suit?"

"God, Avni, you are so impossible sometimes. Why do you jump to conclusions? He is not old-fashioned at all. I have met him. You asked for my suggestion, so I'm giving it. If you are comfortable in jeans then wear jeans," Mrs. Sharma replied.

"Fine, I will see what to wear," replied Avni in a calmer tone this time, "If he is even a bit like that snobbish Dheeraj, nah, Ma..."

"Ya, just walk away, okay," her Mom said over the phone.

She sounded exhausted. It was like Mrs. Sharma was going through a couple of do's and don'ts before her daughter finally agreed to come along. She was at complete loss when it came to what her daughter wanted.

She just could not understand why Avni was running away. A couple of times she had asked her, *"Avni is there someone? You can tell us," she had asked. You know we are fine with all this. We are not caste conscious. Even if it's a different religion, Avni, at least tell us nah, beta. We will see what we can do," she had added.*

"No, Ma, I don't have anybody. I know you are completely fine with it," Avni had said and continued, "Di had a love marriage too, it's not that."

"Then you want to just be a loner all your life?" her mother asked

"No, Ma," Avni would say getting irritated, "I don't know. Not now that's all, okay? I don't know, don't ask me."

That used to send Mrs. Sharma back to square one; at a complete loss for whatever it was her daughter wanted to do with her life. She used to worry herself a lot over it.

Even after Avni agreed to meet Ansh over the phone, she called her father saying they were being unfair to her, but Uma knew this guy was so good. She couldn't lose this opportunity of not making them meet each other. She knew Avni would say yes the moment she met him.

After this long conversation with Avni, trying to explain they only wanted her happiness, an exhausted Uma looked at her husband.

"What do we do... what does she want, Arun?" she asked her husband.

"Don't worry, it will be fine," Avni's father was always relaxed about his daughter's behaviour for he knew it was a human tendency to resist, and especially these days it did become tough for kids like her to accept marriage, but they always came around.

Mrs. Sharma's main concern was just that, Avni did not seem to be coming around any time soon. She just hoped breakfast would go smoothly the next day.

* * *

Avni kept shifting in her seat as she sat in the cab the next day, she was on her way to Greater Noida for the breakfast.

"Where are you?" her dad asked over the phone.

"I will be there in no time," Avni said cutting the call. As she put her head back, she dozed off.

Avni was too meet a family friend's distant relative – Dinesh Uncle. He was coming to see her in their family friend's house for his son. As she was sitting in the hall with him, she realized he was quite snooty as soon as he began to speak. Avni did not like the tone he spoke in. It sounded like he was showing off.

Avni soon was made very sure of the fact that Dinesh Uncle was a person who took great pride in everything he had and owned.

He ranted on about his son, "I am telling you, Arun, he will do wonders. He will be at the top, you know. Right at the top."

When he finally stopped much to Avni's relief about his great family achievements, he looked at Avni.

"So, beta, where have you done your college from? I heard you are working in a bank too," his eyes bore into Avni like if she gave a college's name that was not an Ivy League according to him, he would just reject her for she would not be worthy of his son.

"If it's all right I will be serving breakfast in a while," Sneh Aunty interrupted, much to Avni's delight. Avni sighed in relief and got up to help Sneh Aunty.

"So, Arun," Dinesh Uncle continued boisterously while breakfast was being served.

"That building you have, it's in a prime location. In fact in one of the most posh locations," he said.

"Yes, my father had bought it long while ago," Avni's father replied.

"So how much is it worth? I am sure in crores," Dinesh Uncle said and Avni saw his eyes gleam when he said, "crores."

She definitely did not like that look.

"Well. I have never thought of selling it so I never bothered finding out," Mr. Sharma replied sounding a bit uncomfortable.

"Yes, yes of course, but I am sure Avni will be getting a share of it," he asked greedily.

"No," Avni blurted. She was so angry at him for even asking something so atrocious.

Everyone looked at her. "I mean, even if Papa meant to give it to me and Didi, we would not take it," Avni continued looking up, "It's my Dadaji's property and we want it to stay with Papa."

"Oh yes, of course I understand, was just being curious, beta. Lovely daughter you have got there, Arun," Dinesh Uncle said looking a bit disappointed.

Avni looked at her father, who gave her the biggest smile. She smiled back too.

That property was given to her father by her Dadaji and it was very close to her father's heart; there was no way she would let it go away as a piece of dowry. Education was supposed to make some difference to people's thought process, Avni thought. Quite annoyed, Avni had four aloo parathas in anger. The only way she could think of to keep her mouth busy and refrain from saying anything more.

As Avni was leaving, her mother told her to go down and she would be back in a minute.

"Why? Are you discussing how much that property is worth?" Avni blurted out. She could not seem to keep it to herself anymore.

"Avni. No. No way," her mother replied holding her hands.

"Okay, I will be down with Papa," Avni went down to her father.

After five minutes her mother came walking towards the car.

"So you gave it?" Mr. Sharma asked.

"Gave what?" Avni asked impatiently.

"Remember how you had dislocated your shoulder once and then had a hairline fracture on the same place later on." Uma said.

"Yes," Avni replied, having no clue of where it was leading.

"It still does hurt you, nah, when you lift heavy things?" Uma said.

"Yes, so?" Avni asked.

"Well, Sneh Aunty had mentioned it to Dinesh Uncle long time back... generally," her mother said stressing on generally like she was justifying on behalf of Sneh Aunty. "So, Dinesh Uncle wanted to have a look at the X-rays and the reports to see how your shoulder is."

"WHAT!" Avni shouted looking from her mother to her father. "You gave it to him!?" she asked.

"Avni, he just said he knew some good doctors abroad. He could send your reports and help us," Uma said.

Avni sat back putting her hand over her head, "So you thought he was helping me, Ma," Avni took a deep breath, "he has taken those reports to show to those doctors and ask them, "So now do you think this girl with a not-so-perfect shoulder is worthy of my perfect son!"

"Avni, stop it please," her father spoke finally. Avni kept quiet, but she could not stop breathing heavily out of the anger that was brewing inside her.

She hadn't been this angry in a long time. Avni thought of the possibilities and realized, they might not hear from them after all. First of all her college wasn't good enough. Secondly, hopefully Avni thought her shoulder might add to it and lastly, thanks to Avni, she thought smiling to herself, Dinesh Uncle now knew there was no way he would get a piece of that property. She sighed a relief, one more down she thought to herself.

She was suddenly woken up by her phone ring. She got up and looked around. She saw her mom's name on it.

"Avni, how much longer?"

Avni finally got the hold of herself, sat up straight, rubbed her eyes and spoke. Why did she dream about Dinesh Uncle all of a sudden, she had no idea.

"Mom, two minutes and I will be there," she said widening her eyes trying to wake up.

"Ansh will be here soon. So make your face all right, Avni," her mother said when she walked in.

"Hmmm... so that's his name, Ansh. That Norway guy?" Avni replied, realizing her *kaajal* had spread all over her face.

"Yes, and stop labelling him the Norway guy. That poor kid has got a name. Ansh, okay."

As Avni looked into her purse for make-up wipes she said, "You really seem to like this Ansh, nah, Mom?"

"Well, what's there not to like? He is sweet, very respectable, *bahut pyaara baccha hai,*" her mother said.

Avni rolled her eyes and thought, her mother had never really told her anything like this before. Mrs. Sharma really seemed to like this guy and if Avni said no, she would have a tough time getting 'Ansh' off the discussion board.

She turned to head straight into her bedroom. She was halfway into her room when she heard the doorbell ring. "Uuugghhh," she groaned and turned back towards the hall. She stopped by the kitchen and as she heard the noises in the hall.

These meetings always made her nervous and she had never gone this far before.

This was the first, well second guy she was meeting. *First actually,* Avni corrected herself, *with an open mind*, she thought as she closed her eyes and took a deep breath.

"Okay, calm down," Avni said to herself and walked out.

Avni never forgot first impressions. It was very true, according to Avni, that first impressions do tend to be the last impression most of the time.

That is probably why she could never forget how Ansh looked when she first met him. He was tall for starters and really fair, Avni thought, as she walked towards him. There was something very pleasant about the way he looked. As Avni tried getting a closer look, she realized that he was wearing rimless specks and had very short hair just like an army man.

He was standing by the door talking to Avni's father very "respectfully" as her mother had quoted, and then he shifted his gaze towards Avni who was standing in the middle of the hall.

All of a sudden as all three of them looked at Avni, she realized she was standing there with a very silly smile on her face.

"Avni, this is Ansh," Avni's mother said as she brought him forward. He had a bouquet of orchids in his hand, which he handed over to Avni as he came to her.

"Thanks," Avni replied taking the bouquet with both hands which were trembling.

She looked down as her face suddenly turned hot and was completely red in no time.

Why was she blushing? She had no idea. *Oh my God, I am going red and he is seeing that, this is not good,* she cried in her head.

"Hi," Ansh said, holding his hand out to Avni.

Avni just looked up for a minute and said, "Hi." It was almost like a whisper because she could not seem to speak or move anymore out of nervousness. Not knowing what to do next. Avni turned towards the table to keep the bouquet down.

Orchids, thought Avni, smiling to herself, *quite thoughtful*, and then turned back.

She tried looking at him closely as she attempted to overcome the shyness that had engulfed her completely. She scanned his look; a bottle green T-shirt, the collars of which were put upright over a green striped shirt, which was rolled up to his sleeves.

Avni thought, *his dress sense is smart* – making a tick. *The way he is sitting and talking to her parents seemed like he was a very confident guy* – making another tick.

She then shifted her eyes down to his shoes.

Hmm, Converse not bad, again he seems like an easy-going guy, Avni went on inside her head, making yet another tick against her mental list. *Not bad,* she thought to herself, thinking of her mother's choice.

"Avni, come sit here, *beta,*" her mother said looking up at Avni.

The moment Ansh looked up at her smiling, she looked down again.

She just could not seem to look straight at him. "Yeah," Avni said sheepishly and she sat on the couch beside Ansh.

Hmm... Avni thought, *he smells really good too.* Making yet another tick mark on her checklist.

As they were left alone, at first Avni kept looking at the showpiece by the table. She never thought it could intrigue her so much. When she realized she was staring at it for too long admiring its pattern and design, Avni looked up. He was looking right at her, smiling. She turned hot red and looked down immediately.

This is completely embarrassing and awkward, Avni thought. She did not know what to say for she did not want to sound foolish. *What a complete waste of time,* Avni was thinking… when finally.

"So," Ansh spoke breaking the awkward silence, "how are you?"

"I am doing well," Avni replied smiling up at him.

"So umm... what do you do?" Ansh asked.

"I work in a bank. I am in the HR department and we handle..." and before she realized they had spoken for half an hour about books, music and almost everything under the sun. Soon Avni found herself at ease with him, she was chatting with him like he was some old friend of hers.

It's not that bad really, Avni thought to herself… *meeting a guy.* She was now sitting more comfortably on the sofa.

"Ansh, Avni. Breakfast is served," her mother came into the hall.

It was a pleasant breakfast. They had a few laughs here and there, he seemed to be quite an adaptable guy as he gelled very well with her and her parents.

After about an hour or two he said, "Well, Aunty, it was really nice meeting you, but I think I have to go now. I have a meeting scheduled," he said looking at his watch.

"Of course, Ansh, go ahead," her mother replied, "and it was really nice seeing you as well," she said smiling, looking from Ansh to Avni and then he just bent down to touch Avni's mother's feet.

"No, please Ansh, don't... it's okay. You don't have to," Avni's mother said as she stepped back putting her hand over his head.

"Bye," he smiled at Avni. Avni smiled at him and they bid him goodbye.

"So...?" her mother asked the moment she closed the door. She had this amused look of glee all over her face.

"Well, he is nice." Avni said shrugging her shoulders, trying to downplay the whole thing. Hoping her mother would not catch her going red again.

"That's it?" her mother asked.

"Yes, Ma, he is nice. He is sweet and nice," Avni said.

Her mother smiled to herself for she thought her daughter finally came up with a "nice" for some guy; it was a start.

As soon as Avni got back home, she thought of sleeping but after ten minutes she realized she could not sleep as a restless feeling engulfed her. *She had to talk to someone... but who?* Avni thought. Everyone she knew was in office or college at this time.

She wasn't all that close to anybody in her office. There was one person Avni thought of, getting out of the bed to find her cell. She dialled the number.

"Hi, Avni... my God, long time," came a voice from the other end.

"Yeah, I know, Nidhi, long time."

Nidhi was one of her grad college friends, they were very close back then. They used to always make it to ladies' nights around town. Drive around crazily with full blast music on, singing along. In fact, Nidhi was the first person Avni had tried a cigarette with. She still remembered how they laughed choking over it.

"Nidhi," Avni continued "I met this guy today."

"In office? Really? I thought you were not interested in a relationship anymore," Nidhi replied.

"No, Nidhi, as a marriage proposal," Avni said.

"Haha, Avni Sharma. You actually have started meeting guys after all the fuss. Good start," Nidhi said.

"Yeah well, the thing is you know every time I used to refuse meeting these "guys" my mom used to get so upset but then I finally thought that I should keep my parents heart and I will start meeting them at least. I mean no harm. I could always say no later," Avni said.

"Yeah, so you met a guy for the first time?" Nidhi asked

"Not really… remember Rishil… but I was just 20 then, it was just a laugh, nothing more," Avni continued. "Anyways, meeting this guy has left me confused," Avni finished sitting on her bed frowning to herself.

"Really? Oh my, Avni! You like him, don't you?" Nidhi asked, sounding a bit excited.

"No, I don't like him! I just met him," Avni said. "Okay, you know he is smart and umm… quite decent-looking, you could say he is cute. He is fun to talk to, and now I don't know how to say no," Avni said frowning to herself again.

"Hmmm, or you don't want to say no, Avni," Nidhi added.

"No, not like that. I don't know. How do I know if this is the guy? I mean I hardly spoke to him for half an hour. I hate this, I am not ready, Nidhi, not now," Avni said sounding more and more confused than ever.

"Well, you don't have to say yes now, Avni. Meet him once or twice, you know. Weigh your options. If you still feel the same then get yourself up for it. You know, Avni, a lot of my school friends, they also go around meeting these guys and with one of them they feel it.

You know the connection," Nidhi said.

"Hmmm... the connection," Avni said thinking hard.

She did not know if she felt any kind of a "connection" but she definitely could not seem to overrule Ansh and it made her upset with herself. This was not her plan, she was supposed to meet him and just say no, but he had to turn out to be a "nice" guy, as her mother had quoted.

Also, much to Avni's surprise she had agreed to meet him again! She had told her mother upon being asked several times. Her mother had then called Ansh and told him that Avni was okay with seeing him again. Avni had told her mother of a restaurant she could meet him for breakfast, which was conveyed to Ansh by Avni's mother diligently. She never thought her mother would be so excited fixing up a "date" for Avni.

"Stop hassling yourself over it. It's fine. Just go meet him. He is a sweet guy, right, so just go have breakfast with him and see how things go," Nidhi said on the other side of the phone.

"Ya, okay," Avni took a deep breath, "thanks, sweetie, for the talk. Take care," Avni said as she cut the call.

By the end of the day Avni kept closing her eyes trying to picture his face but she had completely lost his face. She just could not seem to recall it.

Well, no surprise there, she thought to herself. She had hardly looked at his face, all she looked at while talking to him were his shoes and his arms. She then suddenly realized how stupid she must have looked talking to him like that.

As she went through her cupboard for the umpteenth time, she could not decide what to wear. As she kept staring at her cupboard thinking of how few clothes she had. She saw her sister's name buzzing on her cell.

"Hi, Di," Avni said dully. She was tired, thinking of what she was to wear the next day.

"So I heard, just spoke to Mamma," her sister continued, "how is the guy? Dad really seemed to like him and from what Mamma told me you liked him too."

"No, Mamma just keeps saying. I did not like him, I just told Mom that, he is well... nice."

"Hmmm, that's still something coming from you, Avni," her sister said.

"Ya, okay," Avni said getting even more confused by the minute, for she could not decide what she wanted to do or what she should be feeling, "Anyways, Di, I have got to now, bye," she said as she ended the call.

After trying on a dozen dresses, "Okay, now I am really tired. For the last time, how is this?" Avni said half-panting. She was completely exhausted.

Roshni had this weird smile on her face since she heard about Ansh. Avni looked at Kriti.

"This is nice. I like the skirt. Remember we bought this in Bangkok and my, the way we bargained with that crazy woman," Kriti said.

"You know, I have put on weight," Avni said looking down, "this skirt is tight," Avni said looking up disappointed.

"Oh come on, Avni, it's not. It's a pencil skirt, it's supposed to fit your body like that," Kriti said pointing her hand at Avni.

"Yeah, I guess so," Avni replied looking down at her skirt, not looking very convinced. "Okay," she said finally looking up, "so it's decided. I am wearing this," Avni sighed in relief as she turned to go in.

Roshni finally said, "I don't get it."

"What?" asked Avni looking at her.

"Well. Why are you trying so hard to impress this guy?" she jeered.

"I am so not," Avni retorted.

"Then it must be someone else trying on a thousand dresses like she has a date tomorrow," Roshni teased as she looked at Avni.

Avni opened her mouth to say how ridiculous Roshni was being but then she realized that she indeed had spent most of her evening after work just trying on dresses.

"Ya actually," Avni said to herself, sitting down. *Why was she fussing over it so much?*

She walked over to Avni and snuggled on the bean bag with Avni.

"Avni, it's okay. There is nothing wrong with the way you are reacting, "It's going to be fine, Avni," Roshni said.

Avni nodded.

"Anyways I will go hit the bed, crazy day tomorrow," Avni said looking at both her roomies and went inside to get some good sleep before her breakfast with Ansh the next day.

Chapter V

Avni was getting thoroughly worked up. She was late! *As usual,* she thought to herself rolling her eyes. She tried to hold still. Her hands were trembling and there was no way she could put her eyeliner right that way.

"Okay, Avni, relax," she said to herself, closed her hands into fists a few times and put her eyeliner. She checked the time on her watch as she wore her heels. She was still running late.

God, I hope I get an auto in time, she thought.

"I am leaving, bye you guys," Avni shouted rushing out of the house. She had no time to wait for the lift. So she decided to take the stairs.

My feet sure are going to hurt today, she thought, looking down at her heels and she began running down the stairs.

Luckily she got an auto real quick.

"Thank you, *bhaiya*, now make it fast and take me to Sheraton. Quick," Avni squealed looking at her watch again.

The auto drove through the traffic just like Avni instructed and dropped Avni at Sheraton in half the time. As Avni got out, she saw a white Skoda taxi just wheel past her and she realized Ansh was sitting inside.

She sighed in relief, realizing she was not late after all but her heart started pounding like a jackhammer. *God,* Avni thought, as she tried recollecting his face but still couldn't see his face in her mind, but she did soon as Ansh walked up to her.

Was this how he looked? Avni thought to herself, *no*, she fought inside her head.

There was something different. He looked different! Avni thought.

"Hi, Avni," Ansh said smiling at her.

Avni kept looking straight at him. *How could he look so different to her and seem all different? He looked older all of sudden.*

"Avni, are you alright?" Ansh asked.

"Ya, ya of course," Avni said finally looking down wiping the sweat off her eyebrows.

All her enthusiasm and excitement plummeted. For some crazy reason, Avni did not feel the "connection" she had the day before.

Avni turned and started walking, "Umm, the entrance is right here and the buffet will be served a little ahead and left from the entrance," she spoke as she walked in without looking back at whether Ansh was following her or not.

As she reached the dining hall where the breakfast was being served, she realized he was indeed following her quietly all the while. In order to rush things, Avni put her office bag on the first table she found empty.

"Let's sit here," she said hardly looking up at Ansh. "Shall we go get our breakfast?" Avni continued.

Avni knew she was sounding weird to him but something seemed so off. She went through the buffet in a hurry and picked up whatever she liked and looked around once. Ansh was picking up muffins, he looked across at her and smiled.

Guilt flooded over Avni. She did not know what to tell him anymore. It was such a mess all of a sudden. Avni sat down at the table. A few seconds later Ansh joined her. Avni shifted uncomfortably in her seat. Ansh looked at her with utmost concern, but did not say anything.

Avni just looked down and started gobbling her food to finish it as fast as possible and get over with the breakfast.

"You really seem to like baked beans," Ansh started, as he tried making conversation with Avni. He looked at her for a while and then said, "If you will excuse me, I will just come back in a moment," he got up and walked away.

As he walked away Avni put her spoon down and rested her head in her hands. She was such an idiot. Of course, he would understand.

The way Avni was acting all flustered up, avoiding eye contact with him. She had put him off by her behaviour and now Avni did not know where he had gone.

After about ten minutes, Avni started to get worried. She looked around to see if he was coming but he wasn't there anywhere. Avni soon realized he had probably stood her up. *Not his fault,* Avni thought playing with her baked beans with the spoon.

She must have given him all the negative vibes to do so, she thought. She would just finish up her breakfast and leave. *Quite an adventurous breakfast*, Avni sighed to herself.

When Avni was almost about to finish her breakfast, about twenty minutes later, she thought she saw a glimpse of Ansh walking in. She looked around properly to see. It was indeed Ansh walking up to her smiling.

He was holding a bouquet of carnations and orchids in his hand. Avni was taken aback. She thought he had left but he was right there standing beside her with a bouquet of flowers. As he reached out to give them to Avni, he said.

"I am sorry. I must have sounded like a jerk, leaving you like that but I just had to get you these," he said looking at the bouquet, "I do not know Delhi much, so I had a hard time searching for a flower shop nearby, there aren't many around here," he said looking sheepishly at Avni.

"That's okay, not a problem. Thanks," Avni said still very surprised at what just happened.

"I see you were all ready to leave," he continued looking at Avni's plate.

"Oh no. I was just a bit hungry," Avni said. Thinking of how horrible it would have looked if she had left.

They spoke a bit, only this time Avni a lot more conscious and awkward than before.

The flowers overwhelmed her, it was a beautiful gesture but he still looked different to her *and old,* she revisited. As she did, without giving it a second thought she asked, "So, how old are you?"

Ansh looked up and replied very calmly, "I am 29."

Oh my, Avni thought. *Five freaking years. That is old. No wonder. Di is 29. That's like a whole generation gap.*

They had a quiet breakfast.

As she was about to catch an auto, "Can I drop you off, Avni? I have a car here," Ansh offered.

"No, I am fine," Avni replied smiling, "My house is not very far from here," she said.

"It's seriously okay. Please, let me drop you," Ansh insisted.

Avni had no way of getting out of this. She sighed and sat in the car. She mostly looked out of the window and as and when she looked at Ansh, he was looking right at her, smiling.

"Ummm," Avni said getting very uncomfortable. "So, what are you here in India for?" Avni asked finally.

"Well, I am here to take training sessions for some employees we are planning to deploy abroad," he answered.

"Hmmm," Avni replied looking down shifting her feet.

She was thinking really hard on what to say next. She looked out of the window and realized her house was finally here.

"Just take a left and drop me by the corner. Yes, right here. Thanks," Avni said as she looked at Ansh.

"No problem at all. Have a good day. Take care, Avni," Ansh said. Avni just smiled at him and got out. She stood by her building, till his car drove away and then walked to her apartment thinking how crazy breakfast had turned out to be.

How in the world would she explain her parents why she did not want to go any further? Avni wondered for she herself did not know what was wrong. He was still sweet and nice to her, and getting the flowers for her was very nice, but something did not feel right – like that inner call, remembering her father's words.

Avni spent the day thinking about how her morning had gone. It was making her more and more restless by the minute.

"Hmph," she frowned hitting the remote blaming the TV for not showing any good programmes, and picked up her phone.

"I don't understand, Avni. You were all positive about him yesterday and now all you want to do is get out?" Nidhi asked as Avni explained her ordeal.

"Ya, I know but you know today it did not feel right. Have any of your friends ever got mixed signals?" Avni said, sitting on her bed scratching her eyebrows.

"No, I have not heard of anyone getting mixed signals, Avni," Nidhi replied.

"Why me?" Avni replied sounding confused, "Does it happen that at one time you feel completely positive and another just the opposite?"

"You know you should try meeting him once more, probably the whole marriage thing got you worked up this way. Just meet him one more time and see how it goes if you still feel the same way then you know what to do," Nidhi said.

"Yeah okay," Avni said not paying attention to half the things Nidhi said for she was too busy fighting with herself in her head.

Ten minutes after she got off the phone, it buzzed.

Avni immediately picked it up, "Ria, great. Can you come over? I am going crazy."

"How do I explain it to my parents?" Avni said holding Ria's hand like she was now the only saviour Avni had got.

Ria smiled at Avni, pressed her hands and said, "Look Avni, if you don't feel it's right then don't go ahead with it," she said smiling at Avni.

"I am so stupid," Avni said looking up at Ria sheepishly.

Ria giggled, "No, you are not, Avni. You are just a bit confused, that's it and anyone can get confused about things like this. But please be very careful before taking a decision. I don't want you making the same mistake I made."

"I know, Ria. But you know I feel in all my confusion and in my attempt to clear my head, I might be playing with someone else's feelings," Avni replied looking down again.

"I know, Avni, but there's no other way," Ria replied shrugging "or if you don't want to string him along anymore, then just call it off. Tell your parents."

"I can't," Avni said, "I am not able to get the guy I met at my house out of my head, as much as I want to say no. I want to see which part of me is right. God, I am being so selfish, aren't I?" Avni replied, almost horrified at herself.

"No, you are not. Just one more meeting. That's it. Even if you do say no after that, Avni he won't be heartbroken all his life!" Ria assured her.

"Ya, you are right," Avni replied.

For the first time Avni was dreading her mother's call for she did not know what to say, but she could not evade the call, which came the next day. Avni was in her office, drowned in her work, when her cellphone buzzed.

"Ma. What?" Avni sprung up. She felt the blood rushing to her head. She went speechless for a minute.

"Avni, are you there?" her mother asked.

"Ya," Avni said still trying to comprehend what her mother had said. And when she did she said, "No, no. Ma, no. This is all wrong!" Avni protested. "His parents? No, Ma, I can't take this. Why are his parents coming?" Avni went on.

"They just want to see you, Avni, that's it. Ansh is going back in four days and they just wanted to see you," his mother replied.

"Exactly, Ma! Why? I am still not sure," Avni retorted.

Mrs. Sharma took a deep breath, "Avni, I know, but it's not final we are just meeting the parents, nothing is final, okay, so please just relax," her mother assured her.

Avni was in a big fix and she had no idea how she was to get out of it.

Why were his parents coming? Why did he have to call his parents? Did he get a positive vibe after all? I don't think so! Avni thought, recalling the breakfast. *Then why was it all happening so suddenly?* Avni suddenly felt like she could not breathe anymore, she was getting suffocated.

"Ma, I don't know. I am not ready to meet his parents yet, so please just say no somehow. Ma, please I can't do this," Avni said.

"Okay, *beta.* I will see what I can do, but there is no harm in just meeting once, Avni... really," her mother replied trying to be calm with her daughter.

"Okay fine, Papa. Let them come," Avni had finally given in, talking to her parents for the umpteenth time in the day on this topic. She was tired of saying no again and again – it was like talking to a wall.

Her parents were insistent about Ansh's parents coming and there was no way Avni could change their mind.

All they kept saying was, "You are just meeting his parents, Avni, no big deal. It will not get final till you say it is. The last choice will always be with you and no matter what we are with you."

She did not seem to trust her parents anymore. She could not believe, the first guy she agreed to meet a few days back, things had gone so fast that she was to meet his parents now.

The next day Avni asked Smita if she could leave a little early the next day.

"Is everything okay, Avni?" Smita asked.

Smita was Avni's manager and she just got a wee bit curious about Avni being away from office so often.

"Yes, Smita, everything's fine. Just family you know," Avni replied shrugging.

"Hmm okay then, looks like someone's getting a long weekend," Smita said smiling at Avni looking at Avni's calendar.

Avni had applied for a leave on Friday, the day Ansh's parents were arriving. She just held her arms close to her chest and closed her eyes at the thought of it.

"You okay?" Smita asked again.

"I am fine," Avni said opening her eyes and loosening her hands.

She smiled at her manager and walked back to her desk. Avni sat down with a heavy heart, she could not seem get herself to work. She kept analysing and re-analysing the whole thing again and again.

How did she let it go this far?

She had always had a way of getting out, she thought tapping her pencil on her head to make it think harder. This is why she avoided meeting anyone at all, for she knew if she ever did there would then be no end to it. She sighed heavily.

She told herself to just let it be for some time and get back to work. It would help getting her mind off things for a while.

As Avni was walking up to her apartment, her legs felt like there were suddenly filled with rocks. She just couldn't get her legs to move. Of course she could have taken the lift but Avni was so lost in her thoughts today that she was halfway up the stairs when she realized that she could have taken the lift. Tired and exhausted she left like a lost warrior, who had no other choice but to surrender. She sat down by the stairs and looked around.

"I like my life, why are you taking it away from me? I like this, my job, however tiring it is," she said out loud to no one in particular. She liked going to work every day she thought looking at her ID hanging around her neck, her flat, her freedom. She was so happy; she looked up as if she was talking to God.

This is not how I thought it would be, Avni thought. I was supposed to get an inner call or some "connection", at least a tiny feeling inside which would have told me this is it.

Avni pulled a little of her hair with her fingers. *Weren't people supposed to feel nice and happy and excited?* If not in love already, she should have felt something at least by now.

She sat there mulling over the same things over and over till she finally got up and walked up to her apartment dragging her legs, which seemed even heavier than before.

"Hi," came Kriti's voice as Avni opened the door.

Avni did not bother to respond. She was so engrossed in her own world; she went straight into her room without acknowledging her roomies to drown herself in her never-ending grief.

"Hello," Avni answered her cell in her sleep.

"Ma, I slept early today. No. I mean, ya, I ate something before

I slept," Avni replied to her mother yawning, "I am fine, Ma. Ma, I don't think my decision will really make any difference. You want tomorrow's lunch to happen then, it will. No. I know you want my happiness. Yes, Ma. Yes, you have never forced me for anything, but this feels like it. No, Mom, can we cancel it? No nah, then why talk about it? Making you feel bad, what about me? No, I don't want to say no to him. I just wish I had some more time. Ma, it's okay, it's fine. I am very sleepy. I will see you tomorrow... hmmm, goodnight," Avni finally kept her cell.

She had given in, she was too tired of fighting with her mother every single day. She was tired of saying no. She was tired of blaming society for not letting her make a choice in her own time. She remembered her mother saying once.

"You cannot be forty-fifty years old and still not be married, Avni?"

Her sister had once said.

"Marriage is fun. It's like living in with the person you love, with your parent's permission."

She used to make it sound like marriage was so uber cool, but then that's exactly the point. Avni thought, *living with a person you love,* and Avni at this point had no feelings at all whatsoever for Ansh.

Oh dear God, she thought to herself as she disappeared beneath her blanket.

Chapter VI

At her house in the morning, Avni sat by the dining table.

"Avni," Uma said holding her hands, "I know you are upset. You know he is a nice guy," Uma said.

"He is nice, do I have to marry him for that? I don't think so," Avni said looking at her mother.

Uma looked at her daughter with concern, "Avni, his parents are coming today."

"I know, Mom," Avni said resting her head on her hands.

"Avni…" Uma said and stopped.

Avni took a deep breath, she wiped a tear that stood right outside her eyes.

"Okay, you don't trust us, nah, Avni, at least trust your sister. You know she won't give you bad advice," Uma said.

"Avni, I am sorry if you feel we are forcing you, but trust me by the end of it all, it will be your decision. You never said no to him," Uma said.

"Mom, of course I did not say no, but can I at least take some time in deciding," Avni said looking up at Uma.

"Yes, you can," Uma said as she pressed Avni's hands, "I think I should call Priya, You will feel much better with her being here," Uma said.

Avni nodded.

Uma walked off and made a call, she looked at Avni. Avni just looked up forced a smile and started walking towards her room

"Avni, *beta,* we still have a lot of time. Why don't you go to the parlor, get your hair set and all," her mother said.

Avni stopped halfway. It was best for her to get out.

"Okay," she said as she picked up her purse and left.

As the time of their arrival neared, all three of them got busy getting ready.

"Avni, are you done? They will be here any moment," her mother asked as she peeped into Avni's room.

Avni was wearing a blood red silk suit. It was a *patiala salwar* and the *kurti* reached a little below her knee. Avni always felt like she looked like a typical Punjabi wearing this suit, her mother used to laugh at this thought of hers. It had some dull gold leaf-shaped patterns on it. She was wearing her gold and red bangles when her mother peeped in.

"Yes, I am almost ready," Avni replied. She was in a better mood now.

Mrs. Sharma walked up to her daughter and smiled looking at her.

"What? Stop smiling like that, Ma," Avni said looking from her mother to the bangles she was wearing, "You are making me conscious."

"Oh my, really. Your mother is making you conscious now," Mrs. Sharma replied. "*Achha* anyways, come out quickly, Avni," her mother said walking out of the room.

Avni went back to wearing her bangles and doing her face. Once she was done, she walked out to the kitchen. As Avni neared the dining table, she was amazed at the variety of dishes her mother had prepared in no time at all.

Mrs. Sharma had been up all morning working round the clock, from cleaning up the whole house to going shopping for all the vegetables and cooking so much food to Avni's surprise.

"You made all this!" Avni said as she looked around.

"Yes. Why Avni?" her mother replied, wiping the kitchen floor.

"Ma, leave that. I will clean up the kitchen," Avni said realizing she had been so lost in her thoughts she had completely forgotten to help her mother.

"No, Avni. You will get your clothes dirty, don't do any work now. Just go and sit in the hall with Papa, okay," Avni's mother replied.

"Are you sure, Ma?" Avni asked

"Avni, yes go now sit *araam se,*" her mother replied smiling at Avni.

As Avni turned to go to the hall, her mother stopped her. Mrs. Sharma held Avni's hand from behind.

"Avni," she said. Avni turned around and looked at her mother's eyes, there was concern written all over it.

"Ma, what happened?"

Mrs. Sharma took both of Avni's hands in hers looked down at them and said, "I know this is not how you wanted things to be, Avni, but trust me it's for your good. We only want to see you happy," Avni looked down at her own hands in her mother's now and took a heavy breath.

She had decided not to bother herself about all of this and just think of it like a family dinner with some friends but now as her mother spoke, it started to dawn on her.

At Avni's silence, Mrs. Sharma continued, "It will be your decision, Avni. It will be yours, I promise you."

Avni closed her eyes and nodded. She whispered an okay, for no other words came out of her mouth. Her thoughts started engulfing her once again. Ansh's parents were coming to see her, to see how their maybe, would-be daughter-in-law looked.

Daughter-in-law, Avni thought, this was not helping her in any way.

Good things, Avni, think good things, she stared into space for a moment and not one good thought came into her mind. *Okay,* Avni breathed heavily probably she was too worked up at the moment to get any positive thoughts. The best thing to do now was to go to the hall and sit with her father. After about ten minutes, "Dad, when will they come?" she said looking at the door every two seconds.

"If you keep staring at the door like that Avni, they won't pop up from nowhere. They will come," her father said, "by the way what's making you so impatient, *beta*. You know Uma told me. You weren't really up for this," her father said looking at her.

"Huh?" Avni said looking at her father for a second and looking back at the door like if she looked away any longer they would pop up from nowhere just like her father had said. After a few seconds she realized that her dad looking at her.

"I..." Avni looked up at her father like she was making a plea, "I don't know," she said finally looking down.

Mr. Sharma smiled and as he opened his mouth to speak the doorbell rang. Avni jumped in her seat.

Mrs. Sharma screamed from inside, "Oh dear, they are here. Arun, go receive them. I will be out in a minute. Avni, you come inside, *beta.*"

She looked at her father, he gestured her to go inside quick. He brushed of his suit, straightened up, breathed heavily and walked forward.

Avni walked inside, her heart was now thumping so hard she couldn't hear anything else. She walked into the room where her mother was getting ready.

"Avni, are they here? Okay, I am going," she said pinning her sari on her shoulders. "It's looking fine?" Mrs. Sharma asked looking at the mirror now trying to adjust her *bindi*.

She took one last look at herself in the mirror and then turned towards Avni who was standing in the corner of the room.

"Why are you standing like that, Avni?" her mother said, amused, "Anyways come. Let's go," her mother said.

Avni walked towards and sat on the bed. She then looked up at her mother and said. "But Papa told me to go inside."

She felt so much better inside the room, so much calmer. She did not want to go back into the hall. It was just too scary. How was she supposed to behave or talk? Was she even supposed to talk too much or just sit quietly smiling at everybody? How was she supposed to greet them "namaste" or "hi" or just a smile? Suddenly there were a bunch of questions surfacing in Avni's mind.

Why did I not talk to Mamma Papa about this, I had all morning!

"Avni, *kya hua?* I wanted you to help me with my sari that's why I called you in, but now I am done so *chalo, beta,* they must be waiting. *Achha thodi lagta hai,*" Mrs. Sharma replied looking at her. She held Avni's hand and took her into the hall with her.

As Avni walked towards the hall she saw glimpses of his parents and sister and as the voices became clearer. Avni dug her nails even deeper into her mother's hands.

"Shouldn't I come later on?"

"Oh, Avni, those old days have gone. Where you would have come later on with the tray of snacks and tea, it's different now," her mother said walking so fast as though she was going to miss a train.

It's different now! Avni thought. *Well, I'll be damned,* she said to herself sarcastically.

"Avni," her mother said, "it will be fine. Now just smile, okay."

Avni had never walked into her own hall with so much apprehension. *Just normal people,* Avni kept repeating as she walked forward. Her mother left her hand and walked towards a lady. Avni guessed it was Ansh's mother.

"Hi. So nice to see you," Avni's mother greeted Ansh's mother and gave her a hug.

"We meet again," Mrs. Sharma said as she smiled at Ansh's mother.

Ansh's mother had worn a light red sari. She had just a small red *bindi* on her face and nothing else. *Simplicity* was all Avni could think when she looked at Ansh's mother.

"We had to meet. How could we not come? We had to meet Avni," she said looking at Avni, smiling from ear to ear.

"This is Avni," her mother introduced her.

His mother nodded, looking at Avni with so much happiness inside her, for a moment it seemed like Ansh's mother would have burst into tears, but then she took Avni hands in hers and pressed them hard, "So nice to meet you, Avni."

Avni was soon introduced to Ansh's family, his father, sister and his brother-in-law.

All of them greeted Avni with almost the same amount of excitement as his mother. They all looked at her with so much glee which made it even harder for Avni to look up. There was one family member who was beyond herself with joy when she met Avni.

Avni had never seen anybody so happy after meeting her. It was Ansh's five-year-old niece. She looked no less than a doll.

All she wanted to do was talk to Avni for hours together. Kanchan, Ansh's sister and Aarika's mother turned to Avni, "Don't mind my daughter, she usually talks a lot."

"It's okay. She is really sweet," Avni looked up and smiled.

As she did for the first time since they walked in, she noticed Ansh. Avni was amazed at herself for not seeing him since they came in. He was sitting at the corner talking to her father.

As Aarika pulled Avni's *kurti* to engross her into further talks, Avni wished she'd stop. For she now looked at Ansh very differently from her last encounter with him at breakfast.

From where Avni was sitting, she could just see his side profile at most. He was engrossed in his talks with her father. *I don't believe it,* Avni thought to herself. *This doesn't even seem like such a big deal anymore.* He seemed just like he did when she met him first.

Why is this happening? Avni thought, every time she met him she ended up with a different feeling.

She decided she must clear her mind about what she really felt about him and find a way to talk to him. Just then the doorbell rang.

"That must be Priya, our elder daughter," Avni's mother explained as she got up to open the door.

Finally, Avni thought. She had always given a lot of importance to how her sister felt towards almost everything. So it mattered a lot to what her sister had to say about Ansh.

"Hi, Ma," her sister broke into a hug as she saw Mrs. Sharma.

Priya then looked around and greeted everyone.

"This is Priya, Avni's sister," Mrs. Sharma said, she held her arm and took her inside the kitchen.

Avni too got up, "I will just come, Aarika," Avni said and went inside the kitchen.

"Hi, Di," Avni hugged Priya, as they broke apart, Avni asked, "So?" she asked curious to know her sister's answer.

"Well. He is cute." Priya said looking at her mother who agreed instantly. "He is nice, what's all the fuss about, Avni?"

Avni did not know what to say next. She could not figure out if she was to be happy for her sister had liked Ansh or sad. Probably Avni had kept her sister as a last resort who like Avni could have taken her time to decide, but here in just one look she had approved of him.

Avni sighed, "That's not helping me, Di," Avni mumbled looking down at the plate of *samosas* she was about to take out.

"What's not helping you, Avni?" Priya asked.

"Can't you see it's all happening so fast? It's all just too soon," Avni replied. "I mean I have no time to breathe."

Priya looked at her sister trying to read her face trying to figure out what she was saying, "Avni, okay. You know what," Priya said holding a glass of juice. "I will go and have a little chat with him and then we will see how it goes and I know I will still like him and so will you." Priya said as she gestured Avni to carry the plate of *samosas* and come out with her.

"Hi, Ansh, Priya," she held out her hand towards Ansh. He looked up, shook her hand and smiled at her. "Papa, if you don't mind now, we kids will talk. Don't worry, Ansh, I won't bore you a lot," her sister continued and sat beside Ansh.

"Oh no, not at all, Priya, please," he replied.

Mr. Sharma then walked up to Ansh's father and sat beside him. She heard him say something like, "kids nowadays."

"Avni. What are you looking at?" her mother asked from behind.

"Ma, you startled me. You were sitting in the hall?" Avni asked looking halfway at her mother. She then realized she would not have noticed anyway, for she had been standing with the tray in the doorway of the kitchen for about ten minutes looking at Ansh and

Priya.

"Give me the tray, *beta.* I will take it. Why don't you go sit with your sister?" her mother nudged her, "Go, Avni. Here, give me this," her mother said taking the plate from her hand.

Avni walked ahead to go sit with her sister.

"You know actually," Priya interrupted before Avni could sit, Avni why don't you take Ansh down for a walk?" her sister asked.

"Huh? Me? Walk?" Avni stammered.

"Yes, walk. I am sure you would like that, right, Ansh?" Priya asked him.

"Sure," Ansh said smiling.

"Yes, Avni take him down, show him around," Avni mother interrupted. Ansh's mother nodded in agreement.

It's then that Avni realized everyone was looking at them, they had all started noticing her the moment she had walked towards Ansh eager to know what would happen next.

Reading Avni's discomfort, Mr. Sharma said, "Okay, if not down, Avni at least show him around the house."

"Okay," Avni replied.

Although she had been waiting to talk to him, Avni got cold feet as he got up. As she took him inside to show him "the house" she could feel everyone's eyes on their back. They only started talking again once both of them were out of their sight.

She took him out to the balcony, "This is the balcony," Avni said thinking how lame that must have sounded. As usual, Avni could not get herself to look at him so she stared at the pool and the garden below.

"So, how are you doing today?" Ansh asked gently.

Avni looked up at him for a second and then back at the garden, "I am doing well," she replied. "I had to ask you something," Avni said.

"What?" Ansh asked.

"What made you call your parents, Ansh? We just met. I wasn't even ready for this," Avni said looking at him.

"Oh," he said looking at Avni, "I am sorry, I had asked your parents. I did not know you were not ready yet."

Avni looked away again.

After a long pause, Ansh continued,

"You know, it is my bad. I should have talked to you directly. I am so sorry, Avni. I did not realize I am rushing you into this," Ansh sad looking at her.

Avni took a deep breath. Of course he should have spoken to her.

"You should have come to me, Ansh. I would have told you I needed time," Avni said still looking out at the garden.

"I am sorry, Avni," Ansh replied, "Look, you can say no after this, if you want. I never meant to force anything on you," Ansh said.

"I did not say I want out. I just need time," Avni said finally looking up at him.

"Okay, I understand," Ansh said nodding.

"It's not final yet, Avni, so…" Ansh said.

"Yeah. It's okay," Avni said looking at him.

"So… ummm. Are you okay?" he asked.

"Yes, I am fine," Avni replied looking at him, "Look I don't know you so well yet, Ansh, and marriage is a big decision," Avni continued.

"Yes, I do understand that," Ansh replied, he looked at Avni for a while and then continued, "Why don't we start now, getting to know each other?" he said smiling at her.

"Okay, we can do that," Avni replied shrugging her shoulders, "umm, what can I ask you?" Avni thought out loud.

"Do you like travelling?" Ansh asked.

"I love travelling. In fact I always wanted to go travel the whole of Europe," Avni said. "What about you?" she asked looking at him this time.

"I like travelling a lot too. Seeing different places. Meeting new people, getting to know about their culture," Ansh said.

"So, are you spiritual?" Ansh asked.

"Yes, very. People might think I am crazy but yeah I am a very spiritual person. You?" Avni asked.

"Yeah, to an extent. I too am and, yes I am a bit religious, have a small temple back home in Norway," Ansh said.

"Hmm, that's sweet," Avni said smiling. Avni thought of asking something this time.

"Cuisine, I like..." Ansh started when both of them blurted.

"Italian."

He looked at Avni.

"How did you know?" he asked.

"How did I know that I like Italian?" Avni went on sounding a bit confused.

"Oh, I thought, how did you know I too like... " he stopped and smiled to himself. "So we have a lot in common," he said finally.

They spoke a lot about the different things, travel destinations around the world, fashion trends, gadgets. Avni was amazed at the knowledge he had about different gadgets but soon realized there was no surprise there as he was just a major gadget freak!

"You know I used to tell my sister, no one can be a bigger freak than you. I mean... you know in gadgets," Avni said laughing, "but now I think. You could give her serious competition," Avni said.

"So... tell me about your work?" Ansh asked.

"Work. Well it's fun you know, but ummm you know I have realized I can't do a 9 to 5 job all my life," Avni said jokingly. "I want to start something of my own, put my hard work into my own creation. I don't know what it is for, I haven't reached a conclusion yet but I have a few things in mind and am working on them," Avni said.

She was surprised at herself for she had not really discussed this thought with anyone before.

"Hmm, that's really interesting, Avni," Ansh replied.

"Cool. So you are a double income theory kind of a guy?" Avni asked.

"Hey no. I don't mind the thought. The more the merrier but not if it's killing her, no. She could blow all our money up opening something which doesn't work out by the end. I would still be glad that she at least tried," he said looking at Avni telling her things indirectly.

"Really. You wouldn't mind. Really?" Avni asked, not really believing every word of his.

"Yes, completely," he smiled at Avni.

At this point of time Avni had developed a complete opposite view about Ansh then what she did when she met him last at breakfast. She was so at ease with him that she could go on for another hour just talking to him about random things. They had so much in common, that Avni now had a zillion more topics in her mind pushing their way through and screaming in her head for Avni to pick and discuss them first. He seemed quite amiable as she spoke to him, someone who had a fair knowledge about various things. He also seemed very genuine when he spoke to and suddenly he did not seem all that different to Avni but yes, Avni knew deep down it still wasn't enough to look at Ansh as her possible husband.

"So do you like to go to parties?" Ansh asked.

"Yes, once in a while, did a lot of it in college," Avni said.

"Yes, I don't go clubbing that much either. Been there done all of that," Ansh said.

Avni hesitated for a moment and asked, "So do you... umm... drink?"

"No. I don't drink. You?" he asked instantly.

She did not know how to reply. At this point of time she did not want anything to go wrong. Avni thought, *he doesn't drink and if she told him she did things could get a tiny bit awkward.*

"Me neither. I don't drink," she said finally and instantly felt guilty about lying to him.

"Hmmm, okay," he nodded smiling at Avni.

"Ansh, we are leaving," Kanchan said as she peeped into the room.

"Hi, Kanchan, come sit," Avni offered.

"I would have loved to but we have to leave now. I am sure we will keep meeting now, so next time," Kanchan said smiling at Avni.

All of them walked back into the hall and as Avni looked at the clock by the side table she realized it was quite late. They all shared warm byes and goodbyes. Kanchan and Ansh's mother hugged Avni before they left. Just as everyone was bidding their goodbyes, Ansh tapped her on her shoulder and asked her to come aside. Avni looked at her family who were busy talking to his, and walked with Ansh a little further.

"Avni, I won't lie to you," he took a deep breath and continued, "I like you."

Avni turned completely red and looked down.

"I am leaving for Norway in a few days, I just wanted you to know how I feel," Ansh asked.

Avni took a deep breath, she looked at him, *Did she want to say no to him? No, she did not. Could she say yes to him? Yes, she could, but he wasn't asking her out on a date, that she would readily have said yes to. He was asking to marry her; that was a big deal.*

All Avni could say was, "it's so sudden."

"I understand," Ansh said looking at her, "It's a bit fast."

"I just need some time to clear my head," Avni said.

Ansh nodded.

As they got back, "It was so nice, Avni. We are so glad to have met you," Kanchan said as she walked out.

Avni smiled and bid them all goodbye. She closed the door as she looked back. Her family was standing there with their arms folded, looking at her. It was very obvious, the smiles they were trying so hard to hide from Avni.

"Okay. What? Stop looking at me like that," Avni said trying hard to stop smiling for she did not want to give out any signals to her family yet.

"We noticed. The way you were looking at him," Priya said nudging her mom by letting her know she really did see the "look" in Avni's eyes.

"Oh come on, Di," Avni brushed her off.

She tried to get past her family to her room, who were standing in a straight line like a barrier.

"Avni," her mother stopped her finally, holding her arms as she tried walking past them. "Tell us something nah, *beta?*"

"You spoke to him for almost an hour and a half. You realize that. The last time you spoke to a guy was just for fifteen minutes," Priya said.

"Last time. I was just 20 and that whole thing was nothing but a big joke for me," Avni said.

"Avni," Mrs. Sharma said, "they would like to know by tomorrow how you feel?" her mother asked.

"What? Tomorrow. Ma, why? See that's why I told you I don't want to meet. Now they want to know by tomorrow," Avni shouted.

"Avni. Please stop your melodrama. Ansh is leaving in three days time, they just wanted to know if we are positive. He is nice for starters, if you don't believe yourself at least trust me, Dad and Mom. We have seen a lot more. We can judge. Ansh is a very nice boy," Priya finished.

"I knew you would do this to me," Avni started.

"Avni, we are not doing anything to you. We are just trying to make you realize what's right," Priya said.

"I know he is a nice guy and all. I still need time and I told you I need time and see now what you guys have put me into. Tomorrow!" Avni exclaimed.

Mrs. Sharma opened her mouth to say something but Priya nudged her mom to let her talk as she about to reply, "Look Avni, You can say no," Priya said.

"I don't want to yet, I need time. You had a love marriage so don't pretend like you know what it like is to be in my shoes. Three freaking times I meet him and I am supposed to decide if he is the one I am supposed to spend my life with! You know, it even sounds ridiculous."

Avni flared up. As Priya opened her mouth to speak, Mr. Sharma called hearing the commotion in the hall between the two sisters.

"Avni," her father called from inside.

"Yes, Papa," Avni replied and walked into her parent's room.

Avni sat down beside her father on the bed, he looked a bit tensed. It worried Avni too.

"Papa, what happened?" Avni asked.

"Avni, before anything all I want to know is do you like the guy. Tell me honestly whatever comes to your mind," Arun asked.

"Papa..." Avni started "he is a nice guy. He is sweet, nice to talk to. He is nice," Avni said thinking of her conversation she had with him in the balcony.

"So I take that you like him," her father asked.

"I don't like him like him, Papa," Avni said.

"Yes, I meant to say that you don't resent the guy right," her father said.

"Yes, of course not," Avni said. There was nothing in him for Avni to resent.

"Avni," Mr. Sharma started as he held his daughter's hands. "We have spoken to so many families, seen so many guys. You, of course, did not meet many of them but my point is we have seen enough to know who is the best match for you. When I met Ansh for the first time I knew he is a wonderful boy," he paused and then continued, "I can't think of anybody better for you and his family. They are so simple, not someone who would treat you badly or anything, even his sister is so sweet, just like you, Avni. I can't think of anything better – it's a small family, just perfect," her father finished as he looked at Avni.

Avni looked into her father's eyes, every part of him was hoping Avni would believe him.

"I know, Papa, everything you are saying," Avni said. She could not deny or counter any of what her father had just said. It's like every word he said seeped into her mind in complete agreement.

"Papa, I know but they want to know by tomorrow, even if I say yes, don't you think it's all too fast?" Avni asked.

"Avni, sometimes in life things happen just like that," Mr. Sharma said snapping his fingers. "But when a good thing comes to you too fast doesn't mean you push it away," he finished.

Avni sighed and looked down at the floor not knowing what to say next.

"If you need time, Avni, I can tell them that," Mr. Sharma said.

"Yeah, I mean, Papa, I need time. I will tell you but I need some time to think," Avni said.

"Yes, okay, that would be fine, we will talk about it later," Mr. Sharma said. "Go sleep, Avni, It's really late, Goodnight."

Avni smiled back at her dad and got up to leave.

"Avni," her mother came in, "Go sleep, *beta.* Goodnight."

"Goodnight," Avni said and walked to her room.

As she walked out to go to her room she could hear her parents talk

"Why does she need time now? What does this girl want? Some prince charming who will come riding on a horse," her mother said sounding tired.

"Haha, Uma, you can really make me laugh sometimes. Don't you see, she hasn't said no yet. She needs time, don't you think it's a big deal for Avni to even be needing time, I know she will say yes. Trust me," Avni's father replied.

"Okay, if you say so. Oh all my worries will be over the day this girl says yes," her mother sighed.

Avni sighed too from outside their room.

How in the world would she decide!

Chapter VII

"Nidhi, I know, I felt so different today, you know," Avni said.

She was sitting on her bed with her legs folded and was rocking gently as she spoke.

"Yes, Ria exactly... hey, I need you guys to talk to me..." Avni said.

It was two in the night and Avni just could not go to sleep, so she decided to keep her two friends awake the whole night so that she could analyse and discuss her feeling towards Ansh to make her big decision by tomorrow.

"And no, Ria… you so cannot sleep. You have got to listen to me," Avni said.

"Okay, Avni, listen to yourself, and you will get your answers, you haven't spoken a single word against Ansh. You enjoyed talking to him, you are amazed at how much you guys have in common, your parents love him, your sister likes him which is unlikely as it's very tough to impress Priya Di. You like Ansh, just say yes and let me sleep," Nidhi said it all so fast, as though she would lose her flow if she went slower.

"I don't quite think so," Ria said, "it is too fast. Okay, he might be a nice guy but you just met him. So what if he is going to Norway? Avni, remember I did the same thing. I don't want you taking your decisions in haste."

"Do you want to say no and let a guy like Ansh get away?" Nidhi asked.

"No," Avni replied before she could even think about it.

"That doesn't mean she should say a yes tomorrow, Nidhi," Ria argued.

"Then he will be off to Norway, Avni. He won't keep waiting for you, what if he finds someone else," Nidhi said.

"If he really likes her, then he will wait for her to decide," Ria argued.

Avni did not want to say no. He was a nice guy but she couldn't get herself to say yes either. *What if Nidhi was right? What if she told him she needed time and he found someone else? Argh, why was the idea of someone else even bothering her?*

"What if he had asked you out on a date," Nidhi went on.

"He is not asking her out on a date, they will get married if she says yes," Ria retorted.

"You know, Ria, I know you have been through hell but that doesn't mean you turn into such a pessimist," Nidhi argued.

"I am not being a pessimist," Ria said, "That's rude, Nidhi. I am only looking out for Avni."

Oh God, Avni thought as she put her head into the pillow on her lap.

"Please guys, stop it. You are not making this any easier for me," Avni said.

"And Norway. Think about that girl," Nidhi said jokingly.

Avni laughed to herself. It was tempting, but oh how silly would that be.

"Avni, just think over it clearly and you will know what to do, but please be smart about it," Ria said.

"Yeah, thanks guys, go to sleep it's almost two-thirty, bye goodnight," Avni said

"Bye, Avni," they both shouted in unison.

"Whoa... ow..." Avni said rubbing her ear.

As Avni kept the phone, she sat by her room all alone with a huge task daunting over her.

The decision. How does one decide? she thought.

She got up to go to her sister's room when she realized it was three in the morning. Avni looked at her cell.

Should she call Ansh up? It was too late but how did it matter? This was important. She had told him she needed time, then why tomorrow?

She fiddled with her phone for a while.

Should she meet him once before she took her "decision"? Talk to him. Tell him she drinks. What a stupid thought, but then she remembered her sister telling her. "You didn't tell him. Avni, you kind of deceived him, it's important for him to know."

Yes, it was important for him to know. She took her cell typed his name. *It's too late, Avni* she thought and suddenly she saw his name flashing on the phone. She picked it up.

"Hi, Avni, sorry for calling so late," Ansh said, "I know you must be tensed now, this was uncalled for. I did not realize my parents spoke to yours and asked for a decision tomorrow. Guess this is what a communication gap means. I am leaving in a few days and my parents are in such a hurry they want to finalize everything before I leave. They apparently like you a lot, though I am not surprised there," he continued, "I told you I will give you time and I meant it."

"Yes, this is a bit of shock, I really don't know how to get my feelings together with so much happening at once," Avni said.

"I know, we will wait this out," Ansh said.

His voice calmed her down instantly, "Thanks."

"I guess you should sleep now, goodnight," Ansh said.

"Okay, goodnight," Avni replied.

She took a deep breath; she couldn't get herself to think straight. She did not want to make a hasty decision. *What was happening to her? Did she like him or was it just as a friend? Did she just enjoy being in his company or was it something more? She couldn't keep him hanging like that, it wasn't fair. Should she just say yes, or take some time. What if he changed his mind by then or found someone else? Oh man, now what?* She sat up for hours before finally putting her iPod on and dozing off to a dozen love songs figuring out if she could picture Ansh in them.

Avni woke up startled as she heard a dog bark.

"Ughh," Avni said thinking it was the stray dogs outside.

She got up and called out to her mom, "Mom." After about five seconds, "Maaa," Avni shouted. That's when it hit Avni – what had happened last night, suddenly she felt like a heavy stone had been placed on her head.

"Oh God, I still don't know," she sat up straight.

Avni walked out, her sister's door was locked. Avni walked up to her parent's room, they weren't there.

"That's strange, where would they go this early in the morning?" Avni said out loud. She walked out to the hall to see if they were sitting there, but she couldn't find them. Avni did not want to be alone. She felt she would hyperventilate if she was left alone and had nobody to talk to.

She roamed her house pointlessly searching for her parents knowing they weren't in the house till she heard noises at the front door. She sighed with relief and ran out.

"Ma, Papa. Where did you go?" Avni had never felt so happy seeing her parents. "And what is all this?" Avni said looking down at their hands holding big bags full of vegetables.

"Well, we went for a little shopping," her father said.

"For?" Avni asked still looking down at their hands.

"Groceries, if you do decide, you know and if we have to call them over," her mother went on,

"But no rush, *beta,* if you have decided otherwise, we are fine, we just thought we would not have to run at the last minute."

Avni knew deep down that even if it was too fast, it was all good and he was a good guy. She knew he was ready to give her time but what if he changed his mind in that time. She didn't want to get married at first, but she did find a sense of comfort with Ansh. She had gone back and forth a million times in her head and had no idea what to do.

There was no denying there. Avni could not get herself to say no. She had no reason to, so instead, "Ma, wouldn't you have to invite them, if you want to call them for lunch," Avni said finally taking a deep breath.

"Ya, We… would," Mrs. Sharma stammered looking from Avni to Mr. Sharma.

Avni could sense the excitement growing in her voice.

"Yes, we should invite them, nah, Avni," she asked to reconfirm.

"Ya... umm... ya... Ma," Avni said.

With this Mrs. Sharma wrapped her up in a hug.

"Oh Avni, you have no idea how happy we are. So happy, you will be so happy, Avni… such a nice boy, such a wonderful family," she said and her eyes filled with tears. "Okay, now we have a lot of work to do, wake Priya up. Arun, you call them and tell them congrats," Mrs. Sharma said ruffling Avni's hair.

"Go, Avni, wake Priya up, I have so much to make in so less time," her mother said getting all flustered up all of a sudden, "And oh we have to call everyone too. Tell them to come for lunch," she said.

In no time her house had turned into a chaotic mess. Her sister was running around to see which sari each of them had to wear.

"Ma, they are not even pressed. Will I get a *dhobi*?" Priya shouted.

"Priya, we can iron them later. You come here and take care of the food," her mother replied.

"Avni, move! Why are you standing in the way?" Priya said as she rushed to the kitchen.

"Shall I do something?" Avni asked.

"No, you just sit here," Priya replied as she walked out.

Mr. Sharma was busy calling up his brothers telling them to come over for lunch.

She heard her mother call her name.

"Yes, Ma, coming," Avni said as she walked to the kitchen.

"Avni," Kitty slammed right into her.

Avni's extended family had just arrived. Her *taiji* and her two *chachis* and of course their respective families.

"Meghna, Bhavya. Please take Avni into her room and get her ready. There is no time, they will be here any moment, her sari is lying on the bed," Mrs. Sharma said wiping the sweat off her brow.

Her mother looked completely exhausted but she still had this glee on her face like she could go on for the whole day.

Before Avni knew three four hands caught her arms and dragged her inside the room.

"Wha... wait," Avni protested as she walked towards her room.

Once they were in the room and closed the closed the door Avni looked around to see who all were responsible for literally dragging her into the room on her mother's order.

There were three of them. Meghna, her sister-in-law, who was married to Kitty's elder brother, Bhavya, another *bhabhi* of hers and Kitty.

After all the hugs and pats and all kinds of jokes about her finally liking a guy were made, they finally started getting Avni ready.

"You know this is like the first close family wedding we will be having since we got married. Kitty, I and Meghna have been deciding for months now," Bhavya said.

"Deciding on what?" Avni said as she got up to tie up her hair so Meghna Bhabhi could start her make-up.

"Deciding on what to wear of course, we don't want to end up wearing the same colours or same saris," Meghna said. "This is so exciting, I have so much to shop now finally, I will get a different set and sari for each function and ooooh I will wear a *lehenga* on your wedding day," she chirped.

"Bhabhi, relax it's just my *roka* today, wedding will take ages," Avni replied, closing her eyes to allow her Bhabhi to do her eye make-up.

"Oh really," Bhavya said as she sat beside Avni, "You really think so, your wedding will happen so fast now, you wouldn't even know?"

"Yeah, we all are so ready to throw you out already," Kitty remarked.

"Yeah whatever. Shut up, Kitty. Please, Bhabhi," Avni said trying to open her eyes. "Oh sorry," she said realizing her eyeliner had not dried up yet, so she continued with her eyes closed, "No, Mom said it's just *roka* now, I will have a lot of time before the wedding."

"We were all told the same thing. I am telling you, you will be married by the end of this year," Meghna said.

Oh man, Avni was fine with the *roka* but getting married by the end of this year!

She closed her eyes real tight hoping against all odds her wedding date would be next year.

"Where are the pins? Avni, the pins?" Bhavya asked.

"I don't know, no clue. Ask Ma," Avni said.

"Oh dear, Kitty, go ask Uma Aunty for pins, how will we tie her sari?" Bhavya said gesturing Kitty to go fast.

"I am here. Oh God, Oh God, What's the time? Please help me get ready," Priya scrammed in from nowhere with her sari in hand and her hair all messed up.

"Meghna will help you with that, I will get Avni ready," Bhavya said.

"Okay cool. Meghna, I am here," Priya said as she sat down with her chin up and eyes closed.

Priya continued, "There is such a chaos in the kitchen, the ladies in the kitchen are going crazy," shaking her head and then continued. "They just called saying they will be here in twenty minutes, you should see Dad, Avni. He is so freaking tensed, just sitting in the corner by himself, now it feels like there is a wedding at home."

"Priya, you didn't iron my sari. How will I wear this now?" Mrs. Sharma came running in.

"Ohh... ya. Ma, wear something else nah now, sorry," Priya said with her eyes closed as she allowed Meghna to do her make-up.

"Oh God, this girl, now what do I wear at the last moment?" Mrs. Sharma went on as she walked out.

"Aunty," Bhavya called out, she looked back, "I will help Aunty with that, Avni is almost ready."

She then looked at Avni, "Avni, you sit right where you are... I am coming," Bhavya said as she rushed out after Mrs. Sharma.

So somehow in half an hour they all managed to get ready. Avni's soon-to-be *sasural* were to arrive at any moment. All the elders were in the hall waiting anxiously. Avni's mother kept walking in every five seconds to see if Avni was okay.

"You stay right here, Avni, and come out only when we tell you to," Mrs. Sharma kept saying.

"Ya, okay," Avni said, she was so nervous she couldn't stop her hands from strangling each other.

"Avni," Meghna said as she pulled one strand of Avni's hair back. She had been fussing over Avni's hair for about fifteen minutes now.

"It's fine, Bhabhi," Avni said getting more tensed by the minute.

"They have come," Kitty's face said as it popped into the room for just a second and then disappeared.

"Oh my God, Bhabhi," Avni said looking up at her. Avni felt like she was going into a battlefield and suddenly she couldn't breathe.

"Avni," Priya walked in. "They have come, he is looking so nice. Avni, don't be tensed, it's fine," Priya said looking at her sister's face, "Just smile, leave your hands and smile and enjoy, it's your day." Priya said as she walked Avni out of the room.

"You ready?" Kitty asked as she walked out.

To think of how they all got the food and themselves ready in half a day – only Indian families during a wedding can be that fast, Avni thought as she looked down at her sari. It was baby pink with glitter work all over and a *pista* green border that ran all along the edges. Avni nodded, she took a deep breath, closed her eyes for a second and told herself it will all go on fine and walked ahead.

As she walked into the hall, she saw that lovely garlands had been put up everywhere. All her relatives and her family members were beaming at her. Avni was so confused that she did not know where to go or what to say or whether to smile too much or not, so she went to stood near her *chachi*.

"Avni, oh sweetheart, you both look so nice together, go, go sit beside him," her *chachi* said as she pushed Avni slightly forward. Avni was so dazed and just looked around until Priya got hold of her and made her sit beside Ansh.

"What's wrong, Avni? Are you alright?" her sister whispered in her ears.

"Yes," Avni replied looking down. She knew the hall was filled, with her family and his of course but she just couldn't look up.

"Smile, Avni, everyone is looking," Priya insisted and she went and stood at one side.

Avni looked up she saw her family. Aunt's uncles, cousins with gleeful smiles, gesturing at her that they looked good together. She then saw her to-be family standing on the other side looking at her with equal excitement.

Avni looked down blushing, being the centre of attraction was kind of embarrassing.

"Hi," Ansh said, looking at her.

It was then that Avni realized Ansh was sitting beside her. He was wearing a purple shirt, it had stripes of the same colour, just a shade lighter.

She turned her head a bit and looked at him, "Hi," she whispered and looked away again.

The thought of sitting beside Ansh for their *roka* ceremony slowly began to sink into Avni, but no matter how hard she tried none of it seemed real to her anymore. The *tika* ceremony started Avni was so dazed all the time she did not realize how many people came forward to bless them both, apply *tikas* and give them gifts. She kept smiling and taking the gifts as and when her sister told her to.

Even when Ansh's mother came and handed Avni her *shagun,* she looked up at her and smiled blankly without registering it in her mind that she was her to-be mother-in-law.

Once everything was over. Ria, came over from nowhere.

"Avni, oh my. Hi, Ansh, we finally meet," Ria said as she sat beside Avni.

"When did you get here?" Avni asked looking at her.

"Avni, where have you been? I have been right here in front of you all the time and you kept smiling at me too," Ria said, "Where are you lost, Avni?" she asked.

"I have been thinking the same," Ansh said looking at Ria.

"Hmmm, he is right here, Avni. Why are you so lost then?" Ria said teasingly.

"I don't know, I am so zoned out," Avni said. She then looked at Ansh. "I am sorry, this whole thing, it's just making me very nervous," she said.

"Hey, it's okay, relax, I understand, it will all be fine," Ansh said smiling at Avni.

"I really wish Kriti and Roshni could be here but their clients from US had to come in this week," Avni said looking at Ria.

"Ya, I wish they could have been here too," Ria said. "Well I will leave you two and go say hi to Kitty," Ria said as she got up and went.

Ansh looked down at Avni's hands, "You seem very nervous."

"Yeah. I don't know, I ummm just, it will be fine, just nerves," Avni said looking down.

"Avni..." Ansh started asking when...

"Ansh, isn't it?" Avni's uncle came and sat beside Ansh, "So tell me, *beta*, what do you do?"

Well there started the normal interrogation every groom had to go through with the bride's family.

Avni looked around. A bunch of her cousins were sitting at one corner looking at them like they were enjoying a movie show, they raised their eyebrows at Avni as she looked at them. She made a face at them and turned away.

"So how is it going, *beta?*" her mother came by and squeezed Avni's arm.

"I am fine, Ma," Avni said.

"Then stop playing with your hands, Avni, and smile. Why do you look so tensed?" Mrs. Sharma asked.

"No, Ma, I am fine," she smiled at her mother.

"Are you happy?" her mother whispered.

"Yes, Ma," Avni replied.

"Hi," Kanchan said, "Do you mind?" she asked as she sat down.

"No, no not at all, *beta,* go ahead, I will just come," Mrs. Sharma replied smiling at Avni.

"So how are you feeling, Avni?" Kanchan asked smiling at her.

"I am feeling... nice," Avni said looking down.

"I know you are very nervous, Avni, but you don't have to be. We are so happy, I am so happy to get a sister-in-law like you," Kanchan said.

"Thanks," Avni said as she looked up at Kanchan and saw her face smiling right at her.

"Guys, lunch is served," Priya came in, "Shall we?" she said looking at Avni and Ansh.

As Avni and Ansh sat by the table with their plates, everyone stood around them looking, waiting to catch each and every word exchanged between them.

Avni decided to look down at her plate and eat quietly.

"Avni, aren't you going to say anything?" Meghna started.

Avni looked up and tried shushing her Bhabhi.

"Oh come on, Ansh, why don't you say something?" Bhavya asked.

Oh dear, Avni thought, *it was great pulling someone's leg, but when you were on the receiving end it felt horrible.*

Avni and Ansh finished their lunch with great difficulty. It took them almost an hour, for every five minutes one of Avni's cousins kept butting in. When all her cousins finally left them to eat in peace, Avni was relieved.

Moments later, Kitty came over, "Avni, come with me, they are about to leave."

"Leave?" Avni asked.

"Yes, my darling sister, how I understand you want Ansh to stay on for longer. So, before they do we thought..."

"What?" Ansh cut in.

"Hi, Ansh, you guys sit and talk for a while before it's time for him to go, okay," Meghna said as she came in, "take him inside, Avni," she said pointing to Avni's bedroom.

Avni looked at her both her *bhabhis* and her cousins standing, "No, it's fine we will talk here."

"Avni, we were just having some fun, which we are entitled to, isn't it, Ansh?" Monu Bhaiya said as he patted Ansh's shoulder.

"Oh sure," Ansh said looking at her cousins.

"So, we aren't that bad. Now go before it's time for you to leave,

Ansh," Meghna said pulling Avni up and pushing her to go into her room.

Avni gestured Ansh to follow her as she walked into her room. As Avni sat down by her bed, she smiled sheepishly at him.

"So, we are here finally," Avni looked up.

"Yes, I was surprised, when I heard you said yes," Ansh said.

"Yeah, I know, my mind was all over the place yesterday, I still don't know if I am thinking straight," Avni said.

"What?" Ansh said looking at Avni.

Avni just smiled to herself, shaking her head, she continued, "We still need time. I like your company, but this whole marriage thing, to get into that space I need time," she said looking at him.

"Yeah," Ansh said looking at Avni, "we both need time to get there, Avni and I am ready to give you all my time."

"This is weird, isn't it?" Avni asked looking at him.

"Not so much to me, but yes, it is a bit. I hope we cross that bridge soon," Ansh said.

"Me too," Avni said looking at him this time. Being in the hall surrounded by everyone made it easier for Avni to talk with him, but sitting in her room all alone… Avni's mind screamed out that she was now engaged to the man sitting beside her and for some reason a part of her was still fighting to accept this.

"Avni, look you don't have to look at me as your fiancé or your future husband or whatever, just treat me as your friend and that's all," Ansh said after a long silence between both of them.

"Yeah, that would be better, to start with," Avni said.

"I am sorry, guys, but that's all the time that you will get. Ansh has to leave now, Avni," Bhavya said as she walked in.

"Okay," both of them said as they walked out to the hall.

As Avni reached the hall, she saw all of them standing and bidding goodbye.

"Oh, here they are," Mrs. Sharma said looking at them.

As Avni walked past her sister, Priya whispered, "Avni, touch your in-laws feet, your sister and brother-in-law as well okay, go now!" Priya said as she pushed Avni forward.

Avni did as her sister said. She touched their feet, got their blessings and looked up to see Ansh was doing the same, only he had a longer line.

"So, we will take your leave now," Ansh's mother said folding her hands. "Avni, come, *beta*, let's go," she said jokingly.

Everybody laughed, Avni's uncle spoke up, "Not yet *ji,* not yet."

Avni also smiled looking down. Hoping that "not yet" was a long way off.

Avni dozed off right after the *roka,* it was more mentally exhausting for her. She was, however, rudely woken up by her sister.

"Avni," Priya screamed into Avni's ears. "Avni, wake up, it's Ansh on the phone," Priya screamed, shaking Avni.

"Hmm... what?" Avni mumbled with her eyes closed pulling the blanket over her face.

Priya caught her blanket and pulled it down.

"Avni, it's Ansh. Get up. Ma, she is not getting up," Priya said calling out to Mrs. Sharma.

"Okay, okay, I am getting up," Avni said getting up. She stretched her arms. "Where is the phone?" Avni asked.

"Here," Priya handed her the phone placing it in her hand.

"Hello," Avni said rubbing her eyes.

"Hi, Avni, how are you?" Ansh said on the other end.

Avni finally sat upright and spoke.

"Hi, I am fine."

As Avni looked up she saw Priya and her mother were sitting right beside her with a funny look on their face, waiting to know what they were talking about. This made Avni completely conscious so she decided to converse with as few words as possible.

"So, I was wondering, if we could meet up tomorrow?" Ansh asked.

"Yes, okay," Avni replied.

"You want to go see a movie or something?" he asked.

"Okay," Avni replied.

There was a silence for about two seconds from his side before he asked.

"Are you okay?"

"Yes," Avni said looking up at the two of them, who were now trying hard to figure out what they were talking about.

"Hmm okay, so we could have lunch at The Leela and then we can decide," Ansh said.

"Yes, that would be great," Avni replied.

"Umm... about 12:30, would that be fine? I will pick you up then," Ansh said.

"Yes, okay, see you tomorrow, bye," Avni said as she kept the phone in a hurry.

"Oh God, Avni, he is your fiancé for God's sake, not some guy from a call centre. Where all you say is 'yes', 'okay'," Priya said imitating Avni.

"Di! Ma, look at her," Avni whined looking at her mother.

Mrs. Sharma who was more interested in her daughter's conversation with Ansh asked, "So?"

Avni looked at her mother for a moment. She had never seen her so excited, "Well, we are meeting tomorrow for lunch," Avni said looking down.

"Oh wonderful," Mrs. Sharma exclaimed as she ruffled Avni's hair and walked out.

"Great... where?" Priya asked.

"The Leela," Avni replied.

"Not bad, huh. The Leela and all for lunch," Priya added teasingly.

Avni looked up and gave her sister the look that said *I am so not in the mood for this now.*

"By the way, how does it feel, Avni, getting engaged?" Priya asked sitting beside her.

Avni looked at her, she opened her mouth to speak but stopped for she herself did not know how she felt. Reality had really stopped hitting her. Her engagement with Ansh had still not sunk in.

Avni felt very normal – she wasn't upset she was getting married nor was she happy or excited. She was just normal and that started bothering Avni. *Ansh was now her fiancé,* she kept telling herself, but her brain kept laughing it off like her engagement took place in an alternate reality.

"Avni?" Priya said as she held Avni's hands.

Avni had been staring at Priya for about ten minutes now, "Oh sorry, I am a little dazed," Avni said.

"Okay, you rest then, but first come and have some dinner then just sleep, you have a long day tomorrow," Priya said.

"Yeah indeed," Avni said thinking of her lunch date with Ansh the next day.

Chapter VIII

"Hey sorry, I will be ready in no time," Avni said talking on the phone and setting her hair at the same time looking into the mirror.

"Okay, not a problem, just give me your flat's address and I will be there," Ansh replied.

"Sure, just tell me where you are I will direct you," Avni said now looking around for her *kaajal*. "Hmmm... umm... okay, you take a right from the first signal you cross, dead end left, I will come down," Avni said.

Avni put the phone down in a hurry, made a quick calculation and realized Ansh would be here in fifteen minutes. She had enough time to get ready. For the first time Avni thought she would be ready in time.

"So, when is he coming?" Roshni asked.

"Well, he will be here any moment," Avni said looking at her watch and scanning her face in the mirror.

"Yes, you are looking absolutely fine," Roshni said from behind.

"He is here, I am going," Avni said looking at her cell flashing Ansh's name.

"Don't forget to bring him up once you guys come back, we have got to meet him before he leaves for Norway," Roshni called out as Avni rushed out of the house.

"Ya okay," Avni replied before closing the door behind them.

Avni closed her eyes and breathed heavily telling herself, *It's just a normal lunch, he is just a friend,* and with that thought she got out of the lift and walked towards Ansh.

Ansh was standing at the entrance of their building. As he saw Avni approaching he walked towards her smiling, "Hi, Avni."

"Hey," Avni smiled looking up at him. *Just a friend* she kept repeating in her mind to avoid any outburst.

"Shall we?" Ansh said as he opened the door of the car and gestured Avni to sit.

Avni sat inside and adjusted a bit to her side as Ansh sat beside her.

"So how are you doing today? Did you sleep well yesterday?" Ansh asked.

"Yeah," Avni said looking out of the window.

Avni kept looking at him from time to time to register in her mind that the guy sitting beside her was indeed her fiancé, but again for some funny reason her mind had become completely numb to any information relating to Avni's engagement. It refused to react to any information being fed when it came to Ansh. *Oh dear,* Avni thought as she breathed heavily.

"You alright, Avni?" Ansh asked.

"Yeah, I'm fine," Avni said and found herself staring at the red design on his T-shirt. She couldn't get herself to look at his face again.

"So, Delhi seems like quite a pleasant place. I haven't been here much," Ansh continued.

"Oh ya, it does. It's a very pleasant city," Avni said half smiling to herself. "But the traffic is really horrible," she said looking out at traffic. There were frustrated drivers in trucks, buses and cars honking and screaming at each other. "It just keeps getting worse every year," Avni continued.

"Hmm, ya... it's like how Bangalore is now too," Ansh replied.

"Auto rickshaws are even worse. These drivers. Oh God. They are so freaking stubborn," Avni said now looking at a lady arguing with an auto rickshaw driver yelling at him from the looks of it creating quite a scene on the road.

"You can't really blame the lady you know," Avni said as she saw Ansh looking at her side.

"Yeah, I know, I've gotten into quite a few of those with these guys," Ansh said.

"I used to have a tiff with them almost every day," Avni said looking at Ansh.

"Really how?" Ansh asked.

"Okay, so once when I was going to college," Avni started now shifting towards Ansh sitting more comfortably in the seat. Avni had once again let her guard down in front of Ansh and spoke to him just like an old friend would.

"So, you know any place we could go shopping?" Ansh asked once Avni's jabbering finally ended.

"Shopping, loads. But what do you have to buy?" Avni asked.

"Just something for my family and some friends back in Norway," Ansh replied.

"Okay, there's CP, it's the closest. We could go there. I am sure you will get something there," Avni continued.

He just nodded at her.

As the driver halted the car, Avni got out and walked towards the entrance.

"So, what do you want to buy? There is so much over here," Avni continued as she opened her bag to be checked by the guards.

"Okay, which is the shop you like the best?" Ansh asked.

"Umm," Avni looked at him. She was not very sure if they were here for her shopping or for his family and friends. If they were here for her shopping, it could be very odd if they ended up buying something expensive.

So, she kept in mind not to mention any super exclusive store, the safest name she could think of was, "Any... umm... Shopper's Stop," Avni said pointing out in front and walking towards the store.

"Okay, Shopper's Stop is cool," Ansh said walking behind Avni.

As they entered the store, the aroma of the perfume store hit Avni.

"God... that's why I love walking into stores like these," she said sniffing in every kind of smell that came her way.

"Perfume section. Okay, we will go here first," Ansh said walking towards the perfume counter.

Avni followed him, "Who do you want to get perfume for?" Avni asked thinking hard who could it be.

"Which brand?" he asked looking around.

Avni looked at him again, she so wanted to ask is it me you are buying for but what if he wasn't. It would end up being quite awkward for both of them.

"Umm, Burberry. I like this and Nina Ricci, Gucci is nice too," Avni said looking around.

"Hmm, okay we will start with Burberry," Ansh said looking around for Burberry. "There, come," he said.

After twenty minutes of sniffing twenty odd perfume bottles, also taking in large amounts of the coffee beans smell, for Avni very obviously kept losing her sense of smell every now and then, they finally narrowed down to two.

"Okay, so are you sure?" Ansh asked.

"Pretty much," Avni said looking at the two bottles.

She couldn't get through smelling even one more perfume. They had all started smelling the same to her.

"Okay. Could you get these two packed?" Ansh said smiling at the lady who assisted Avni.

"Who are they for?" Avni asked finally.

Ansh looked at her and smiled, "Well, that's for you."

"Wha..." just what Avni had dreaded. "I thought it was for your family," Avni said.

"Well I assumed if I told you it's for you, you wouldn't have gone through so much pain in selecting the perfume you really liked," Ansh said looking at Avni.

"Ohh, thanks. Ansh, that's really too much, but thanks," Avni said smiling.

She looked at the gift and said to herself, *this is from your fiancé.*

She kept saying thanks to him all the way back to the car and till the hotel, for every time she said thanks she felt a little less guilty. It also made her talk a lot more to him.

"Sir," the driver said.

Avni, in all her chattering, did not realize that they were at the entrance of The Leela already.

"Oh, okay," Avni said as she got out looking at an elderly man dressed traditionally who was holding the car door open. Avni and Ansh walked towards the dining hall. Avni was walking normally besides Ansh and was talking to Ansh quite chirpily about the disco she had been to quite a few times in her college days. They were soon given their table outside.

"Thanks, this is nice," Avni said sitting down as the lady pulled out the chair for her.

"I am glad you like it," Ansh said looking at Avni.

Avni looked at him and saw him smiling right at her, this made her nervous and she looked down again.

"Sir, drink?" a waiter came over.

"Ummm, red wine," Avni blurted before she could stop herself. She had forgotten she had lied to Ansh about not drinking.

"Okay. One red wine for the lady. Any..." Ansh said casually looking at Avni.

"I am sorry. I should have told you," Avni said looking down feeling guilty for not telling him before.

"It's okay. Please. I don't mind," he said, "it's okay."

There were so many things she wanted to tell him, but if Avni blurted out all of them. She remembered her sister saying, "Avni, no matter what. You should tell your fiancé about your past, not with all the details, but he needs to know."

Probably this is not the time, Avni said to herself, smiling at Ansh.

Shopping in a mall with hundreds of people around was quite normal but sitting alone with him for lunch made Avni a little conscious.

Reading into Avni's silence, Ansh said, "We don't have to treat this as a date, you know," smiling at her.

"I don't know what to make out of this anymore," Avni said shifting in her seat, "this is..."

"All so sudden," Ansh finished, "yes, I know."

Avni smiled. She shifted her gaze unknowingly towards the dessert section.

"You like something there?" Ansh asked.

"No. Yes, I like chocolate mousse a lot," Avni said nonchalantly still looking at the dessert section.

"Hmmm," Ansh replied.

They had a pleasant lunch talking about general things here and there. Shared a few laughs over how nervous they were yesterday.

"I blanked out for a while," Ansh said.

"You did!" Avni said cutting in again, "Me too and not for a while, most of the time. I was so zapped," Avni stopped as the waitress bought a chocolate mousse cake.

"For you, Ma'am. Hope you are enjoying your lunch."

"Yes," Avni said looking down at the cake, "thanks."

"So, here is your cake," Ansh said handing Avni the knife to cut the cake.

"Oh my. Thank you so much," Avni said taking the knife. *That was very sweet of him.* So, yes Avni was smiling, as she took a piece of the cake on her plate.

"Thanks," Avni said again eating the cake.

"I am guessing it's good enough," Ansh said looking amused at Avni devouring the cake.

"Oh, I am so sorry," Avni said feeling stupid for just serving herself with the cake and eating. "I didn't realize..."

"It's okay. I was just kidding," Ansh said as he took the knife from the table and served himself. "So umm. You want to take a walk or something around here?" Ansh asked Avni who was still busy looking at the cake she was eating.

"Okay," Avni said looking up. "I am sorry, old habit, I can't seem to look up when I am eating," Avni said. "Actually, there is this bowling alley over here. We could go there if you like," Avni said.

"Okay. Bowling it is then. Just give me a few seconds. I will be back in just a minute," Ansh said as he got up and walked inside.

Avni sat there looking at him till she lost sight of him.

That is my fiancé, she repeated in her head. No reaction. *Oh God! I am engaged. He is my fiancé. The only guy I will ever be with.*

Nothing.

Have you gone deaf inside? Avni shouted in her head. She pinched herself real hard, "ow," she screamed. No, she was definitely not dreaming, nor was she in any alternate reality. It was very much happening to her. She did get engaged and she was out on a date with her fiancé – someone she hardly knew and was meeting for just the fifth time. The most disturbing part for Avni was that her mind and body had gone numb to this fact.

"Shall we go, Avni?" Ansh walked in.

"Yeah okay," Avni said walking inside with him.

As they passed the desk, the receptionist bid them goodbye, "Have a nice day."

Avni smiled back at the receptionist and a couple of other waitresses who stood there giving Avni envious glances. She wondered why it was, did they know they were engaged how could they she didn't have any ring yet.

Was it written over their faces? Was it so obvious?

"The bowling alley is this side, right?" Ansh asked.

"Yes, it's down and to the right," Avni said looking around, "Okay, there are the stairs," Avni said. "Oh dear. We will have to wait," Avni said as they walked in.

"No problem. We will sit here till then," Ansh said pointing towards a lounge at the side. "I will go put our names down," he said walking away.

"Yeah, okay," Avni said sitting down by the couch in the lounge.

As Avni sat down, all of a sudden, it was like Avni's mind had been switched on from nowhere Avni's mind started buzzing with thousands of thoughts. All that she had been repeating to herself exploded in her head screaming real loud, wanting Avni to do something about it.

She looked around to find Ansh; instead her eyes fell on a bunch of college kids by the bowling alley. They were laughing over something and seemed to be having a great time.

You will never have that again, Avni. Going out with a bunch of friends, having fun all day, doing crazy stuff, a voice inside her said. *It's all gone, Avni,"* Avni sat up straight to shake off that thought but she couldn't help looking at them.

Lucky them, came the voice again, *not engaged, nowhere near being married. No pressure. All you will do after marriage is be clad in a sari and sit in one corner without making any noise."*

Of course not, Avni said fighting her inner voice. *I am going to have a good time.*

But Ansh is the serious kinds, argued her inner voice. *You think he will ever go out and scream around and have fun like you do. Welcome to the adult world, Avni. There will be questions about everything now. Where you are going? Who are you with? You think you would be able to wear whatever you want or behave however you want to?*

Avni tried shsshing the voice inside her which didn't budge.

"Okay. They said it will take twenty minutes. That should be fine," Ansh said as he sat beside Avni.

Avni looked at him so scared like she had seen a ghost.

This is the guy you are going to get married to. What do you feel towards him... do you love him? No! And you are getting married to him, laughed a voice inside Avni.

"Avni, are you alright?" he asked looking at her.

Ansh had suddenly lost all his charm. He did not look even a teeny bit pleasant to Avni. She was engaged to him, now he was just a guy who stood between her independence, her life, her friends, her fun everything. All of it had started hitting her finally, and so hard she couldn't take it anymore. Before Avni knew it tears dropped from her eyes.

"Avni, oh my God. What happened?" Ansh asked sounding tensed, "Did I do something?"

Avni looked away. *She was engaged. Oh God! To a guy she hardly knew. Forget about liking him. She was still getting to know him.*

"Excuse me, I have to go," Avni said as she got up and walked away as fast as she could towards the washroom. The moment she entered the washroom, she rummaged her purse to find her cell. She dialled Priya's number. It began to ring.

"Hello."

"Di," Avni said sobbing.

"Avni… what happened?" Priya asked.

"Di, I can't get married. No, Di, I can't do this," Avni cried.

"Okay, Avni, what happened? What went wrong?" Priya asked.

"Nothing. It's my mistake. I was wrong. I made the decision too soon. I am sorry… I can't get married," Avni said sobbing.

"Avni, first of all stop crying, please, where are you?" Priya asked.

"In the restroom... at The Leela," Avni said.

"Oh, dear God, okay, calm down," Priya said.

"Ya okay," Avni replied trying to control her sobbing.

"Now, Avni, what happened? Did he say something," Priya asked calmly.

"No, Di, he didn't. He didn't do anything. I made the wrong choice and now I don't know what to do," Avni said as she held her head.

"Okay, Avni. No problem. Avni, listen to me. Take your time, give yourself some more time. Trust Di okay, if you are still not ready, I am there okay, I won't let you sit for the *pheras* till the time you are ready," Priya said weighing every word.

"I don't think I am ready," Avni said.

"Avni, I promise. Give me fifteen days. Let me come back from my office trip," Priya said

"Oh, you are on your way," Avni said calming down a bit.

"Ya, I am at the airport. Let me come back. We will sort this out. You trust Di, nah?" Priya said.

"Yeah," Avni replied, "What do I do now?"

"Avni, go to him now please, he must be worrying over where you went. Does he know you are crying?" Priya asked.

"No, he doesn't," Avni lied biting her lip.

"Okay, then go and trust Di. I will make it alright," Priya said.

"Ya," Avni replied. She cut the call, washed her face, put her smile back on her face and walked towards where Ansh was waiting for her.

As she walked towards the couch Ansh was sitting on, guilt struck her when she saw him with his head in his hands. She knew deep down that whatever was happening with her, he was nowhere at fault, but unknowingly he was still standing in the way.

"Hey," Avni said sheepishly as she sat down beside Ansh.

He looked up at Avni, "Are you alright?" he asked looking worried.

"Ya," Avni nodded looking away.

"Avni, can I ask you something?" Ansh asked looking at her.

Avni nodded still looking away.

"Was it entirely your decision?" he asked.

Avni looked at him. His face looked so worried.

"I just want to know, Avni. Was it your decision?" he asked again.

"Yes, it was my decision," Avni replied looking down.

"You were not forced?" Ansh asked.

"No," Avni said knowing that no one had forced her into this. It was entirely her decision and still it all seemed so wrong. "I just got bit nervous, I am sorry for this," Avni said looking at him to help him get over his worries.

"Are you sure, Avni? Look, I don't want you doing under any kind of pressure," Ansh said.

"No, it's all good, umm can we get out. I don't feel so good," Avni continued.

"Okay, Avni... you know if you want to go back home, I can drop you back, no issues at all," he said.

Avni did want to go back home that very instance, but then she looked at him. It would look rude on her part to leave. So she decided to stay a little longer, "No, it's okay. I will stay."

"Avni. Are you sure you are okay?" Ansh asked scanning Avni's face again.

"Ya, please. Don't worry. I just got worked up a bit," Avni said looking down.

"Please don't be, Avni. Okay… where next?" he asked.

"I don't know," Avni said. Nothing came to her mind except going home which she couldn't do. "We could go for a drive," Avni said finally.

"Okay, cool," Ansh said as he got up to call the driver.

She checked the time. It was going to be 4. *Just another hour,* Avni thought, *then I would get back home.*

"The driver will be out any moment, shall we proceed?" Ansh asked.

"Yeah okay," Avni said as she picked up her purse.

"Actually, Mom told me I have to buy you a sari," Ansh said as they got into the car.

"Okay," Avni said as she adjusted herself in the car.

The drive was probably the most awkward drive Avni ever had. She kept looking out most of the time every time she looked at Ansh. She saw him looking right at her smiling. After a while he asked once more.

"Avni, are you fine?" he looked worried.

Avni did not know what to say to Ansh anymore. She felt horribly guilty about acting like that. Her engagement had hit her not softly or lightly, but like a firing bullet at her face. All this while she thought she had control over this whole thing. That no matter what she could sway away from her marriage, enjoy her life till she could but now it was completely out of control. She was engaged! And every time she went over it she couldn't figure what made her come so far. It was an impulsive decision, she made at the spur of the moment.

Why? she wondered again.

"I am sorry. Just got lost in my thoughts," she replied waving her hand in the air. "I am fine, trust me."

"Okay," Ansh replied not looking very convinced, "Lot of traffic out here. It will take us ages to reach there. Do you know any place nearby?" Ansh asked.

"Well. There is one on the way," Avni said thinking she did not need another sari.

"Okay," Ansh looked ahead, "Driver, Sarojini Nagar. We need to go there. How long would it take?"

"*Sirji*, about twenty minutes with this traffic," the driver replied looking back.

Ansh looked at Avni for approval. Avni merely shrugged and turned away.

"Okay, take us to Sarojini Nagar," Ansh said.

"Ummm, so what kind of movies do you like?" Ansh said after a long silence to start some kind of conversation.

Avni felt she should really give him a break and not make it any harder on him so she replied, "Umm, any kind, not horror though. I am terrified of them."

Ansh giggled to himself and for some odd reason Avni liked that sound.

"Hmm, so you are terrified of scary movies. So which ones are you terrified of?" Ansh asked.

"Mostly *Exorcist*. Especially those stairs, they horrify me," Avni said looking scared just thinking of that scene.

"Yeah, that was very scary and umm *Grudge*," Ansh said, "*The Burp,*" Ansh said looking at Avni.

"Don't remind me. I couldn't sleep for days together," Avni said closing her eyes.

"*Paranormal Activity,*" Ansh went on.

"No, I haven't seen that because it's so scary and the worst part it's true," Avni said looking at Ansh.

"No, it's not. It's said that it's true, that's why so many people watched it," Ansh said.

"No. It's true. It happened," Avni replying sounding very sure.

"And you were there watching her get pulled out of her bed? How do you know?" Ansh asked.

"Pulled out of bed! Did someone get pulled out of bed? No, of course not, I wasn't there... okay," Avni thought for a moment, "it's not really true. I mean it's fake," Avni asked looking at Ansh.

"Of course, it's fake. I meant it's just fiction. So, you wouldn't mind watching it now?" Ansh asked.

"No. Someone getting pulled out of bed, I wouldn't be able to sleep on my bed. What if I get pulled out of it?" Avni replied clearly alarmed.

Ansh giggled again. "You have a funny imagination," he said.

"You have no idea," Avni replied shaking her head.

Avni suddenly stopped and looked at him again. This short conversation had made her forget what was boggling her so much ten minutes back.

I am engaged to him. This time she didn't flip out.

"*Sirji,* we are here. Where to go?" the driver asked.

"Umm... *accha,* tell me any shop where we can get saris?" Ansh asked.

"There is one Mysore Silk Udyog around the corner," the driver replied.

"Okay... umm, is that fine?" Ansh asked looking at Avni.

"Anything is fine by me," Avni said shrugging her shoulders. She never shopped for saris before so she was fine with any shop.

After about an hour or so Avni walked out of the shop with a beautiful silk sari. It was black with a maroon border and *pallu*, she decided it on after trying on a dozen of them.

"So now... home?" Ansh said looking at Avni.

"Yeah, home," Avni said shrugging.

"Okay cool," Ansh replied opening the car door for Avni.

As they reached Avni's home, she tried to grab the cake, her purse and the gifts for about five minutes when finally Ansh agreed to help her carry them up to her apartment.

"Thanks," Avni said for the third time as they walked out of the lift on to her apartment floor.

"Uh, I will just ring and check," Avni went on, she had to see if her roomies were in a state to welcome guests or even if her house was in a state. "Yeah hi, I am outside the door. Ansh is with me. Is it cool for us to come in?" Avni asked over the phone.

"You are kidding us, right? We have been waiting for him since morning and the house never looked better," Kriti replied.

"Okay," Avni said as she kept the phone. She looked at Ansh. "Okay, come in," she said as she unlocked her apartment door.

The moment Avni walked in she realized Kriti really wasn't joking. The apartment had never looked better. Both Roshni and Kriti were sitting standing by the table wearing a smile Avni had definitely never seen before.

"Guys..." Avni started.

"Hi, Ansh," Roshni moved forward with her hand held out. "I am Roshni. So nice to meet you."

"Yeah same here," Kriti too moved forward and literally stumbled in excitement, "Whoops... sorry," she continued, "I am Kriti."

"Hey," Ansh replied shaking both their hands after depositing Avni's gifts on the table.

"Ooh gifts," Kriti said, "nice," she said looking from Ansh to Avni.

Avni closed her eyes. As if what happened wasn't enough.

Ansh kept the cake by the table. Kriti continued, "And cake... cool," she said smiling even wider now.

"Kriti!!" Avni said giving her the look to shut up.

"Oh come on, Avni, such a whiner you are," Kriti continued as she turned toward Ansh, "Sit, please, it's your home."

As Ansh sat on the bean bag. Kriti dragged another bean bag and sat beside him, "So, how are you liking it?"

Ansh looked at her and then at Avni for a second, "Yeah, umm liking all of this very much," he replied.

"Would you like some?" Roshni said as she held a glass of lime juice.

"Yeah, thanks," Ansh said looking at Roshni.

Roshni too sat beside him looking at him to say something.

Ansh looked at Avni again as if asking for help.

"Okay guys, that's enough. Ansh, don't you have to go? It's getting late," Avni said looking at Ansh.

"Yeah," Ansh said looking at his watch. "It's actually quite late. So umm, I guess I will make a move," he said looking at Roshni and Kriti.

"Ya cool," they both said in unison.

"Okay," Ansh said getting up, "Bye, it was nice meeting you both."

He then walked towards Avni, "It was really nice today. Hope you enjoyed it too," Ansh said looking at Avni.

"Yes. I umm… enjoyed, today was nice," Avni finally said.

"Okay, then hope you enjoy the cake," he said looking at the box by the table.

"Sure. Thanks," Avni replied.

"Please, Avni, no thanks," Ansh said as he walked out.

"Yeah, bye, take care," Avni said, "By the way what time do you leave tomorrow?"

"My flight's at 1 p.m. to Mumbai. I will drop by tomorrow morning before you go to office, if you don't mind," Ansh said.

"Yeah, no. I don't mind. Sure, bye," Avni replied as she closed the door behind him.

As she turned around she saw her two roomies standing right by the door with the silliest smiles on their face.

"Oh, please guys you can really wipe those stupid smiles off your faces," Avni said as she walked into her room to change.

They came running behind her smiling even more than ever, "So..."

"So?" Avni looked back shrugging.

"Oh come on, Avni," Roshni rolled her eyes as she held Avni's hand and dragged her on to the bed to sit. "You know what we are talking about. How was it?"

Avni got up from her bed and walked towards the cupboard, "Well, it was nice," she looked back realizing this didn't satisfy her roomies one bit she continued, "Okay, it was fun, we went shopping and then had lunch, it was nice. Oh come on, what else do you want to know."

"Like did you guys hold hands? Hug or kiss?" Kriti asked with her voice really shrill.

"No!" Avni retorted, throwing the T-shirt she had decided to wear towards Kriti, "None of that happened okay, it was a normal day,"

"Oh blah," Kriti said as she walked out of the room.

"I don't believe you," Avni said.

"Well, I expected something, you guys are engaged. What's the deal?" Kriti said looking at Avni.

"No deal, I just need time. This whole thing still freaks me out. I can't imagine I am actually engaged," Avni said going through her cupboard.

"Hope you won't walk up to your *pheras* and say it's freaking me out," Roshni said imitating Avni.

"Yeah right," Avni said rolling her eyes hoping by then she would have found some kind of an acceptance. This weekend had seemed so long that her office seemed to be something in a far-off island.

Chapter IX

The next morning, as Avni was getting ready, she kept mumbling to herself.

"Hey guys, I am engaged." "Guys, I have some news." "Guess what? Ughhh," Avni went on. Now how does one break their engagement news in their office. *I will just say whatever comes to my mind at that moment.*

"Okay guys, how would you break the news in the office if one of you got engaged?" Avni asked as she walked out to the hall.

"Umm, hey I am engaged," Kriti said after giving Avni's question a serious thought.

"Yeah, thanks," Avni replied sarcastically, "Couldn't have come up with that one by myself."

"Mail all of them, easier than saying it," Roshni interrupted as she walked into the hall.

"Hmmm, not bad, I could mail all of them," Avni said staring into the space. "I am engaged. Jeez, can you guys believe it? Because I really can't!" Avni said shaking her head.

Kriti smiled, "So can't we, but someone's going to get married!"

"Oh my," Avni thought looking at Kriti.

"By the way how come you are ready so early," Roshni said checking her office purse.

"Ansh is leaving today so before going to the airport, he is just going to swing by," Avni said looking at the watch, "He should be here any minute."

"Nice, how is it not romantic for you yet?" Kriti asked.

"I don't know and you know that is exactly what's troubling me. All of this is supposed to feel nice and romantic, right?" Avni asked.

"Don't worry, it all will very soon," Roshni said walking out, "anyways guys gotta go, bye."

"Yeah bye," Avni replied looking down at her watch again, when her cell rang. "Ooh, he is here," Avni said as she got up.

"Enjoy," Kriti said from behind.

"I will get the lift," Roshni said as they walked out.

"Open, open," Avni said as the lift reached the ground floor.

Roshni smiled at her.

"What?" Avni said.

"Nothing," Roshni said as she shook her head. "Hi, Ansh," Roshni said as she saw him standing at the apartment gate.

"Hey, how are you?" Ansh said as he stood up straight watching them both.

"I am good, sorry I have got to go, but hope to see you soon, have safe flight, bye," Roshni said as she half hugged him and left, "Bye, Avni," she called out as she left.

"Bye," Avni replied, she then looked at Ansh.

"Hey," Ansh said looking at her.

Avni smiled.

"So, umm did you sleep well?" Ansh asked.

"Yeah I did," Avni said looking down.

"I got something for you," Ansh said as he looked at Avni.

"For me? You already got so much for me," Avni was surprised, feeling bad for accepting so much from him at once.

He smiled excitedly as he got into the car and came out with a package.

"Oh my," Avni said looking at it, wondering what it was this time.

As he put it in Avni's hand, "Something you wanted," Ansh said.

There are so many things Avni wanted she thought as she opened the package. Avni ripped off the wrapping slowly till she could see the contents. Avni's eyes widened in amazement.

"Oh my God," Avni said as she kept looking between the package and Ansh.

"You like it?" Ansh asked.

Avni ripped it open in no time. It was an iPhone.

"Oh my God. You didn't have to," Avni said opening the box.

"Of course, I did. I know you wanted it," Ansh said.

"I did, but I was just mentioning it casually to you. Oh my God. This is too much," Avni said looking up, "I… I can't accept this."

"Avni, please," Ansh said holding her hands.

Avni smiled, looking down at her new phone, her hands were now trembling beneath it. She had turned completely red. Avni had never felt so flattered before. It was too much for her to accept.

"I can't, Ansh, this is too much," Avni said.

"Avni, please, if you even take me as a friend, you will accept it," Ansh replied.

"I don't know, Ansh," Avni said looking at him, "You already got me so much and now this, it's a little too much for me. I was saving up for this anyway."

"I know, you told me, look you can use those savings for something else you need," Ansh said, "please keep this," Ansh insisted.

She took a deep breath and kept the box on top of the car.

"I... uhh... um. Can I hug you?" Avni asked shyly. She was so overwhelmed. It just came out of her mouth before she knew it.

"Sure," Ansh said and held Avni lightly for a second.

In that one second, Avni wished she could just stay there forever. *Was it happening? Did she start liking him? Or she was just happy because she was gifted an iPhone? Was she just being selfish or did she genuinely start feeling something towards him?*

She really didn't know yet, but yes she did feel she could stay like that for a long time.

"I have got to go," Ansh said looking at Avni. He was smiling like never before. "I will see you soon for sure, take good care of yourself and enjoy your new phone," Ansh said as he got inside the car.

Avni nodded and smiled, "You have a safe flight and take care."

She stood there looking at the gift; *this was completely unexpected,* she thought. She took a deep breath and walked back into her apartment as her cab was still a while away.

Avni kept looking at her iPhone and didn't realize when she walked into her office building and towards her desk.

"Hey, Avni," Sunaina said as Avni walked towards her desk. "Where were you Saturday night? We had a team dinner."

Whoops, Avni thought. She had completely forgotten about that. Anyways how could she have remembered? She had got engaged the same day!

"Yeah," Avni said rubbing her forehead, "Something important had come up that day."

"Really like what? A date," Sunaina jeered.

"Nope... I... umm... okay, I got engaged," Avni replied.

"Oh yeah right, you got engaged, good one," Sunaina said waving the pencil at her.

"No... seriously, I am engaged," Avni said looking at Sunaina.

Sunaina looked at Avni laughing, "Really, you expect me to buy…" she stopped halfway when she realized Avni was indeed serious.

She got up from her chair, "Oh my God. You aren't kidding," Sunaina said raising her voice with every word. She hugged Avni. "When, what, how? When? All of a sudden! How?" Sunaina asked looking at Avni.

Avni laughed, "I will tell you all about it."

"Ya, you better. I need to know," Sunaina said. She looked around.

"Guys," she screamed, "Avni's engaged," holding Avni's hands.

"Sunaina, what..." Avni started.

"Oh come on, everybody will know sooner or later. We so need a treat from you," Sunaina said excitedly.

"Yeah," Avni said smiling at her colleagues who were mouthing congratulations to her.

"Oh my God, this is big," Sunaina went on. She then shifted her gaze to Avni's hands. "Where's the ring?" she said looking up.

"Oh no, it was just a *roka*. Ring ceremony will be later on," Avni said rubbing her ring finger.

The entire day whoever came to their bay stopped to congratulate Avni. Avni was embarrassed shaking hands with random people and saying thank you. Her cell buzzed with a name she would now be seeing quite often on her cell's screen.

"Hello. Hi Ansh, yeah okay, that's great. When is your flight from Mumbai? Okay great, yeah. A bit busy, no that's okay. Ya okay, sure call me once you leave. Okay, take care bye," Avni said as she kept her phone.

"Umm," Sunaina cleared her throat looking at Avni

"What?" Avni asked widening her eyes.

"Nothing," Sunaina said returning to her work. After a while, Sunaina looked up, "Oh come on. You can tell me at least. When are you getting married?"

"I don't know. It's not fixed yet, but yeah not anytime soon which I am very sure of," Avni said hoping it really would not be anytime soon.

She kept saying the same to everyone possible over the next few days. She even told Ria about it.

"Ria I swear, I am so not getting married this year," Avni said.

She argued with her mom, "Mom please, I don't care what the pandit*ji* says, you will tell him to pick a date for next year."

"What if Ansh and I had met next year. Ma, no I have told everyone I am not getting married anytime soon because I am still need time to know him. No... okay, ya... bye," Avni would keep the phone and frown for hours.

She tried talking over the phone to her father over the next couple of days.

"Papa. Please tell Mamma. I am getting so worked up here. Ya okay, I will calm down. He is nice. No, he doesn't have a bad temper. No, he hasn't said anything to me. No, Papa, he doesn't have anyone else in his life. He is nice," Avni paused, "I need time. I know I said yes. I still need to know him. Papa, I still don't know him. It's so scary to think I will be marrying someone I don't even know yet. Okay. I know it will take time. Okay, bye," Avni would then frown again knowing talking to her father was in vain.

She thought talking to Ansh would help.

"You know, Ansh. I really hope we have a long courtship period. It will be so much better for us you know at least till next year," Avni would say. "Yeah, you think so too. Great," Avni would reply sighing a relief, not realizing only Ansh would agree to whatever she said, but unfortunately it wasn't entirely in his hands to decide the date.

God, I swear I won't ask anything more, somehow make me fall in love with Ansh. Oh God, I am still not in love with him, Avni would worry, *or please delay the wedding date.*

No matter how much she tried convincing everyone all of it went in vain and Avni realized that when her mother called her weeks later, one dreadful morning when she was in office.

"Hello. Oh my God, okay they are out," Avni said straightening up as if her board results were just announced. She took a deep breath.

"Okay, I am ready tell me. What? No... no... not that one... next... oh," Avni voice dipped with every word. She held her head, "So December 12 it is huh, Ma," Avni whined.

"Oh come on, Avni, stop whining, what is wrong with you? It's almost like the end of the year. Now call up Ansh and tell him," Avni's mom said as she kept the phone.

"December 12," Avni repeated.

Oh my, I am getting married, and I am not excited one bit. Great! Avni said to herself.

Why was she supposed to call Ansh? Wouldn't he know by now? Avni thought looking at the phone. She juggled it for a while and dialled his number.

"Hi," Avni said.

"Hey. I heard about the dates, too bad it had to be this year," Ansh said trying very hard to hide his excitement.

"Yeah, so," Avni said dully.

"Ummm, we will have to start thinking about your visa and how to get you here by next year," Ansh said.

"Ansh," Avni said and then stopped.

"Yeah, Avni, anything wrong?" Ansh asked.

"I don't know. It's all going too fast. I hardly know you. We have just been talking on the phone for a month," Avni said thinking. She couldn't even remember his face.

"I know but it's still a good five months to go. We have a lot of time. Avni, whatever it is that you want to know. I am an open book. I will give you all the time in the world," Ansh said.

"It's not that, Ansh. We talk a lot on phone and it's great but I just hear your voice every day. I don't see you in front of me. It's weird to think I am getting married to you in five months," Avni said.

After a long pause Ansh spoke, "You know you are right. We have just been talking on the phone. We hardly spent three days with each other before I had to go. We need to spend some time together. You are right," Ansh said.

Finally, he understood where Avni was going. She needed to spend time with him, probably this could help her feel towards him.

"You know, Avni, just give me a few minutes, I am going to call you back," Ansh said.

"Anything wrong?" Avni asked.

"No. Just a few minutes," he said and hung up.

Hopefully he is convincing his parents to postpone the dates a little.

After a few hours he called.

"Hey, what happened? You said you would call in five?" Avni asked.

"Sorry. I had to talk to my seniors regarding something. So here is the plan. I will be coming to Delhi for about two months. I will work from India, so in that time we will spend as much time as we can with each other. We will go around, get to know each other better. I am sure after that it won't feel like you are marrying a stranger," Ansh finished.

"Wow, really, I mean would that be okay for you?" Avni asked.

"Of course, it's fine. Don't worry about all that. It's been taken care of," Ansh said.

"That's great then I mean, Ansh, thanks. That's great and you are not a stranger to me now. Just that we still have to get to know each other," Avni said.

"Yes, I know so you can start making a list of places you want to show me around," Ansh said.

"Yeah, there are loads of places I can take you around here," Avni said lightning up.

"Okay, so I will book my tickets and will call you in the night, okay," Ansh said.

"Ya, okay bye," Avni ended the call with a smile on her face.

Just as she was getting back to her work, her cellphone buzzed again. She had a message from an unknown number. Wondering who it could be, she read the message – "*Hi, Avni, I just heard about your engagement. I see you have finally moved on. Anyways just wanted to congratulate you. Hope everything else is well on your end. Sidharth."*

Avni just stared at her phone, she kept looking at his name, a name she had loved watching pop up on her phone once, a name she had written a million times with hers in random books and papers. Today that same name stung her so hard, she could still feel the sting in her heart.

Her eyes blurred for a moment. *No Avni,* she thought to herself, *You are over this chapter, he cannot and will not affect you anymore,* she said to herself as she pressed her eyes shut and opened them again sitting up straight in her chair. Life was full of such irony, he was congratulating her on her engagement, when they had spoken about theirs own a million times before.

"You know what I would like?" Avni had said as she had rubbed her fingers sitting at a rooftop bar with Sidharth.

Sidharth had kept his beer down, he had wrapped his arms around

Avni, "I am all ears, what kind of ring would you like?"

"Umm, a diamond one of course," Avni had said smiling at him.

He smiled and nodded.

"White gold, I don't like yellow gold on engagement rings," Avni had said.

"Hmm... okay," he had said listening to her every word, "white gold, diamond ring it is, but hey if I get a little late don't you find someone else to put a ring on your finger," he had said holding Avni's face.

"Never, Sidharth, you and only you will put a ring on this finger," Avni had said looking at her fingers, as she hugged him.

A tear rolled down Avni's cheeks as she remembered that night. She looked at her ring finger, he had ruined it. He ruined everything. Why? Avni didn't know. For a long time she recalled all things he had said, all the things he had promised but she realized there was no point. He never meant any of it, even if he did, he was just someone who thought he needed more than one woman in his life.

Avni still remembered the dreadful day, she had realized he was cheating on her. She re-lived that night in her head.

"How could you?" Avni yelled with anger, as she threw the book lying beside her at him.

He ducked as the book came at him, "Avni, please just listen to me. It was just this one time. It was a mistake, I am sorry," Sidharth said.

"One time! One time!" Avni screamed, "These messages tell me something else," Avni said as she held his phone.

"Okay, probably not one time, it was..." Sidharth stopped, searching for words to save himself.

"Probably just a dozen more times," Avni said throwing his phone at him, "Thank God I did not have balance and chose to use your phone instead, but guess who messaged? You had plans tonight!" Avni screamed.

"I... no... I... Avni, look can we sit down for a second," Sidharth stammered.

"You were supposed to have your uncle over tonight, this is your uncle, Sidharth?" Avni yelled as she walked towards him. "I can kill you right now, what have you done, Sidharth," Avni screamed as she shook

him, "Do you even realize what you have done?"

"Avni, I am so sorry, please. It was an honest mistake," Sidharth said trying to hold her.

"No, Sidharth, this is not a mistake and I can't forgive you," Avni cried as she pushed him away.

"Avni…" Sidharth pleaded as he looked at her.

"It's over, Sidharth. Everything, I am done!" Avni said as she shook her head in tears.

"You are breaking up with me?" Sidharth asked as he just stared at her.

"Have you left me with an option?" Avni yelled as she looked up at him.

"We can get past this, Avni, let's talk this out," Sidharth said as reached for her.

"Past this?" Avni said as she picked up his phone, "No, because if we do, if not her someone else will come. It won't stop, Sidharth," Avni said looking at him.

"Avni, please, it will never happen again," Sidharth said.

"You were supposed to meet her tonight, isn't it?" Avni asked.

He just looked down.

"Answer me, Sidharth, was she supposed to come here tonight?" Avni asked looking around at his flat.

Sidharth stayed silent.

"You not saying anything has told me a thousand things, Sidharth," Avni said, "We are done, and since she will be here soon I guess I should leave," Avni said finally as she walked out.

As she thought of it all, she got up and walked out, she needed to breathe. She was over this, over him. Avni had never looked back after that day, no matter how much it hurt. She couldn't get herself to forgive him. No matter how much he tried, Avni didn't relent. She could have taken anything, but another woman was something she couldn't live with. She had left all of this way behind, then why the hell was it stinging her so bad again?

Ansh, Avni think of Ansh, Avni repeated to herself, *He is a nice guy.*

Sidharth was too, what if she fell in love with Ansh and he did the same? another voice within her instigated.

No, Avni, she argued in her head, *Ansh wouldn't do that.*

Even Sidharth wasn't like that. You never thought he would do that, she reasoned within herself.

No, I can't do this to myself and to Ansh, it's unfair, Avni shook her head and then held it in her hands. *I closed this chapter a long time ago, I can't let it ruin my present,*" Avni said decisively.

She had to let this baggage go to let Ansh in. She had to let go of this fear. *Not all guys are jerks, Avni, and definitely not Ansh,* she reassured herself as she looked at her finger, *he will put a ring on it because he will stay true to you.*

It was almost the end of the day, she took deep breaths, and walked back into her building to pick up her things and head home. When Avni got back home, she realized Kriti and Roshni were out grocery shopping, so she just sat by the TV and randomly switched channels till Ria called.

"Hi, Avni, I just heard from Priya Di about your wedding date. That's great, Avni. I am so happy," Ria stopped for a second and then continued, "I… oh… so, it's not next year but hey it's almost next year, I mean it's in December," Ria said trying to convince Avni.

"Yeah, I am sorry, I shouldn't be sounding sad about this," Avni said dully.

"That's okay, you will get used to it," Ria replied.

"Anyways, I think my mom and I will be going to different venues next week. You know book the garden and all that," Avni went on half-heartedly.

"Okay, that's nice. Hey, have you asked Ansh what kind of wedding he would like? You know it's his wedding too. You are going to choose the venue and all," Ria said.

"Yeah, I didn't. I should have," Avni said.

"Okay, then call him now, bye." Ria said.

"Ria…" Avni said as Ria was about to cut the call.

"Ya..." Ria replied.

"Sidharth messaged, congratulating me on my engagement," Avni said, closing her eyes.

"Really, how did he get your number?" Ria asked.

"No idea, I had changed it right after that and I don't know," Avni shrugged.

"Anyways, so what did you reply?" Ria asked.

"Just thanks," Avni said.

"Avni, are you sad hearing from him?" Ria asked.

"No, why would I be?" Avni said sounding defensive.

"Avni, I know you. I can make out from your voice. Look I know how much he hurt you but you have to stop letting him bother you now," Ria said.

"I know, exactly, I thought I had left this behind me and now I see his message and it screws my mood up. I hate it, Ria. I don't want to care, I hate it so much," Avni complained.

"Stop thinking about him, think of Ansh," Ria said.

"Yes, I know. Ansh is so nice, I don't want to think about this," Avni said.

"Then don't, stop doing this to yourself and go call Ansh," Ria said.

"Yeah, okay, see you, bye," Avni replied.

As she got off the phone with Ria, Avni called Ansh right away,

"Hi," Ansh said.

"Hey," Avni replied.

"So what kind of wedding do you want?" Avni asked, "I am going to choose the venue. You know these places get booked months in advance," she said.

"I always liked open garden weddings," Ansh replied "So anything would do as long as it's a nice garden," Ansh said.

"Okay, garden it is," Avni replied thinking it sounded so casual talking about their wedding venue.

There was no excitement in her; she was going through some kind of a routine drill. Talking to Ansh did take her mind off

Siddharth and eased her a bit. She knew she had to look forward, but probably she was pushing herself too hard.

Avni used to talk to Ansh till wee hours in the morning at times but she still felt nothing, like she was talking to a friend.

Why was she not feeling attracted to him yet? She still didn't feel the excitement one was supposed to feel. *She was engaged for crying out loud.* Avni knew that Ansh was sweet and way too decent and she didn't know why it bothered her at times. She had tried talking to her sister about it once when she was in office a few days later.

"You have a problem just because he is decent and doesn't want to have 'fun'? Marriage isn't only about fun. Let me tell you, missy, when you land in the slightest of trouble, a college cool boy is not going to stick around, but Ansh would, no matter what. Avni, please realize that, haven't you learnt enough already with what happened earlier," Priya said.

Avni sighed, "I know."

"Avni, please you have got to switch off your judgmental button. Stop judging him for every single thing. He is trying his best, isn't he?" Priya asked.

"Yeah he is. He really is trying his best," Avni said remembering how much he was.

"Then give him a chance, Avni. Start afresh. Accept him for whatever that he is. Trust me, you will start liking him soon enough," Priya continued. "Or if you can't like him, we will say no."

"I don't even know if I want to say no. I mean he is nice, there is nothing wrong with him. I will give this time. Ya, love you, bye," Avni said, feeling encouraged.

I'm probably just stressed about the whole thing, nothing else, Avni thought, as she logged off her computer and got ready to leave for the day. She was pondering over the whole thing while in the cab when suddenly,

"Avni."

"Huh?" Avni looked around.

"Where are you lost? Your home's here," her colleague, Naina, said making a gesture with her hand for Avni to get out.

"Oh yeah," Avni said trying to make sense of where she was. She used to be so lost in her thoughts lately, most of the time people had to jerk her back to reality. As she turned entered her building, her phone rang.

"Hey, Ansh, yeah right time. I just got off the cab."

"Sure. No problem, bye," Avni said as she kept the phone.

So, they were not going to have the usual "night talk" as Ansh had some dinner plans. Avni was too tired anyways. She hadn't been sleeping properly for days as she used to talk to Ansh till late in the night, trying to convince herself she was into him but in vain. She would finally get a full night's rest today.

"Hi guys," Avni said as she put her bag by the table half-yawning.

"Hey," they both said in unison.

"So, what's up with this show?" Avni asked as she sat down in front of the TV.

"No phone coming from Mr. Norway today," Kriti teased making a phone gesture with her hands.

"Nope. He has dinner plans," Avni said nonchalantly.

"Ooh. You should be careful," Roshni said from behind.

"Hahaha ya," Avni said.

"Don't let the flowers fool you," Roshni said.

"Ya, I won't, don't worry," Avni said smiling to herself.

She just couldn't imagine Ansh out with someone else. *What if he was,* she thought, *no Avni, I can't put him through that test because of my insecurities, he's too nice for that sort of a thing.*

"You know what guys. I guess I will go to sleep now. It's been a while since I got a good eight hours of sleep. Goodnight guys," Avni said as she got up and walked towards her room.

"Cool, goodnight," they said together.

Avni got up dazed. She thought she heard someone crying, now she wasn't sure if it was someone in her sleep. She rubbed her eyes and looked around. No noise. It was definitely a dream. Why was that woman crying all of a sudden? Avni was talking to her about the wedding preparations in Norway, and she just started sobbing out of nowhere; her dreams were definitely getting crazier by the day.

She checked her watch; there was still an hour for her alarm to ring. As she tried closing her eyes again, she heard sobs. She sprung right up and looked around.

"Roshni," she shouted from her room, after a few seconds Roshni walked in with concern written all over her face.

"Hey, what happened? I heard someone crying?" Avni asked.

"It's Kriti, now that you are up, you should come talk to her," Roshni said walking out of the room.

Avni got out her bed and followed Roshni out of the room towards the hall. She saw Kriti hiding her face in her hands.

"Kriti, what happened? Oh my God, your eyes are swollen. Are you alright?" Avni asked as she walked up to her.

She just shook her head and hid beneath her hands again. Avni looked at Roshni.

"You know about Arvind and Kriti," Roshni said shrugging her shoulders.

"You have been in a relationship for so long. What happened? I can't imagine Arvind doing anything," Avni said as she put her hands around Kriti.

"Oh, he didn't do anything. He is such a sweetheart, as always," Kriti said sobbing.

"Then what happened?" Avni asked as she sat down beside her.

"My parents, they have liked this guy for me. He is a distant family friend," Kriti said looking up.

"Oh Kriti, they have just liked this guy. Have you met him? Have they said yes? Has he even seen you?" Avni asked.

"No," she said shaking her head.

"Then talk to your parents. Look, Kriti, whatever it is, at the end of the day they are your parents. I am sure they will understand," Avni said.

"No, you don't get it, Avni. It's not that easy. I come from a very strict family. I can't imagine telling my parents I like someone. They will kill me. Not literally, but you know what I mean," Kriti said.

"Kriti, you will never know unless you try talking to them," Avni said putting her hands on Kriti's shoulder.

Avni looked at Roshni to help her.

"I tried telling her the same thing. But you know, Avni, I have met her parents. It's not going to be easy," Roshni said, "Arvind is from Andhra and she is from Gujarat. It will be very hard to convince them."

"It's like a whole new culture," Kriti said wiping her tears.

"Kriti, nothing will happen if you just sit here crying. You have to try. Why don't you try talking to your mother or your sister first? See what they say," Avni said.

"You know, I hate myself for this but I don't have the guts to do it. I am so scared," Kriti said.

Avni heaved a sigh, "Look you have to try. If you can't, Kriti, you have to accept the truth and see this new guy," Avni said.

"Oh, I don't know what to do. It's not like I saw where Arvind is from before I fell in love with him," Kriti said as she broke down.

"Oh, Kriti, of course you didn't. Nobody does. They are our parents; they just want our happiness. If they see your happiness is with Arvind, I'm sure they will oblige," Avni said.

Chapter X

Weeks later, Avni was sitting in the meeting room with her team discussing the next quarter projections, when her phone beeped. Her mother had messaged, she opened it.

"A what!" Avni almost shouted looking at her phone.

Everyone looked at her.

"Avni, are you okay?" Sunaina asked.

"Yes, sorry," Avni replied looking around. "It's just. I am sorry but I have a family emergency, may I be excused?" Avni asked.

"Ya, sure," Smita, her manager said.

"Thanks," Avni replied excusing herself from the meeting. She called her mom as soon as she came out.

"Mom! I was in the middle of a meeting when you messaged. You don't message such stuff. Why? Why?" Avni asked.

"Oh Avni, stop being so dramatic again," her mother replied, "You need to do this so that you are better accustomed once you are married."

"Oh Mom, is it so necessary?" Avni asked.

"Avni, I don't understand what the whole fuss is about," her mother said, "always whining for everything. What will your mother-in-law say?"

"Oh, Mom please," Avni said. She hadn't even thought about how it would be living with her in-laws. She hadn't even spoken to them much.

She sighed, "Mom, you know how I become when I skip one meal," Avni said raising one finger as though her mom could see it. "One meal and I go crazy, you are telling me to fast for the whole day."

"Yes, I am. Your mother-in-law would like you to keep it," Uma said.

"Hmm," Avni said, "did you not tell her how crazy your daughter gets when she is hungry?"

"Well, I don't think she would have wanted to hear that," her mother said. "Grow up, *beta,* sometimes actually a lot of times we have to do things we don't like just to make someone else happy. Especially when you are married," her mother said.

"Oh, Mom," Avni whined, "Okay, What is this *Teej* thing anyway?"

"I will tell you all about it once we meet. They have sent a sari for you to wear that day," her mother chirped.

"A sari, Mom! Isn't a fast enough now you are putting me in a sari all day?" Avni asked.

"Oh God. What will this girl do in her *sasural?* I am getting dizzy thinking about it," her mother said.

"Ya, well I never thought of fasts and saris and *bindis* and all. Will I have to do a lot of that, Mom?" Avni asked.

"Yes, on these occasions. It doesn't harm you and it's our culture, something that will be expected of you," her mother replied.

"Hmmm," Avni said thinking about her future standing in a bling sari with a red *bindi,* doing namaste in continuous repetition like a mannequin.

"Avni!" her mother shouted.

"Oh my God, Mom. Why are you shouting?" Avni asked.

"I am because you weren't replying. Where are you lost?" her mom asked.

"Nowhere, Mom. I was just… I will do it," Avni gave in. "I have to go now. I actually walked out of a meeting," Avni said.

"Oh okay, go then, Avni," her mom said as she kept the phone.

Wow, so now I am officially keeping fasts for a guy I hardly know, Avni thought to herself.

Of course, they did talk everyday, so there was quite a lot they knew about each other but so many things she still didn't.

Did he frown a lot? Or how did he sit when he was tensed or relaxed?

What does he do first thing in the morning?

Did he like watching TV or did he just read books?

So many things still unexplored… she thought as she walked back into her meeting room.

"I am keeping a fast on something called *Teej*," she said to Sunaina as she walked out the meeting.

"Hahaha, what?" she said grabbing Avni by her arm, "What is this *Teej*?" she asked looking perplexed.

"Don't ask, I have no freaking clue," Avni said shaking her head.

"Ooh fast for your to-be-husband. Why the smug face?" she asked.

"I don't know him so well yet," Avni stressed, "and doing all this. Shouldn't it come from within?"

"You know anyone better you want to get married to?" Sunaina said.

"Ughh, I know. So weird isn't it. He seems so perfect yet why does my heart not fall for him. Why am I not in love?" Avni said raising her hands as if she was asking God.

"That's because you are a big whiner," Sunaina said smiling at Avni.

"What?" Avni asked, "my mom thinks the same," she muttered.

"Well, you are, but the real reason is because love is not something you force upon yourself. You are making it so hard like I am sure every time you talk to him in your head you are like I have to love this guy because I am getting married to him," she said.

"Pretty much," Avni replied.

"Love is an emotion, it just happens. It takes its own course. Can you let the pressure go and just be with him? Stop waiting for yourself to fall for him and you will," Sunaina ended as she sat down by her desk.

"Look who is talking about love?" Avni added smiling at Sunaina, "Why don't I ever hear of a someone from you?"

"Ya, well. I don't score very well in that department, but I am happy being a single woman," Sunaina replied as she raised her shoulders.

"Ya, I have heard that before, you don't need a man to complete you," Avni said looking at her.

"Exactly, and my parents are okay with it now, so it's all good for me," Sunaina said.

"Ya, good for you," Avni said sitting down.

After another day of her never-ending work day she finally dialled his number.

"Hi," Avni said as he picked up her phone.

"Hey," he said. "How are you? I was just going to call you."

"Really?" Avni said, randomly going through her mails at the same time.

"Yes. I will be in India in a week's time from now," he said sounding excited.

"Oh ya," Avni replied sitting back, "so you are coming next week?"

"Yes. It will be so nice to see you," he said.

"Yes," Avni replied wondering how it would be to see him after so long? She was engaged to him but didn't know how she would react seeing him, however, something inside her was twirling as she heard the news.

A part of her wanted him to come right away and a part of her didn't know what she wanted.

Would they behave like strangers or friends or something more, she didn't know. By the time Avni reached home, the battle which ensued in her head just made her jittery.

"Hey guys, you know what?" Avni burst as soon as she walked in. "Ansh is coming next week."

"Wow, that's great," Kriti said as she stuffed a bunch of chips in her mouth.

"Yeah, isn't it," Avni said sitting down, "How will it be?" she said looking at them.

"How will what be?" Roshni said as she snatched the chips

packet from Kriti, "Won't it be great?" she asked.

"Yes, it would be, right?" Avni asked, "I am getting so nervous. I don't know what to do. What will I say or do?" Avni said walking up and down hastily.

"Well you talk to him all night and day on the phone so I think that area is cleared. What you want to do with him? That is totally up to you, I mean how can I tell you that?" Kriti said smiling at her.

"Oh, shut up," Avni said as she threw a pillow at her.

"You asked first," Kriti said in her defense.

"By the way, what do you want to do to him?" Roshni asked teasingly.

"Oh my God, guys, I am going in," Avni said as she walked into her room.

She could hear them both laughing. She had turned red. For some funny reason she couldn't stop blushing. For the first time in months she recalled that hasty hug she had given him when he was leaving. She couldn't help smiling to herself. I guess it was great that he was coming over, this way she could get a lot of her thoughts and feelings towards him sorted.

* * *

"Sunaina, am I looking fat?" Avni asked.

"Avni, you so are. What are we going to do now?" Sunaina said looking at her.

"Oh, come on, really?" Avni said looking down at herself.

"Well you asked me this question for the tenth time today and I told you nine times you aren't fat. So this time I thought you wanted to hear something different," Sunaina said looking back at her computer.

"I just wanted an honest opinion," Avni said.

"I gave you one. You did not take it apparently. What is with you?" Sunaina asked looking at Avni. "Seriously, I don't get you. Sometimes you act like you don't give a damn and look at you today," she smiled at Avni.

"I don't know," Avni said sitting down, "I am seeing him after so long. It is either going to be very awkward or..."

"Very magical," Sunaina said looking at her.

"Yeah," Avni said rolling her eyes.

"By the way. How many more days will you be in office?" Sunaina asked making a sad face.

"Aww, I will miss you too," Avni said looking at her sad face, "two weeks and I am done," Avni said looking around at her office, "Oh I am going to miss this place."

Avni had given her resignation and was on her notice period this past month. She thought it was best since Ansh was coming down, and after he left she wanted to spend time with her parents before she left for Norway.

"Well, are you really going to miss this place? I don't think so, since Ansh would be here. I am sure he will fill the void very easily," Sunaina said chewing the end of her pen.

"Fill the void, Sunaina, seriously. Come on, this place has been my second home for so long now. Of course, it's also because we spend all our freaking time here finishing the work that somehow never seems to end," Avni said looking back at her mails.

"Where do they come from? I just emptied them," Avni said taking a second look at her computer.

"Beats me. Trust me, if I had the answers," Sunaina said looking at Avni.

Another long tiring day of Avni's office ended. Avni found so much solace every time she sat in the cab and put on her earphones to drift into a world of her own.

Of course, she still tried real hard to picture Ansh in most of the songs but over time she had forgotten what he looked like.

As hard as Avni tried she could never put a face to her imaginary man in the songs. He was also uncannily always wearing the same shirt, the shirt he had worn when he came with his parents, a white shirt with pink stripes of different shades.

"Madam," the guard called out to her as she was walking up to her apartment.

"What?" Avni asked looking back.

"There is a parcel for you, if you can sign here," he said.

"Can you take it upstairs, I will sign here," Avni said looking at the size of the parcel.

"That's it, right here," Avni said as she walked into the apartment, she directed the guard to put it on the table, "thank you, *bhaiya,*" she said as he walked away. Before she got to open the parcel. She heard sniffs from her room. She looked around and realized Kriti and Roshni weren't in the hall, which was where they were every day when she got back. She rushed to her room.

"What happened?" Avni asked as she entered the room and saw Kriti on the phone crying and Roshni standing silently behind her.

"But... Arvind, I am so tied. What do I do? He is coming day after. No, I don't want to see him... Why would you ask me that? Of course, Arvind, I love you and only you. You know that. Understand my situation… It's so difficult... Ar… Hello... Arvind... Hello... You there... He..." Kriti just looked at her phone, "he cut the call," she said looking at the phone, "he just cut the call."

"Oh, Kriti," Avni said as she went up and hugged her.

"How do I explain it to him that I love him but I am so scared," Kriti said sobbing in Avni's arms.

"Kriti, you shouldn't be scared. If you really want to be with him, you will have to try," Roshni said, "Look, I know your parents but I also know your father adores you. Kriti, he might give in for your happiness but we will never know unless you don't try talking to them."

"Yes, Kriti, you can't live in regret for the rest of your life," Avni said, "I am telling you. Talk to your sister first, then we will see how to go further, make her meet Arvind. She will realize how nice he is," Avni said holding Kriti's hands.

"Ya, I think I can talk to Di first, oh only if she doesn't kill me," Kriti said hiding her face beneath her hands.

"She won't silly, she is your sister after all," Roshni said sitting beside her.

"So, it's decided. We are going to invite your sister over and talk about this," Avni said.

"You guys will be there?" Kriti asked looking at them.

"Yes, you know to protect you in case you sister does think of killing you," Roshni said smiling at Kriti.

"Oh, you guys," Kriti said as she hugged them both.

"By the way, if we are done here, I have a parcel waiting for me outside," Avni said.

"What! Why didn't you say so?" Roshni screamed as she ran out.

"Oh my God, look at the size," Kriti said walking in.

"Will you do the honours already?" Roshni squeaked looking at Avni.

"Yeah okay," Avni said as she unwrapped the parcel.

"Are you kidding me, this is so beautiful!" Kriti said as she held a huge framed picture of the three of them.

"Wow, this is so sweet of him," Roshni said, "Hey, this is the same picture I had sent him a week ago," Roshni said as she took a closer look at the picture.

"You sent him this picture?" Avni asked.

"Ya, we were just casually talking and he asked me if I had a picture of the all three of us," Roshni said, "he is pretty sweet you know," she said smiling at Avni.

"You guys talk?" Avni asked.

"Oh God, after all I said, that's the one thing you are stuck at. Yes, we do. Why you are scared he would start liking me over you," Roshni asked bumping her shoulder into Avni's.

"Oh please," Avni said shaking her head.

"You should call him and thank him, no, we all will thank him," Kriti said.

"Yeah, I should. Give me a second," Avni said as she walked into the room with her phone. She opened her phone and went to her contacts and dialled Arvind instead.

"Hi. How are you? I am good. Yes, he is fine too... I am so sorry for whatever is happening but I've known Kriti so long and if there is one thing I am sure about is that she loves you... and she wants to be with you, but please try to understand, it will take her little time to gather up the courage to go talk to her parents. Of course, I know you will always be there for her… that's exactly why I called you… Arvind, she needs you more than anybody now, you both have to fight this together… Don't let the times test your love… No you don't have to thank me… Talk to her… Tell her what you just told me… She needs you… Yes, okay… Bye," Avni turned around as she cut the call.

She was startled as she saw someone standing behind her. "Don't worry it's just me," Roshni said.

"Oh, thank God. I thought it was Kriti," Avni said.

"I am so glad you did that. You know what the funny part is?" Roshni said folding her hands.

"What?" Avni asked sitting down.

"The way you spoke to Arvind like you understand so much about relationships and love and everything yet you are so confused in your own," Roshni said.

"Yeah. I know, it's always so easy to give advice but so difficult when it comes to your own. I am good now, a lot better," Avni said, "See I am not shaking anymore when I talk about him," Avni said as she held out her hand. Avni joked and continued, "I know him well now, but as a friend. You know you are supposed to be in love when you are getting married to someone. That is not happening," Avni said looking at Roshni.

Roshni hit her head, "Avni, what else do you want him to do? He trying so hard to woo you," Roshni said.

"I know, and yet my silly heart is unresponsive, I hate it," Avni said

"Avni, it will happen. Just give it some time, else if you still feel it's not. You always have a choice, right," Roshni said.

"Yeah, I do," Avni said.

"Anyways, let's go, I am pretty hungry," Roshni said as she got up.

They saw Kriti giggling in a corner over the phone as they entered the hall.

"Kriti, do you want anything to eat?" Avni asked.

Kriti did not reply as she was engrossed in her phone call.

"I guess we should just let her be for now," Roshni said.

"Ya I think so too," Avni said walking into the kitchen.

Avni looked at her phone and called Ansh.

"Hey, I just received the photograph, it's beautiful," Avni said, "and Roshni says thank you," Avni said looking at Roshni who was gesturing at Avni.

"Sure, we will talk later, bye," Avni cut the call.

"So soon?" Roshni said looking at Avni.

"He was in the middle of a dinner with some clients," Avni said.

"Too many dinners, I am worried now," Roshni teased.

Avni just shook her head and smiled.

"Hey, isn't that *Teej* thing day after? That day you are supposed to fast?" Roshni laughed, "You will have to be in a sari all day, huh?"

"Apparently, yes," Avni said, "I just hope I survive the day."

Chapter XI

"Avni, happy *Teej*," her mom chirped on the phone, "Oh I am so happy I am getting to celebrate this with you today."

"Ya, Mom," Avni replied with her eyes half-closed. "Is it my fast day today? I am hungry already," Avni whined.

"Oh Avni, don't whine so much. Just a couple of hours till we do the *pooja*," her mom said. "Okay, we are coming to pick you up so just be ready," she squealed.

"Mom, you are actually happy making your daughter go hungry!" Avni said.

"Oh, Avni. Yes, I am because it's for a good deed, now go get ready we are coming," her mother said as she kept the phone.

"Hey, Avni what's up?" Roshni said walking in with a bread *pakora* in her hands.

"What? What the hell are you guys doing with bread *pakora* so early in the morning?" Avni asked.

"Oh, we were just hungry. We had to have these *pakoras,"* Kriti said taking a bite.

"Want some, Avni? Oh, I am sorry, I forgot you cannot eat today," Roshni said as she walked out.

Avni threw a pillow at them, which they dodged.

"So not fair, you guys. I am so hungry now," Avni said and she dug her face in the pillow.

"Wait till you guys are in my place," Avni said looking up.

"Oh, we will wait, till then we will enjoy our delicious bread *pakoras.* You know, Kriti, what else is great with these… *jalebi!"* Roshni said widening her eyes.

"Oh yeah, okay calling Haldiram. *Jalebi* on the way," Kriti said walking out.

"Uggghhh, I hate you guys," Avni said getting out of her bed.

"Oh, we love you too, Avni," Roshni said grinning at her.

There were days Avni would go hungry till noon and not think about food for once, but since she was on a fast today all she could think of was food, which made her stomach rumble like crazy.

"Oh, you have to stop," Avni said looking at her stomach as she got ready. "How is my staying hungry ensuring a longer life for Ansh," Avni said as she wore her shoes, "Oh I swear, I could eat these shoes!"

"Haha, beats me. You are his better half so your prayers will reflect on him I guess," Roshni said looking up thinking.

"Yeah, they better do, else I will kill him myself," Avni said walking out.

"Yeah, the irony," Kriti said giggling.

"Yeah actually, anyways bye guys, see you later," Avni called out as she walked out.

Avni walked sheepishly into her aunt's house; the functions she had avoided all her life, today she unwillingly had to be a part it.

"Welcome to the perks of being married," Kitty joked, "Enjoy and I will till I can," she smiled.

She could hear giggles from across the hall, *oh God,* she thought to herself. *I can't sit there and sing and dance like that, this is all so awkward*, Avni thought to herself.

"Avni, come in. We will get you dressed and then you can come outside with us," Kavita Aunty said as she took her inside. Kitty kept making silly faces at Avni as she got dressed.

"Oh, come on, Kitty, stop pulling her leg," her aunt said she tied Avni's sari.

"Hope this is not too tight for you," her aunt said looking at her.

"No, I can breathe, so I think I am fine, Aunty," Avni said.

"Okay, then we are done," her aunt said showing Avni the mirror.

"Wow thanks," Avni said as she looked at herself in a sari." It was deep pink *leheriya* sari.

"Okay, Avni, let's go," her aunt said.

She was taken into a hall full of ladies dressed and blinged up. They were all giggling and talking like chirping birds. Avni was welcomed like a new entrant into their gang. They sat and sang for hours, Avni just sat and smiled sheepishly at everyone. At one point she was made to get up and dance to which she refused but was forced to. She just stood and swayed from one side to another.

"This is not how you dance," her distant aunt came and took her hands and started swinging it furiously.

"Ouch," Avni exclaimed.

"Oh, this girl, such a delicate darling you have here, Uma," her distant aunt told her mom, "She doesn't even dance."

"She is new to this, I am sure she will get used to it," her mom replied.

Avni looked at her mom and mouthed, "What the hell?"

Her mom just shushed her and made her sit again.

"Mom, I am hungry, why is everyone still singing and dancing? Let's do the *pooja* and eat," Avni said walking behind her mom into the kitchen.

"Oh, Avni just a little more time. I know my poor baby is feeling very hungry," her mom said holding her face.

"Then can I please have something?" Avni whined.

"No, *beta,* see this is your first *Teej*. Don't ruin it. The *pooja* will start soon then you can eat as you please," her mom said patting her.

When Avni finally did eat, she gobbled up all her food and ate so much she couldn't move an inch. Once all the guests left, Avni lay down on the sofa in the hall.

"Oh my God, I ate so much, I think I am going to puke," Avni said looking at Kitty.

"Couldn't you eat slowly? You were eating so fast like some war had broken out," Kitty said looking at her.

"I was so hungry, you know what it is like to not eat for so long," Avni said.

"No, that I don't, it's okay you will be fine in a while," Kitty said smiling at her.

"Okay, I guess since I can't move at all. I am going to sleep on the sofa," Avni said sliding down.

"Okay," Kitty said getting back to her book.

"Goodnight," Avni said yawning.

Just then Ansh's call buzzed.

Avni looked at it, "No, I can't take this call… very tired," she said to herself.

She messaged him, *"I am sorry I can't take your call now, completely and thoroughly exhausted. May you have a long life. Bye."*

As Avni got up in the morning, she was still completely drowsy. She looked at her phone and saw the time. It was 8 a.m.

"Oh my God, office," Avni screamed as she got up and rushed to get ready.

"Bye Kitty, bye Aunty, bye Mom," Avni mumbled with her mouth full stuffing them with *idlis* her aunt had made for breakfast. She rushed out to catch an auto to get to office.

She looked at her phone as she was in the auto, she saw Ansh's message. The message read: *"Hi, Avni, thanks for the long life ;) Since I am leaving day after, just wanted to know what kind of chocolates would you like from here and if there is any perfume you would like. I can pick it up from duty free."*

"Oh my God," Avni exclaimed, "I completely forgot he is coming."

Avni couldn't seem to concentrate much on her work that day; she kept tapping her pen on the table, which kind of turned into a tune as she kept repeating it.

"Okay, you have to stop it, because it's getting to my head," Sunaina said looking over her desk.

"Oh sorry," Avni said and started to tap it on her head.

"Okay, you have to stop this," Sunaina said as she came over and took her pen away.

"What's the deal?" she asked, "the usual Ansh thing or something different."

"The usual," Avni said looking at her.

"Hmmm, I am all ears," Sunaina said.

"You know he is coming day after! I am not even prepared," Avni said looking at her.

"Is he some kind of exam you are not prepared for?" Sunaina asked, "He is your fiancé, can't you relax!"

"Yeah, I will. He is just a guy so no worries, but no," Avni paused, "he is not just a guy…he is the guy I am getting married to!" Avni said as if shouting at the computer.

"What's your deal, Avni, seriously," Sunaina said, returning to her desk. "He is not a monster, just your fiancé."

"Ya I know," Avni said swinging her pen and getting back to work.

When the day finally arrived, Avni was very jittery. She couldn't stay in one place for more than five minutes. She kept standing, sitting and then walking around. She had already had five cups of coffee and it was just noon.

"So, you are preparing yourself to be up all night with him," Sunaina jeered looking at her sixth cup, as Avni walked past her.

"Oh please, no! I have actually had too much coffee. Oh, I will be like on a different high with so much coffee when I see him," Avni said, "I think you should take this one."

"Okay thanks," Sunaina said as she took the cup.

Sunaina causally checked her phone, "It's almost time by the way, you should log off," Sunaina said.

"Yes, okay, he said he will come by the parking lot and he called an hour back from the airport telling me he will be here in half an hour. Where is he?" Avni half-screamed.

"Okay woman, you have to relax," Sunaina said as she held her by the shoulders. "Sit, relax," Sunaina said, "Are you sure you don't love him? You are acting crazy waiting for him," Sunaina said.

"Hmm, am I?" Avni asked.

"Oh my poor Avni," Sunaina said looking at her, "I think you are."

"Hmm so that's it… I am in love," Avni shrugged looking at her.

"You will know when you see him," Sunaina said, "Now go," she said.

"Okay," Avni said taking deep breaths and walking out.

She stood by the parking lot. Her heart jumped every time a car went by.

Oh my God, what is happening? Why am I getting so nervous? Avni pondered.

She took out her phone to call him just as a white Skoda pulled up and stopped in front of her. Ansh stepped out.

Avni went red and felt her face burning up. He was wearing a bottle green collared T-shirt, blue jeans and had a wide smile on his face.

"Hi," he smiled holding out his hands for a hug.

Avni just smiled as she was too nervous to open her mouth and half-hugged him.

"Shall we?" he said opening the door for her.

"Thanks," Avni muttered as she sat in the car.

As they sat there was an awkward silence between them. Avni looked at him and they both smiled. He held her hand, and Avni blushed a deeper shade of red. They just sat there in silence; Avni could not seem to look up, she didn't know what to say. She had so many things to ask and say but suddenly she was tongue-tied, her mind completely blank. She had no idea how to break the silence.

After a long silence, Ansh finally asked, "Shall we go eat something?"

"Yeah, we can, I am hungry too," Avni managed to speak.

"Okay, you will have to help us because I am so new to this place," Ansh said.

"Oh yes, umm, which cuisine would you like to have?" Avni asked.

"Whatever you like," Ansh said.

"Please you pick. You like Italian, right?" Avni asked.

"Yes, and so do you. It's a win-win situation," Ansh said.

"Okay, so Italian it is, I know a nice restaurant," Avni said, "*Bhaiya,* Lodi Road *lena,"* Avni said to the driver.

She was sitting so stiff all this while, but eased out a little as she shifted in her seat.

"Oh, by the way, how was your flight? You must be tired, jet-lagged?" Avni asked.

"Yes, I am a little tired but not so much. I am used to travelling from Norway now so I don't get too jet-lagged," Ansh replied.

"Oh okay," Avni said as she looked out through the window. This was a little awkward, she was seeing him after more than a month now.

"Avni," Ansh said looking at her. She turned to look at him. "It's so good to see you. You were so right, we needed this – to be able to sit this way and talk to see each other. It makes all the difference," Ansh said.

"Yes, I am glad we could do this, this is really different and nice. I have been talking to you on the phone for so long but it's so different now, because we are face to face now," Avni said looking at him.

Now that he was right there beside her, it was okay. At least she did not shudder at the thought of getting married to him. The more she looked at him, the more she blushed. *Was it just an impulsive feeling since he was here or was she falling in love with him?*

Avni took a deep breath. She did not know yet but she knew she was in a comfortable place now and had all the time to get her feelings sorted. They had a lovely lunch. Their discussion went from Avni's mundane office life to his life in Norway, to how she loves shopping and how much he loves it more.

"Oh no, street shopping for me, I love that kind of shopping. You buy cheap and even if it goes bad in a few months it's cool I mean you go shopping again. That way you always have variety," Avni said twirling her spaghetti in her fork.

"Hmm, I get your point, but I go for quality. I can only get them in good brands," Ansh said.

"You are a brand conscious guy," Avni said cutting in.

"You can put it that way," Ansh said smiling at her.

"First of all, if I become brand conscious I will only be able to afford shopping like once or twice a year," Avni said counting on her fingers.

Ansh laughed, "Don't worry, I'll make you one very soon," he joked.

"Yeah, let's see about that," Avni replied going back to her meal.

They continued their lunch merrily talking. After lunch they walked back to the cab and Avni thought it was best Ansh got some rest.

"I think you should really go rest," Avni said.

"Yeah okay, hey by the way, I have some chocolates and stuff I bought for you. You should take them with you. They are in my luggage," he said turning back towards the trunk of the car.

"Okay, where are you staying?" Avni asked.

"In a guest house near my office," Ansh said.

"Hmm, okay. I will wait here. You can take them out and then I will head home," Avni said.

"But I will have to open my luggage. Lots of things packed together," Ansh said.

"Okay," Avni replied shrugging her shoulders, "I will come up then and wait."

"You sure?" Ansh asked.

"Yeah, of course," Avni said.

Ansh nodded and instructed the driver to head to the guest house. Once they were up in the guesthouse, the awkward silence between them ensued.

"Okay, I will take out the stuff I got for you," Ansh said taking his luggage in the room to unpack it.

It was a small one-bedroom apartment. Had a decent-sized hall a small kitchen to the left, with a small round dining table, Avni noticed as she walked around. It had a room at the end with a small balcony.

"This is nice place," Avni said as she looked around.

"Yes, quite apt for me," Ansh said as he gestured her to sit.

A few minutes later Ansh entered the hall with a bunch of

goodies. There were chocolates, cookies, and this lovely piece of jewellery, which he personally handed to her. It was a beautiful diamond pendant with a pearl in between, it had a pair of lovely matching earrings.

"Oh. Oh my God. It's beautiful," Avni said looking at it, "you didn't have to."

"Please, Avni, come on," Ansh said holding her hands.

She felt a little awkward this time.

"Umm no, it's too much," Avni said slowly sliding her hands out from his.

"It's not. Please, I insist," he said keeping the jewellery beside her.

"All of this..." Avni said pointing out to the array of goodies he had got her.

"Is nothing," Ansh completed her sentence.

She just smiled.

"Avni, are you okay?" Ansh asked sitting beside her on the sofa.

"Yeah totally, why do you ask?" Avni asked still looking at her gifts.

"You are being a little awkward," Ansh said.

"Hey no, you know this will take time," Avni said pointing between them.

"Okay," Ansh nodded, "Look, I understand. That's why I am here," Ansh said.

"You know we are going to get married and sometimes it's difficult to let that sink in," Avni said.

He just looked at her listening very intently.

Avni took a deep breath and continued, "Look you are a really nice guy and I know you do so much for me. You have done so much for me, any girl would by smitten. You know I like you as a person, but not like you like you yet. I hope you know what I mean," Avni said.

Ansh looked at her and then nodded to himself and shifted back from where he was sitting on the sofa.

"Avni, I understand," he said, "I told you we are friends first, but yes we eventually are getting married so it's very important for me that you can see me that way."

Avni sighed and looked down.

He continued, "Avni, please there is no pressure, but you know what. I like you, I really do and I don't want to give up so easily. I will try all that it takes to show you just how much I care about you and want to be with you. I will until you come and tell me it's not working out for you. If it's not working out for you, Avni, I need you to come and tell me. It's very important for the both of us," Ansh said.

He continued, "I will not let you sit in the *mandap* until you are wholeheartedly into this, not even half-heartedly. How we will handle the families is my problem. I will tell them," Ansh said looking at her.

"Oh, you see this is another problem that you are just too nice," Avni said.

"You don't want me to be nice?" Ansh asked.

"Yes, not so much, it will make me feel less guilty," Avni said

He just laughed.

"Okay, then I will be a little blunt now. I am damn tired and I need to sleep. You don't want to see the cranky me, so please excuse me," he smiled.

"Yes, please do sleep, thanks for all this," Avni said picking them up.

"By the way, are you going to office tomorrow?" Ansh asked

"Yes, it's my last week," Avni said.

"Okay, then I will see you once you are done tomorrow. Is that okay?" Ansh asked.

"Yes, sure," Avni replied as she left the guesthouse.

Chapter XII

"Wow, that's a lot," Roshni said rummaging through Avni's gifts.

Her roommates had caught hold of her the moment she reached had home; they took all her packets to look through all that Ansh had got her.

"And this jewellery, my God," Kriti said holding it in her hand.

"Oh, I feel so bad," Avni said hiding her face in the pillow.

They both looked at her, "Bells haven't rung in the background yet?" Roshni asked.

"No, I mean when he just came I was blushing and then I just went back to square one," Avni said, "How can anyone be this stupid and confused?" she said throwing the pillow away.

"Beats me, I would have been totally taken and not be here with you girls now," Roshni said sitting down, looking at her jewellery.

"I am telling you. He has just come, give it time. Now it's all different since he is right here," Kriti said.

"I feel like I am playing with his emotions," Avni said.

"Does he know about your I-still-don't-know status?" Roshni asked.

"Yeah, I told him, and he said that he will still keep trying till I tell him a clear no," Avni said.

"Then he is okay with this," Roshni replied.

"Oh, come on, this is so bad. I feel like such a bitch," Avni said.

"That you are, I don't understand why you aren't giving into him? I mean what's wrong?" Roshni said.

"Come on, Rosh, getting married is not easy," Kriti said patting Avni's shoulder.

"And who are you? Some love guru," Roshni asked Kriti.

"At least I know more than the both of you," Kriti replied looking at Avni, "Have you ever even kissed a guy?" Kriti asked.

"Oh whatever, they are such waste of time," Roshni said walking out.

"Silly woman, anyways come," Kriti said holding Avni's hands, "Maggi time," she said dragging her off the bed.

Avni had to let herself ease out; she had to let things happen at their own pace. As the days went by, Avni could really see Ansh trying in every way, her heart did melt at times but something still stopped her. Was it her fear from her past or her reluctance towards the word marriage? Or just that she was an introvert and getting into such a relationship really took her a lot of time. Or was it that she didn't want to get married yet. She didn't know what was stopping her more.

One such day when Avni and Ansh were out for dinner. Ansh was talking about his work, a project they were trying hard to get.

"It's so difficult to convince the clients, they just sit there and think everything is damn easy but it isn't, there is a lot of work that goes in. I have to make my employees slog day and night to meet their demands."

Avni just stared at him, not processing much of what he was saying. She kept looking at him, the way he was talking, the way he was looking.

He looks good, Avni, he's nice, she thought, *then why?* she thought as she held her head and smiled at him.

"Why can't you fall in love, Avni?" she blurted out loud.

"Huh, what?" Ansh said suddenly. "Who can't you fall in love with?" Ansh asked.

"Uhhh... I... Oh, I am sorry," Avni said as she put her head down.

"Avni, is everything okay, were you thinking out loud?" Ansh asked holding her hand.

She slid her hands from Ansh's, "Ansh, I am sorry, this is so awkward."

"You still wondering why you haven't fallen in love with me?"

he asked.

Avni's heart sank, she hated seeing him like this. She hated herself for this but she had to be honest with him.

"Ansh, I am trying," Avni started.

"And you still can't get your heart to say a yes to us, isn't it?" Ansh asked.

Avni just looked down, "I hate myself so much."

"Avni, you don't have to. At least you are being honest with me. I told you, Avni, if you are not okay with it, we will call it off," Ansh said looking at her.

She took a deep breath. She couldn't just say no either. There was nothing wrong with him.

"Okay," Ansh continued looking at Avni's silence, "We will just put this whole thing off for a few days. I know it's unfair on my part to put the pressure on you to decide, but I think we need some time off from each other."

"Hmm...yes," Avni replied.

"It's okay, Avni. There is no pressure," Ansh said as he asked for the check.

As he dropped her home, she looked at him and smiled.

"So, you will be busy for the next few days. Those clients are coming down?" Avni asked as she got out of the car.

"So, you did pay attention to a bit of what I was saying?" Ansh asked.

"Yes, I did," Avni replied, "Anyways I will see you later. Bye and best of luck," Avni said as she left.

"Hey, how was your dinner?" Kriti chirped as she saw Avni come in.

"What's with you?" Avni asked looking at Kriti smiling at her.

"Love is in the air," Roshni replied shaking her head, "Arvind just left."

"Aah, nice," Avni said dully as she removed her heels.

"Why ain't you chirpy?" Kriti asked.

"I don't know, I hate doing this to him, I hate myself. I hate this whole thing," Avni said as she sat down.

"Wow, what happened?" Roshni asked.

"I was so lost in my thoughts all through the dinner, that I just blurted out loud in front of him that I am trying to fall in love with him but in vain," Avni said.

"Are you?" Roshni asked.

"Avni, is this not working out for you?" Kriti asked, "He is so good."

"Yes, I know, that makes it even more difficult. He is too good and you know," Avni said, "The thing is my heart goes more for these bad boys, those jerks. Like it gets some sadistic pleasure in me liking them."

"Good boys are boring in your head, aren't they?" Roshni said as she went back to her laptop. "You can date the bad ones, not marry them. That is a big disaster."

"I know. Anyways we are taking a few days off from each other, hopefully it will help me figure out what I want," Avni said.

"You know, Avni, I know I said something else earlier but if you really can't figure this out, you shouldn't keep him hanging for too long," Kriti said.

"I know, it's so unfair," Avni said, "I will see how it goes for the next few days," Avni said as she walked to her room, "Goodnight guys."

She heard a faint 'goodnight' as she closed the door and was quickly off to sleep.

Avni checked her phone first thing in the morning. No message. She went through her morning keeping a close watch on her phone. He actually hadn't called or messaged her since last night. Which was odd for her, as he always messaged her in the morning. She remembered, they had decided to take some time off. She got up to get ready and walked out to the hall. She couldn't help looking at her phone every now and then,

"You waiting for something?" Roshni asked looking at Avni staring at her phone mumbling to herself.

"Huh? I... Oh, Ansh hasn't messaged or called since morning,"

Avni said looking at her phone.

"Weren't you guys taking some time off?" Roshni asked eating her toast, "The way you are acting, are you sure your feelings aren't sorted towards him?"

"Yes, they aren't. It's not like I am in love. He always messages or calls, but I know we decided to take some time," Avni replied going back to her toast.

"So, what your plan for today?" Roshni asked

"Oh, I have been stalling Mom forever. She wanted to buy some suit materials we could get stitched for my wedding," Avni said, "So I guess I will go today."

"You are still not sure whether you want to get married or not and you are going for your wedding shopping?" Roshni asked looking at her.

Avni opened her mouth but then thought for a moment, Roshni was right.

"Oh, I know. See even if I am not getting married, they are just suits. I can always wear them," Avni said shrugging her shoulders.

"Hmm, and your job?" Roshni asked.

"Roshni, I don't know. I know I planned this thinking I am getting married by this year-end, but I will see when what happens, whenever it happens."

She could imagine her mother freaking out.

"I have given up. No, Arun, I seriously have given up on her. She has no sense of responsibility. All of this is coming from staying alone. I should have left my job and stayed with her. Who will put sense into her, he was so good. Now what will we do? I am worried sick of her future," her mom would say crying if Avni ever decided to say no.

She spent the rest of the day hopping from one shop to another. They bought plenty of suit materials for Avni.

"Avni, I think we should buy some saris for you now," her mother said holding her.

"Saris, why, Ma? Look we have bought enough today. Can't we buy saris later?" Avni asked.

"Avni, we are out now and it's so difficult to get hold of you,"

Uma said.

"Mom, I don't want to wear saris. These suits are perfect," Avni said looking at the bags.

"What do you mean you don't want to? See, Avni, you are getting married, so it would be nice to see you in a sari once in a while. Besides it's tradition for us to give you saris when you get married," her mother said holding her hands.

"Really, tradition? Mom, can we really do this later," Avni whined.

"Oh Avni, how will we ever finish your wedding shopping this way," her mother complained.

"We will, I promise, but not today let's go, Ma. I am hungry," Avni frowned.

"Well, I can't say no to that now, can I?" Uma said smiling at Avni.

Avni had dinner with her mom and got dropped home.

"Mom, are you sure you want to go back to school now? It's so late," Avni asked as she got out.

"Yes, *beta,* don't worry, the driver is there. There is a function tomorrow in school so I have to go," her mother said as she waved her goodbye.

"Okay, Mom, be safe and please message me when you reach," Avni replied as the car pulled out.

"Hi," Kriti said as she walked in.

"Some pasta?" she asked eating it.

Avni was busy checking her phone.

"Avni!" Kriti screamed.

"Huh, what?" Avni asked looking around.

"I am here," Kriti said waving her hand. "What's with you?" Kriti asked.

"He still hasn't called or messaged," Avni frowned as she sat down.

"But didn't you guys..." Kriti started.

"Yes, I know we decided we will take a few days off, but he hasn't called," Avni whined.

"Then you call," Kriti said eating her pasta.

Avni just sighed as she took the pasta bowl from Kriti.

"No, not mine, take some from the kitchen and wash your hands," Kriti said.

"Kriti," Avni whined looking at her.

Kriti stared at her.

"Okay," she gave in as she walked into the kitchen.

They watched the TV for a while. Roshni and Kriti bid Avni goodnight. Avni stayed on as she couldn't sleep all night, wondering if Ansh was comfortable not talking to her at all, was he not missing her. She didn't realize when she fell asleep on the sofa mulling over her thoughts.

When she got up it was almost half-past twelve.

"Oh my God," Avni said, "Why did you guys not wake me up?"

"You slept really late, Avni. I could hear the TV till around five in the morning," Roshni said.

"Oh, really. Why are you guys not in office?" Avni asked looking at them.

"It's Saturday, Avni," Kriti said looking at her, "seriously, what is wrong with you?" Kriti asked.

Avni checked her phone and frowned.

"Still hasn't called?" Roshni asked.

"No!" Avni whined. "How? Why? What's wrong with him?"

"Avni, you call him," Roshni said applying her nail polish.

"I will have to now, he is not calling at all," Avni complained. "It's like he doesn't care suddenly, what happened to 'I will keep trying till you say a definite no.' Did I say no yet?" Avni asked looking at her roommates.

"Is it really bothering you so much?" Kriti asked filing her nails.

"Yes, it is. I can't stay like this," Avni said.

"Avni, you really crack me up. You can't go two days without talking to him. How do think you will spend the rest of your life if you say no to him?"

Avni sat down dumbstruck. They were right, it had barely been two days and she was going crazy not hearing from him. She was so used to listening to his voice or seeing his face now, that something seemed so off when she did not.

What was happening to her? she thought. *Was she so used to him already? Was she in love? Why was she getting so restless and angry with him for not calling her at all?* She looked at her phone again, *why was heart yearning to see his name on her phone?*

"You think I love him, then why don't I smile to myself and blush and hum songs when I am with him?" Avni asked again.

"Avni, because you are not in a movie. This is reality, and you do blush only you don't realize it," Roshni said looking at her nails, she then turned towards Kriti, "how do they look?" she asked Kriti.

"Ooh nice, I am going to put this one too," Kriti said.

Of course she blushed. Roshni was right. She did start liking him, that's why his not calling her was bothering her so much. But just like that, in a normal way she had begun to like him. *Oh, these stupid Bollywood movies have ruined me,* Avni thought as she held her head.

"I should talk to him," Avni spoke out loud.

Kriti looked at her and said, "Then just go to him, and stop lying to yourself and to him that you don't like him because if you didn't, you wouldn't be eating our heads right now."

Roshni looked at her in agreement drying her nails. "I don't know about love but you definitely like him," Roshni said. "Avni, Ansh is really smart, you know. I think he knew what he was doing," Roshni said going back to nails.

Avni's heart started racing, "Yes, he is smart," Avni thought as she looked at her phone for the umpteenth time. *Did he know I started to like him? Did he know I would react this way? Was this his way of getting me to confess?* Her head buzzed with a thousand questions.

She dialled his number. It kept ringing, nobody picked up. Her heart sank.

"He is not picking up, has he left?" Avni panicked as she looked at them.

"Are you stupid? He must be busy," Roshni said.

Just then a message pinged on Avni's phone. She opened it.

"Avni. So sorry, couldn't pick up. In a meeting with clients at The Leela."

"He is in a meeting," Avni made a sad face, "It's Saturday, what the hell!"

"It's okay, let him finish his meeting. He will call you," Kriti said.

Avni just sat there looking at his message, "I think I will go there."

"And do what, barge into his meeting saying, 'Ansh, I love you'," Roshni said enacting Avni in a dramatic way, "Quite Bollywood-style I must tell you, but you will thoroughly embarrass him and he will definitely lose his clients."

"Oh please, I won't do anything of that sort," Avni said, though she had half a mind of doing exactly that.

"I will just go there and wait for him, by the time I reach The Leela, his meeting should be over," Avni said looking at the time.

She got dressed, ordered for a cab. As she sat in the cab she fumed at how much Ansh was trying to test her patience.

She messaged him when she reached Leela.

"*Since you don't have time for me anymore, I came to The Leela. Ping me when you are done with your meeting.*"

Avni went and sat by the lobby. She turned around as people walked by her thinking she would see Ansh but she did not.

"Humph," she fumed, "this is too much."

Her phone buzzed.

"*Coming out in five.*"

Her heart jumped at the thought.

Avni, don't look or sound too excited when he comes, Avni thought to herself as she calmed herself and sat down.

After five minutes she saw him walking up to her, he was with a bunch of other people. Avni assumed they were his clients. Avni had never seen Ansh dressed up so properly before. He was in a proper suit, was clean shaved, and smelled amazing.

You didn't have to look so good you know, especially when I am supposed to be upset with you, Avni thought to herself.

"Hi, Avni, this is Karen," Ansh said introducing her to his client, "and John and this is Perry."

Avni shook hands with all of them and said hi.

"Nice to meet you," Karen said, turning to Ansh, "It was really nice meeting you, Ansh. I am glad we could do this. I will see you in Norway soon," she said as they bid their goodbyes.

"Yes, thank you for coming and I will see you soon. Bye John, bye Perry. Have a safe trip back home," Ansh said as he bid them goodbye.

"So, you here?" Ansh said looking at her, with his hands in his pant pockets.

"That's all you have to say?" Avni asked looking at him.

"Huh?" Ansh said.

"Oh, forget it," Avni said as she walked away.

She walked a little bit, turned and saw him standing right where she had left him. She fumed and went back to him.

"What has happened to you?" Avni asked.

"Nothing, Avni. Are you alright?" he asked.

"We haven't spoken in two days, does it not bother you at all?" Avni asked.

"Did it bother you?" Ansh asked.

"Did it bother me? Of course, it did. I thought you were into this and not me," Avni said as she turned away.

Ansh grabbed her hands, "Okay, I am sorry, Avni for all this, but I had to do this to find out how you feel. I had to know if me cutting off from you bothers you at all."

"Roshni was right, you are smart," Avni replied looking at him.

"You know, I was thinking you would come to me in a week's time but it's just been two days," Ansh said grinning at her.

"A week, you wouldn't have called me for a week!" Avni screamed.

"Avni," Ansh said as he looked around, "we are in a hotel."

"Yes, I know," Avni said shaking her head.

"Avni, trust me, it was the hardest thing for me to do," Ansh said holding her hands.

"Okay," Avni said looking down.

"Avni, does it really make a difference when you don't hear from me?" he asked.

"Yes, it does. I become my crankier self," Avni said looking at him.

He laughed.

"You are so cute," he said.

Avni blushed.

"I am going red, ain't I?" she asked looking at him.

"Yes, you are. So, Miss Avni, now will you marry me?" he said as he came closer.

"I don't have a choice now, do I," Avni said looking at him.

"You still do, you can go away and never see me again," he said.

"That is never going to happen, because I am staying right here," Avni said hugging him.

"I love you," he whispered.

Her heart skipped a beat as he said that.

"Okay, don't push it now," Avni replied jokingly.

He just laughed and held her tighter.

"Lunch?" he asked.

"Yes, please, I am starving," Avni said.

How much ever she denied it earlier, she was getting used to being with him every day. How much ever she refused to believe it, her heart was finally giving in to him. She knew things were changing, she smiled more now, blushed a lot too, liked holding his hand while walking.

She slowly stopped panicking at the thought of marriage. It was coming around to her slowly and steadily. Being with him made her happy, not worried anymore.

One such day after lunch Avni stopped by the *golgappa* stand she loved.

"Ansh, let's have *golgappas,"* Avni squealed in excitement.

"Oh ya, I love them too, but here?" Ansh asked.

"Yeah, why what's wrong?" Avni asked.

"Avni, is it hygienic? I mean it just on the roadside," Ansh said looking around.

"Yeah so?" Avni asked.

"We don't even know if he washed his hands before serving us," Ansh said.

"Haha, are you for real?" Avni asked.

He just looked at her smiled.

"Okay I get it, it's not hygienic at all. Now that you are saying it, it got me thinking. We never really bothered about it before. I just love this guy's *golgappas* and see he has plastic gloves on," Avni said pointing out.

"Which I don't trust either. I am sorry, Avni, I might come across a bit snooty to you at this point but I can't have it here, is there some other good place which has a proper kitchen?" Ansh asked.

"Oh God, the NRI can't have *golgappas* from the roadside," Avni joked.

"Yeah, you see my stomach can't take it anymore, it has lost its immunity to such stuff," Ansh said.

"Okay, I know a *chaat* place, Koshy's. It's got a proper kitchen, sitting area. It's clean. The *golgappas* are of course not as good but definitely way more hygienic," Avni said, "let's go."

"*Kya hua, madam, aapka golgappa aaj nahi?*" the *golgappa* guy asked.

"*Nahi, bhaiya, aaj nahi,"* Avni said and held Ansh's hand and walked.

She looked back at him, he was just smiling at her.

Avni suddenly dropped his hand when she saw a one of her college friends walking by. She brushed her clothes and started walking with a straight face.

"Hi, Avni, what's up sweets," one of the girls screamed as she spotted Avni.

"Hi, Ruhana," Avni hugged her.

"How are you, babe? It's been so long," Ruhana said.

Avni still remembered every time Ruhana entered the college, it's like the time used to stop for all the guys. Their heads moved in the direction Ruhana did. *Why not?* Avni thought, if she was a guy hers would have too. She was beautiful, smart and funny. Avni knew her from one of the fests, they had worked together for the fashion show.

"I am good," Avni said looking at how she hadn't changed a bit.

"Ooh, your boyfriend?" Ruhana asked.

"No, my, umm... my fiancé," Avni said.

"Oh my God, Avni, you are engaged," Ruhana said holding her hands, "where's the ring?"

"We just had a *roka*, the ring ceremony will be later," Avni said rubbing her fingers. "By the way, this is Ansh. Ansh, Ruhana," Avni said introducing them both.

"Hi, wow, you are so cute," Ruhana said holding his hands, "Oh why didn't I meet you earlier?"

"Hi, Ruhana, and thanks for compliment," Ansh said.

Oh, will you ever change! Avni thought.

Ruhana kept smiling at him and finally left his hands after a few seconds.

"I have to go, so good meeting you two lovelies. Avni, let's plan a date or something it would be great," Ruhana said hugging her goodbye.

"Yeah sure I will, good to see you," Avni said.

Avni and Ansh walked ahead, she looked at him.

"Why that smug look?" Avni asked.

"Huh, what?" Ansh asked.

"She thought you were cute," Avni said.

"Yeah. Can't help with what she thinks, can I?" Ansh asked shrugging his shoulders.

"So, did you think she was cute," Avni asked.

"This is a trick question, right?" Ansh asked.

"No, just tell me. Look she was the most popular girl in college, all the guys were crazy about her," Avni said.

"So, okay she is pretty, no doubt about that, but she ain't the prettiest," Ansh said looking at Avni.

"Oh, you are just putting me on," Avni said.

"You girls are a funny lot you know, she is pretty you are pretty, what's the deal?" Ansh asked.

"She was trying to flirt with you," Avni said.

"She was, I wasn't, Avni. I am with you, not her, and I met her because she is your friend. Shall I be rude to all your friends who are pretty?" Ansh asked casually.

"No," Avni took a deep breath, "I am sorry, you are right, we are a funny lot," Avni said shaking her head.

After walking in silence for a while.

"Umm so, you were jealous?" Ansh asked looking at Avni.

"Me! No! I mean... I didn't like you know… not that I don't like… I mean she said 'oh you are so cute and she held your hands', not that I have a problem you now but…" Avni kept rambling until Ansh just held her by her waist and she gulped.

"It's okay, I quite like it," he said whispering into her ears.

Something very weird tickled Avni from within and she turned completely red.

She kept thinking about this incident for days on end until one day, "Avni, you there?" Kriti asked shaking her.

"Huh... what?" Avni said.

"Oh, for God's sake. Can you wipe that silly smile of your face?" Kriti Asked.

"Smile, what smile?" Avni asked looking around getting a grip of where she is. She was at her apartment, sitting in the hall.

She had been daydreaming so much nowadays, all thanks to Ansh.

"Avni, seriously you have become so wasted in love," Kriti said dramatically.

"No, I haven't, come on what are you guys talking about?" Avni asked.

"Deny it all you want, you are so in love," Kriti teased Avni.

"I am not. It's just… you know," Avni started to ramble again, "Anyways forget about all that, when is your sister coming?" Avni asked looking at Kriti.

"In fifteen minutes, that's why, Avni, please snap out of your dream world, come back to reality and please help me out here," Kriti said pulling her up.

As Avni walked into the hall she saw Roshni arranging the cushions in the sofa.

"Ooh new cushions. They are so nice," Avni said picking one up, "when did you buy them?"

"When you were out busy with your Mr. Norway," Roshni said smiling at her.

"And, Avni, give me the cushion back I am arranging them here."

"Yeah okay," Avni said plopping on the sofa.

"Sorry, no time to sit, go to the kitchen. Just see if the gravy is done. If it is, the *paneer* is kept in the warm water by the bowl. Please, Avni, dice it and put it in," Roshni said looking at Avni.

"Wow, we are having *paneer* today. Hey, isn't that your sister's favourite?" Avni asked looking at Kriti.

"Well, that's exactly our plan, her kind of cushions, her favourite food," Kriti replied.

"Ooh, I hope this works out," Avni said hugging Kriti.

"Ya, we don't have time for that also now," Roshni said tapping her phone, "Avni, gravy, *paneer*," she said pointing her towards the kitchen.

"Yeah, I am going," Avni said.

Soon, there were just a few minutes before Kriti's sister, Ahana, was to arrive. They were all ready, with the food on the table, the flowers in the vase, the curtains all drawn up. Avni had hardly seen their house so clean and well kept.

It was a big deal, they had to make her sister comfortable, had to convince her about Kriti and Arvind. It was a question of Kriti's whole life.

Avni remembered talking to Ansh about it, who had a very practical outlook.

"See Avni, this is a very sensitive situation. Especially since Kriti's family is strict regarding these things. Some families are very particular about which family to marry in. You can only try but not intrude. I know she is one of your best friends and you really want this to work out for her, but that's her family. They will know and do what's best for her."

Avni did agree with what Ansh said and realized there was only so much she and Roshni could do. The rest was up to Kriti and Arvind.

"So, if I was from a different place and you had met me randomly, what would you have done? Would your parents have accepted me?" Avni asked Ansh.

"Okay, I don't enjoy these trick questions so much because I don't know where they come from," Ansh said, "Yes, my parents are strict too and I would have had to convince them."

"What if they did not agree at all?" Avni said cutting in.

"I would have tried harder, but why are we even talking about this? Weren't we talking about your friend?" he paused, "The fact is," Ansh said holding her close, "that we love each other and our parents are totally fine with it, so we are in a complete win-win situation," he said pecking her on her cheek.

"Yes, and you really do have a way of wriggling yourself out of these conversations," Avni said pulling his arms around her.

"Avni, come on not again," Roshni said shaking her.

"Oh," she said looking around at the sofa only this time she and Ansh weren't sitting on it anymore, Kriti and Roshni were.

"Really woman, you can't drift away like this every now and then. I mean I can't imagine you were crying a month before because you did not know how you would marry him and look at you now," Roshni said.

"I am so sorry, this is so embarrassing. My stupid brain keeps drifting away," Avni said hitting her head.

Just then the bell rang.

"Oh my God. I am going to die," Kriti said holding Roshni's hand.

"No, you are not, can you just chill?" Roshni said, "And stop strangling the cushion, Kriti. If you behave like this she will know something is wrong."

"Okay," Kriti took a deep breath.

"Hi girls," Ahana said as she stepped in with a bunch of bags, "these are for you," she said handing them to Kriti.

"Wow, Di, what are these?" Kriti said looking into the packets.

"Just some snacks and sweets and frozen stuff, in case you guys don't feel like cooking. You can always use them," Ahana said.

"Thank you so much, Di," Avni said taking the packets and putting them on the shelf by the dining table.

"Oh no problem, Armaan is just parking the car and coming, can I have some water?" Ahana said looking at Avni.

"Yes, of course," Avni said walking into the kitchen.

"Ooh looks really yummy," Ahana said looking at the spread on the dining table.

"Thanks, Di, "Roshni said, "come sit. It's actually pretty late so we can have lunch as soon as Jiju is here," Roshni said holding out a dining chair for Ahana.

"Ya sure," she said sitting down.

After the delicious lunch Kriti and Roshni had prepared, they all plopped on the sofa with their overfull stomachs.

"Oh my God, this is too much," Armaan said, "my God, you girls can really cook."

"Yeah, we can cook unlike Di who keeps wondering what I eat all day," Kriti said.

"Yes, I do, because I worry about you," Ahana said ruffling her hair, "if only your office wasn't so far away from our place. I would have made you stay with me."

"By the way, Avni," Ahana asked turning towards her, "how is it going with your fiancé?"

"It's going well, Di," Avni said smiling.

"Well! We have to keep snapping her out of her dream world every now and then," Roshni snided.

"Oh please," Avni said.

"You want me to count since this morning?" Roshni said.

"Okay, I got it. I am glad it's going well for you. Kriti used to tell me about your panic attacks. I can understand arranged marriages can get a little scary in the beginning but it all turns out well," Ahana said.

"Yeah," Avni said.

"I know Kriti will feel the same too when her time comes," Ahana continued to hold Kriti's hand.

Roshni gestured Kriti to speak up; Kriti hesitated but she knew she had to so she took a deep breath and started.

"Di, there is something I need to talk to you about," Kriti said.

"Yeah tell me, you need money or something?" Ahana asked.

"No, not money, I... umm..." Kriti mumbled.

"What is it?" Ahana said looking around.

Avni took a deep breath as well.

"Well you were saying that by the time I come to Avni's phase..." Kriti said.

"Do you not want to get married?" Ahana asked.

"No, Di," Kriti cut in, she paused, "Okay, just hear me out please and don't be angry, please. Just hear me out first."

Ahana nodded.

"I met this person in my college. We were friends at first and then best friends and then, we started to like each other and now there is nobody else but him I want to be in that phase with," Kriti said it all in one breath.

Ahana left her hand and put her hands on her mouth, in deep thought.

For two minutes she just sat there trying to process what Kriti just said.

"Di, did I speak too fast... did you?" Kriti started.

Ahana just raised her hand and nodded.

"Who is this guy, what is his name?" she said with a stern voice.

Kriti just looked at her sister with teary eyes, "Oh I knew this was a bad idea."

"Kriti, just answer me," Ahana said.

"Arvind, his name is Arvind," Kriti said looking down.

"And why are you telling me this?" Ahaha said boring into her eyes.

Kriti just looked down.

"Kriti, I am talking to you, your looking away won't help," Ahana said.

"Di, we…" she said wiping the sweat of her forehead, "We really like each other and want to get..." she gulped, "... married."

"So, you think, by telling me I will help you," Ahana said raising her voice.

Kriti nodded.

"Kriti. What made you think I can? Don't you know our family? Dad, *tauji*, don't you know them?" Ahana shouted, "Your staying here alone is such big deal. You know what a big scene was created at home for that?" Ahana asked.

"Yes, I know," Kriti mumbled.

"Ahana, you have to relax," Armaan said.

Ahana took a deep breath, "Yeah, I know. See, Kriti, I can understand you meet someone, you like him, but you have to understand. This will never be accepted in our family," Ahana said calmly, "Do I know this guy?"

"Yes, you have met him once at my birthday last year," Kriti said still looking down.

"Hmm, really Arvind," Ahana tried remembering muttering to herself. Suddenly Ahana's voice changed and she held Kriti by her shoulders, "Kriti, isn't he from Andhra?" Ahana shouted.

Kriti nodded and hid her face beneath her hands. Ahana sat back at the sofa with her hands on her head.

"Kriti, what makes you think mom dad will agree. He is a Telugu you are a Gujarati.

What were you thinking?" Ahana shouted.

"I know, I know, oh this is such a big mistake but I did not think of it when I fell in love with him," Kriti said crying.

Avni went and sat beside Kriti, she put her hands on her shoulders.

"Di, I know you are upset but please just hear her out. He is a very nice guy, we know him well. He is well settled very nice, mature, loves her a lot."

"It's easy for you to say, Avni, you are having an arranged marriage," Ahana snapped.

"I am, but my sister did not," Avni said.

"Then our family is very different from yours," Ahana said looking at Avni.

She looked at Kriti, "If you called me here for an advice then yes, this is a very bad idea. I do not know what you were thinking falling in love with him. You know our family, Kriti. This will never be accepted," Ahana said.

Kriti just sobbed.

"Ahana, it's not impossible," Armaan spoke up.

"Armaan..." Ahana started.

"Ahana, doesn't mean if a love marriage has never taken place if never will. Look, I know our families are very traditional and different but we can at least try," Armaan said.

"Try, Papa will kill us," Ahana said.

"Oh, you are being so dramatic. I know Papa too and I know if there is one thing in the world he really cares about, it is your happiness, both of you," Armaan said, "Ask yourself does it really matter to you if the guy is nice?"

"My opinion doesn't matter, Armaan," Ahana retorted.

"Just tell me?" Armaan asked.

"No, if he is a nice guy it doesn't matter where he is from, but it is a big deal for our family," Ahana said, "and I am not going to talk."

"Okay, then I will," Armaan said and then looked Kriti. "I will only talk to Papa if I meet Arvind first. Only and only if I and your sister feel he is good and will keep you really happy," Armaan said looking at Kriti.

"Thank you so much, Jiju," Kriti said crying.

"Armaan, how?" Ahana asked, he just smiled and nodded at her. Ahana took a deep breath.

"Okay, we will meet Arvind. But, Kriti if I don't feel he will keep you well, I will not go ahead with this," Ahana warned. "And you will talk to my parents, Armaan, not me," Ahana said looking at Armaan.

Armaan nodded "Don't worry, I will handle that part."

"Kriti, are you sure about this?" Ahana asked.

"More than anything in this world," Kriti said.

Ahana nodded to herself, "Okay."

Kriti just hugged her sister. Avni and Roshni too came and joined them.

"Okay, cut it out all of you," Ahana said jokingly.

Once Ahana and Armaan left, they all sighed a relief, looked at each other and smiled wide.

"Oh, if it was not for your Jiju, your sister would have never agreed," Roshni said, "I got so scared in between."

"Same here, it's all up to Arvind now," Avni said looking at Kriti.

"Yes, all up to him and then up to my Jiju to convince my parents. Oh God, if this happens I will be so happy," Kriti said sitting on the bed.

"Don't worry, we have come this far, it will happen," Avni said.

"Don't you have to get ready and go?" Roshni said looking at her watch.

"Oh, I completely forgot," Avni said grinning.

"Oh God, here we go again. Can you stop smiling like that," Roshni said.

"What? I am not smiling," Avni said throwing a pillow at her.

"I am going to get ready. Shopping time," Avni said.

"You better make him regret courting you for so long," Kriti said.

"Yeah, I so will," Avni shouted from her room.

* * *

Ansh and Avni had decided to go shopping. It couldn't get any better. Only her idea of shopping was very different from Ansh's.

"Oh, come one Ansh, this is great stuff," Avni said standing by the shoe shop on the road which had an array of shoes of different kinds.

"Uhh... they are off the road," Ansh said looking around.

"So, they have great *chaps*," Avni said.

"*Chaps*?" Ansh asked.

"*Chaps, chappals*, I mean shoes," Avni said. "*Yeh kitne ka?*" Avni asked a boy sitting by the shop.

"*Yeh 150 ka madam aur yeh 200 ka,*" he said.

"*Dono loongi 200 mein,*" Avni said.

"Avni, what 200, look I will buy them for you," Ansh said holding her hands.

"Don't be crazy, he will give us both for 150 also if I bargain enough," Avni said letting him go.

"What do you mean he will come even lower? How much are these shoes worth?"

He said picking them up, "Avni, they are not even of a good quality," he said looking at her, "this will last you only a few months."

"Ya I know," Avni said, "I will buy another after a few months."

"Okay, this is crazy," Ansh said.

"What is crazy?" Avni asked.

"You, shopping here," he said looking around.

"Look I know this is not your typical mall kind of shopping, but I like street shopping this way," Avni said.

"Avni, please let me take you to a better shop," Ansh said.

"I can get ten shoes here worth one shoe there," Avni said.

"Yes, but of a much better quality, which will last you years," Ansh said.

"What will I do wearing the same shoe for years?" Avni retorted.

"Avni, just come with me," Ansh said holding her hands and walking.

"Where are you taking me?" Avni said letting him go.

"To shop in a much better place," Ansh said.

"No," Avni said adamantly, "I like it here. I have always shopped this way, Ansh. You can't change what I like."

"Avni, I am not changing the way you shop, but you don't have to go street shopping anymore," Ansh said, "look you are my fiancé now so I would like you to shop nicely, wear good stuff," Ansh said.

"I don't wear good stuff, according to you?" Avni asked.

"No, I did not mean that. I meant that I will... um... make you buy better ones you know of good quality, of a good brand," Ansh said.

"I do street shopping not because I can't afford your kind of shopping but because I like it. Of course, I don't have the kind of money you do but I can shop well too," Avni snapped.

"Avni, you are taking this somewhere else altogether," Ansh said, "I am not saying you can't afford it, and it's not about your money or my money. We are together now, it's our money. Avni, these shoes are of bad quality, more than them being bad they are not good for your feet," Ansh said pointing at Avni's feet, "Do you know how important it is to wear good shoes?" Ansh asked.

"Yeah, I know all that," Avni said looking away, "but I have to shop differently because I am your fiancé now."

"Okay, now you are just picking on my words and grilling me for it," Ansh said, "The thing is…." he paused, "Look, Avni, this is not my style. We can buy from a better place. Don't take me wrong, but please don't buy shoes from here," Ansh continued, "It's just that I wanted us to go shopping and this was not on my list," he said looking at her.

"So, now you are embarrassed because I want to shop from here?" Avni said.

"Will you look at that quality, Avni? Please let us buy something nice," Ansh said pointing at the *chappals.*

"Okay, you go buy shoes from where you want to and can afford," Avni stressed, "I will buy mine from here," Avni said.

"Avni, you are being silly," Ansh said looking at him.

"I can't believe you are not letting me shop here?" Avni said looking at him.

"Avni, I won't. We can do better," Ansh said looking around.

"I can do better too, Ansh," Avni said sounding a bit offended, "It's just that I like it here."

"Avni, no," Ansh said shaking his head.

"What is wrong with you?" Avni asked.

"Nothing is wrong, Avni, I would like you to shop elsewhere," Ansh said.

Avni was so pissed off; she couldn't believe Ansh had a problem with this. Why did he want her to wear branded things, why couldn't she just shop here? This was so uncalled for.

"You now, I don't think I am in the mood for shopping anymore," Avni sulked.

"Okay," Ansh shrugged, "it's better not shopping than shopping here," Ansh said looking at the shops.

Avni just opened her mouth in disbelief, "You are impossible, Ansh," Avni said.

"I am not, Avni," Ansh replied, "Look, let's just catch a movie or something and we can go shop in the mall later."

"No, Ansh, I am not in the mood. Let's just call this day off," Avni said as she walked away.

"I can't believe you are making such a big deal out of this," Ansh said walking behind her.

"I am making a big deal, Ansh," Avni snapped as she looked back at him, "What about you?"

Ansh just looked at her, he looked down, shook his head, "I guess you are right, let's just call it a day."

Avni nodded and walked to the car.

* * *

She walked into her house fuming. As much as Avni was happy Ansh was here and it made her come to terms with her true feeling for him, she realized that they both were very different from each other. The things Avni enjoyed, he hated. He was more prim and proper, sophisticated like a typical NRI.

Avni was more casual, relaxed, she loved things off the street whether it was shopping or eating. He avoided it as much as he could. Avni would get a headache sitting too long in the AC and he couldn't stay without it. She remembered one time when they were out on a drive.

"Can we open the window?" Avni said, "it's such a nice weather," Avni said.

"Ya, okay. I will switch off the AC," he said hesitantly.

"Yes, please do. How can you stay with that all day long? Just enjoy the weather, you know I think it's going to rain," Avni said.

"Oh crap, really?" Ansh said looking at the clouds.

"Oh crap? Don't you love rains? They are so beautiful, and I thought you were the romantic one," Avni said shaking her head.

"Yes, I am but not a fan of rain. You won't be either when you come to Norway," Ansh said.

"I am not in Norway right now so I still love it," Avni said, "Ooh that's perfect, stop," Avni shouted.

"Huh, what why?" Ansh said.

"Because I said so," Avni said, "Just stop."

"See, a dhaba. I feel like having a nice masala chai," Avni said pointing out.

"Avni here, no. You know there is a Barista somewhere here," Ansh said.

"Oh, forget about Barista, please this is fun, just come," Avni said holding his hands.

"I don't think this is a good idea," Ansh said getting out.

"You never think it's a good idea," Avni said.

It was 5 in the morning. They were in the middle of nowhere. They couldn't see a soul on the roads for miles.

"What if it's not safe?" Ansh asked.

"You are there, right, why should I worry?" Avni said putting his arm around her shoulder.

There was an old man who served tea for them and went away inside once it started to drizzle.

They were on a rock by the side which was covered by the tent. As they sipped on their hot cups of tea Avni looked at him and realized how uncomfortable he was sipping his chai in a place like that.

"Men and their egos," Avni mumbled under her breath as she remembered that incident.

She finally decided to drop it as it was impossible to get past him on this, it was something they both decided to shelve for a while.

Chapter XIII

A week after their fight, Avni and her roomies were besides themselves with joy. Avni had called Ansh home in a hurry. Arvind had convinced Kriti's sister and Armaan and now they wanted to celebrate.

"Avni, I am not much into clubbing," Ansh said.

"Oh, come on please," Avni, Kriti and Roshni shouted in unison.

"We have to celebrate this," Roshni squealed, "Kriti's sister and her Jiju have approved Arvind. He is through round one," Roshni said high-fiving Avni.

"Yes, I know and that is great. Kudos to him. We are having an arranged marriage and I still got grilled by Avni's sister," Ansh joked.

"Hey!" Avni said.

"Don't hey me. I know what I was going through," Ansh said.

"Anyways, you have to come," Kriti said, "for me and Arvind," she said jumping.

"Are you high already?" Avni asked looking at Kriti.

"Yes, no, I mean I don't know ya, I had the liberty of having a little vodka," she said grinning at them.

"Avni grinning like this I can understand… but you grinning, you are definitely drunk," Roshni said.

"Ansh, please come ya," Kriti screamed again swaying his hands.

"Okay, I will," Ansh said.

"And keep passing us the drinks then," Avni said.

"Yes, but not too much," he said looking at her.

"Oh please," Avni said, "Let's go," she said as she grabbed his hand.

Avni could sense Ansh getting a bit uncomfortable when she

took her first beer, but at this point Avni did not care. All she wanted do was celebrate. It was Kriti's big day, they had invited a couple of their college friends. They all hugged and cheered for both Arvind and Kriti. Ansh sat by the bar in the beginning; he, however, joined Avni on the dance floor in between.

"I did not know you could dance this well," Avni said they were dancing.

"Well, there are a lot of things you don't know about me then," Ansh said as he held her waist.

"I can't wait to find out," Avni continued looking at him.

"I am not going to spill all my beans so soon," Ansh said jokingly.

Avni smiled at him and continued dancing.

When Avni started on her fifth beer, Ansh held her hands as they were by the bar and said, "Avni, you should stop."

"Why? Ansh, please we are all having fun," Avni said.

"I know, Avni, but you have had a lot," Ansh said.

"Ansh, just one last okay," Avni said walking back to the dance floor, Ansh decided to sit by the bar for a while to sip on his virgin mojito.

Ansh was right, Avni was getting high. The music, the sounds were all ringing in her head, and her body was just swaying and moving to the tunes inside her head. She kept dancing when Sahay, one of Avni's college friends, appeared and started dancing with her, till suddenly Ansh came over and grabbed his collar.

"What the f*** do you think you are doing!" Ansh screamed, "I will smash your face."

"Oh, you should have seen her dancing with her ex then," Sahay said.

"You…" Ansh screamed when Avni cut in.

"Ansh, what the hell," Avni said holding him.

"And what the f*** are you talking about?" Avni said looking at Sahay.

"Leave me, Avni, and you… stay away," Ansh shouted jerking her hand off and staring at the guy.

Avni was so high it took a while before she could hold Ansh's hands again.

"What are you doing, have you gone mad?" Avni screamed.

"No, but you definitely have," Ansh shouted, "You are so drunk you don't even realize what he was doing or how you were dancing."

"Ansh, what are you saying, we were just dancing, for God's sake," Avni said.

"He was trying to grab you," Ansh shouted, his eyes were red with anger.

Avni had never seen this look on Ansh. Taking advantage of them fighting, Sahay sneaked away.

"Just because I allowed you to drink and have fun, Avni, doesn't mean you lose your senses," Ansh screamed.

"Allowed me? Excuse me? You allowed me? Who are you to allow me?" Avni shouted.

"I am your fian… Actually, you know what, you are right. Who the hell am I?" Ansh asked, "I have had enough, I am going," Ansh said.

Ansh turned around, "Arvind, bro, drop her back safe," he said putting his hands on his shoulders.

Arvind nodded.

Ansh walked away.

Avni just stood there trying to make sense of what just happened; he had actually walked away.

Avni knew it, he had a problem with this part of her life and he could never accept it. Avni was not the one to change for him. He had to accept her with all of this. This is why she hated marriage. She felt caged.

Allowed me? she fumed in her head.

* * *

Avni got up with a bad hangover.

"Oh my God," she mumbled putting her hands on her forehead.

"Here, take this," Roshni said holding out a glass of lime juice for her.

"Thanks," Avni said taking it.

"Are you okay?" Roshni asked.

"Ya, where is Kriti?" Avni asked looking around.

"She is with Arvind," Roshni said.

Avni slowly remembered all that happened last night, she shook her head and checked her phone, nothing from Ansh.

"Can you believe him?" Avni said.

"Excuse me, believe him? Do you even know what happened last night?" Roshni asked. "Sahay was trying to get cosy with you, and you expect Ansh not to react," she said.

"He wasn't, we were just casually dancing. Ansh just overreacted," Avni said.

"No, he did not. Because if Ansh hadn't come over, I would have slapped Sahay a minute later," Roshni said.

"What? No, Roshni," Avni said sipping her lime juice.

"That's the problem with you, when you drink you remember only half the things," Roshni said, "Why do you drink so much when it doesn't go down well with you."

"Oh please, don't start like Ansh again," Avni said.

"Avni, you are impossible. I don't know why you got a guy like Ansh, but sometimes I feel like you don't deserve him," Roshni retorted and walked out.

"What?" Avni just stared at her and back at her juice. She got up and went after Roshni.

"Roshni, I am sorry. Please listen to me," Avni said holding her.

Roshni turned around, "Avni. What happened yesterday was bad. Look any guy would have gotten this angry. The funniest part was you were so drunk you didn't even realize the gravity of the situation and struck back at him," Roshni said.

"It was because he was so uncomfortable with my drinking from the beginning and he did not even want to come clubbing in the first place. He stopped me in between also," Avni said.

"So?" Roshni asked.

"So? He has a problem with my drinking and partying," Avni

stressed, "Allowed me?"

"Avni, look he doesn't drink, okay. He is a different guy and you know that. It doesn't have to be your way all the time. You have to work this out with him. Besides, you are stressing on something that is completely irrelevant," Roshni explained.

"What if he doesn't like it? What if he says you will never go clubbing again?" Avni said.

"I am sure he won't, he is mature. But yes, if you get drunk like that then I don't blame him. Avni, you are getting married to him," Roshni said, "Grow up."

Avni just grumbled, "We are so different, you know," Avni said sitting down.

"Okay. Isn't that nice?" Roshni said.

"No, it isn't. He likes different things. I like different things. He is very proper and I like having fun. He is nice, I of course like him but sometimes I feel we are two opposite poles," Avni said.

"You should go talk to him," Roshni said, "And get your head sorted, I know his is."

"Roshni," Avni whined.

"Are you actually having second thoughts about this? One fight and you call it quits. Sweetheart, I don't have a boyfriend but I do know this is not how you can remotely survive marriage. You don't run at every fight."

"I am not," Avni said.

"Then go talk to him," Roshni said.

"Yeah, okay," Avni said as she got up to get ready to go to Ansh's guest house.

She kept checking her phone every now and then hoping to see his text or call. Every time she saw her phone screen blank, she realized he was probably really angry and worried if he too was contemplating their relationship.

"Oh my God," Avni shouted out loud while sitting in the cab. The cab driver turned back. She shook her head saying nothing.

She now remembered, Sahay had mentioned her dancing with

Sidharth.

"Oh no," Avni thought, no wonder he hadn't messaged or called.

This is going to be tough, Avni thought as she reached his door and rang the doorbell. After a good ten minutes, Ansh opened the door. His hair was ruffled up, he stood in his shorts, yawning.

The moment he looked at her he froze, then turned around and walked inside, "Come in."

Avni walked in sheepishly.

He just sat by the sofa and looked at Avni.

"I just want to know, if you have a problem with me clubbing?" Avni asked sitting down.

"You came all the way here just to ask me that?" Ansh asked flatly.

"I just want to know," Avni said.

"Avni, I don't want to talk about this," he said as he got up.

"You have to," Avni said getting up too. "I need to know why you got so uncomfortable from the moment we stepped in the club," Avni asked.

"Look Avni, I am a different kind of guy, but," he took a deep breath, "that doesn't mean I won't let you go out. See, I don't have a problem. I let you go and drink," Ansh said.

"Let me?" Avni snapped, "See that's my problem right there. Let me? What do you mean let me? I am your fiancé, do I need your permission for everything now?"

"Avni, you are starting it again, we are getting married, for God's sake. There are things I would take permission from you for, because we are together in this. So, we both decide," Ansh said getting a little angry.

"If I tell you to stop doing something then," Avni asked, "how would you like it?"

"I would not mind it like you are. I would sit down reason it out with you, and if something makes you really uncomfortable we will try to work a way around it," Ansh said.

"So, you do have a problem with it?" Avni said.

"Yes, I bloody do. Because you don't just drink and dance, you get drunk and go crazy on the dance floor. You lose sense of what you are doing and what others are doing to you," Ansh shouted.

"I…" Avni started and then stopped.

"You realize what the guy was doing. I don't think he realized your fiancé was sitting right there," Ansh said getting red again.

"I know what he did was wrong," she paused for a second, "I know I don't remember much of it, but you got really angry," Avni said.

"How else do you think I should have handled it. Excuse me, I think you are trying to grab my fiancé, please don't do it!" Ansh said, "Avni, you have to get a hold of yourself and be careful around your guy friends. They are your friends but they are guys, okay. You can't get so close," he shouted.

"Ansh. Are you…" Avni took a deep breath, "What do mean by close, you don't have girls as friends?" Avni screamed.

"Avni, I do have girlfriends, okay. But I know how to behave. I know my limits," Ansh shouted.

"You have this thing against my life, my friends," Avni shouted.

"Avni, you don't get this, do you," Ansh screamed.

"I do, okay, I got drunk. I shouldn't have and he shouldn't have done what he did," Avni sighed, "but are you also so angry because of something else he said?"

"Yes. I heard that too, Avni. Look, I am a mature guy, shit happens, it was your past. I just… I just wish I had heard it from you rather than from that jerk," he stopped.

He closed his eyes, opened it again and asked, "You used to get drunk like this and dance with him," Ansh looked at her with surprise.

Avni just looked at him.

"Doesn't matter what you did. It was your past, it's gone," Ansh said sitting down again.

"He was such a jerk. He promised me something and then cheated," Avni started.

"Avni," Ansh raised his hands gesturing her to stop talking, "I don't want to hear about him, not now, not ever. It happened, it's the past. Let it just be that way."

They just looked at each other in silence when Avni asked, "Are you okay?"

Ansh just nodded.

Avni just sighed, "Is this working out?"

"What?" Ansh asked looking at her.

"This is not working out, we are so different. We want different things from life. I want to be in a certain way, you want to be in a certain way. I can't be like this. Do this. Don't do that. That's why I resented marriage so much," Avni said sobbing.

Ansh got up again and walked towards her and held her, "Are you kidding me?" he said looking at her, then continued, "Am I stopping you from anything? When did I ever say don't do this? Don't you tell me not to wear that grey shirt you don't like or not to drive too fast, have the music too loud, not to sit on my laptop too much. You think I should feel suffocated?" Ansh asked.

He paused closed his eyes took a deep breath and asked, "Avni, what is marriage to you?"

"I don't know, okay, I don't know what it is, but it's not my piece of cake. I don't deserve you. Roshni was right. You are a good person, we are just different," Avni said turning away.

Ansh held her again, "I don't care who told you what. I know I deserve you and so do you. You don't run away like this, Avni. You sort things out," Ansh paused again and asked, "Do you like me?"

"Ansh?"

"Just answer me. Have you ever had any feelings towards me, Avni?" Ansh asked.

"How can you even ask me that?" Avni asked.

"Why do you want to give it up then? You think it's not worth fighting for," Ansh said bringing her close to him.

"I like you, Ansh," Avni said tears rolling down her face.

"And I love you, Avni," Ansh whispered in her ears.

She just stood there with a warm feeling engulfing her from

within.

"We are so different, we will fight this way every time," Avni said.

"No, we won't, Avni. We will work a way around our differences and if we do I will make up to you always," Ansh said.

"No, you won't. You walked away yesterday and you did not even call or message and even now, I came here," Avni said.

"Avni. I am sorry I was really angry last night and then I just slept very late," Ansh said "but trust me, I will." He took a deep breath, "Avni, you came here because in your heart you want this too," he said tapping at her heart.

"But it's not easy. You want different things from life, I want different things from life," Avni said starting to walk away.

Ansh pulled her back in and held her by the waist, "I know I want this."

"Ansh, think about it," Avni said, "You need a simple, sorted girl."

"No, I want a crazy, foolish one," Ansh replied.

"I am not foolish." Avni said.

"Yes, you so are," he whispered again.

He pulled her closer and kissed the tears of her cheeks, her chin and then slowly her lips. Avni felt a shiver run down her spine. They had always hugged and snuggled, but this was the first time he kissed her and it felt like time stood still.

After kissing her he whispered, "I know I want this, Avni. Do you?"

Avni just smiled with her eyes closed.

"Then we don't want different things from life, do we?" he asked.

"No, we don't," she said as she closed in to kiss him again.

Chapter XIV

"Oh, look who is here finally," Ria said sipping on her coffee.

"Hi, Ria," Avni greeted her. "Oh, oh, dear silly me," Avni said smiling sheepishly as she walked into her house.

"Yes, very silly of you, Avni," Kriti said sitting beside Ria with her cup of coffee.

"You actually stood me up," Ria said.

"I am so sorry, I remember I told you to come over today but you know so many things happened and I had to get them sorted," Avni said holding Ria's hand as she sat beside her.

"I know, I got all the gossip from Kriti," Ria said, "You are crazy, I hope you realize that, don't ruin this for yourself."

"Yeah, I am not going to, don't worry," Avni said smiling.

"So, it's all cool?" Kriti said.

"Ya, I am going and getting some coffee now," Avni said as she got up.

"Hello girls," Roshni said walking in.

"Where have you been?" Avni asked.

"Oh, don't ask, the usual some random guy my dad wanted me to see. Some family friend's son," Roshni said, "Oh, we know him since years, you know the son too. You used to play together as kids," Roshni said imitating her dad.

"Really, you didn't even tell us," Kriti said.

"Because I was trying to avoid it for so long," Roshni said.

"So?" Avni asked.

"So? He is such a show off, such a ba…" Roshni started closing her fists.

"Okay, we got it," Avni said going into the kitchen, "you want some coffee?"

"Yes, please, seriously, Avni! You are so lucky," Roshni said.

Avni just smiled to herself.

"By the way, what happened? All cool? Did you guys patch up? How did it go?" Roshni asked Avni.

"Yes, it's good now," Avni said looking at Roshni.

"Look at us," Roshni said looking at Ria.

"Yeah," Ria replied shaking her head, "It's just us and our dear coffee."

Avni gestured Roshni to stop talking, Ria had recently broken up with her fiancé and Avni didn't want to touch upon it in any way. Roshni looked back at Avni perplexed.

Ria who caught them looking at each other said, "It's okay, guys, I am happy this way," she smiled looking at Roshni as she walked out into the hall.

"Oh, I am so sorry, Ria, it just slipped my mind," Roshni said looking at Ria as she followed her.

"Why? Come one, Rosh, I am over him. Seriously after getting out of that engagement, I realized I am better off not married at all. I mean why do I need someone, or why should I even get married if am of a certain age. I can very well be single and happy," Ria said smiling at Roshni.

"Way to go, Ria!" Roshni said smiling at Ria, "exactly why is there this need to get married," Roshni said and then looked at Avni and Kriti, "I mean you guys found someone deserving enough to get married to and you want to, so it's fair."

"Yes, I do understand, Rosh, marriage shouldn't be something you need to tick off from a list, it should come from within," Avni said, she then looked at Ria, "I am so proud of you, Ria, for coming out of it the way you did. And no, marriage or just being with someone shouldn't define you, you are so much more than that," Avni said as she reached over and hugged Ria.

Ria smiled, "Yes, so stop feeling sorry for me, guys. I am happy now, trust me," Ria said sitting back.

They all nodded at Ria and spent the rest of the day gossiping, teasing Avni and Kriti. Deciding what they would wear for both their weddings. Kriti said she will make sure she didn't get married too close to Avni's wedding, so they could make it to each other's weddings. The conversation soon shifted to what the in-laws would be like.

"Speaking of in-laws, how are yours, Kriti? Have you ever met Arvind's parents?" Avni asked.

"They could be my in-laws if my parents agree," Kriti said crossing her fingers.

"Oh, I am sure your Jiju will convince them," Ria said.

"I really hope so, but yes, I have met them a couple of times. His mom is such a sweetheart, but his father looks a little reserved and strict," Kriti said looking at them, "How about yours, Avni?"

"Oh, I don't know. I just never got to talk to them much. Met them just twice, when they came to see me and then at the *roka*," Avni replied.

She realized she no idea what her in-laws were like. She was so dazed when she met them last, she didn't interact with them much. She knew they were a little traditional. So, she decided to talk to her mother about this when she met her next. She did almost a week later.

"Who isn't, Avni? They would expect you to be a certain way," her mom said sitting her down.

"Like what way, Mom, all this makes me so jittery," Avni said playing with her hands.

"Avni, like you have to behave in a certain way. You can't be so loud and irritated and casual there," her mother said holding her hands.

"Really, why?" Avni asked.

"Oh, how do I make this girl understand? Okay, like you will have to wish them every morning, wear a sari, *bindi*, bangles," her mother went on.

"Wait what, every morning! I mean wishing them is not a problem, but wearing a sari, *bindi* and all... Mom, we are not in the

18th century," Avni said.

"Yes, we are not. Not everyday, Avni but occasionally you will be expected to be in a certain way. Avni you have to grow up now and stop being so stubborn about everything," her mother replied.

"I am not! Mumma, what is this I mean, does marriage change one so much?" Avni said. "See I told you don't rush me. I did not want to get married so soon," Avni grumbled.

"Okay, don't. We will tell Ansh to find someone else he can get married to, someone who has some brains," her mother joked.

"No! Why does he have to marry someone else?" Avni replied.

"Then. What do you want to do?" her mother asked.

"I don't know. I want to get married to him but in another reality without all these formalities and bonds and ties," Avni said folding her hands and frowning.

"You think marriage is a cakewalk. It's a huge responsibly, Avni. You will be going to a new family. You will have to adapt to their ways and accept them as you own family," her mother said unfolding Avni's hands.

"What are their ways, again a list of do's and don'ts," Avni cribbed.

"No, to you everything is about that. Avni, we have our way of living as a family, every family does. That's all I am saying. You are getting married now so you have to understand these things," her mother asserted.

"Okay, Mom, I understand," Avni said just to end their conversation.

It was too much for her to process, this world seemingly upside down, she thought, but like Roshni said the idea of getting married to a guy like Ansh was not bad at all.

In fact, it made her smile every time she thought of it.

She had to ask him anyhow, so a few days later when she was at Ansh's place she went and sat beside him while he was busy on the laptop.

"Hey," she said.

He just smiled and continued his work.

Avni half-closed his laptop.

"Hey!" he said.

"Yes, I did that to get your attention. What are you doing?" Avni asked.

"Some office work," he replied opening it again.

"Ansh, please, listen to me," she said holding his hands.

He shut his laptop and looked at her. "Okay shoot," he said.

"I had to ask you some things," Avni said.

"Go on," Ansh said.

"But you must promise not to get pissed," Avni said looking at him.

"I won't, even though I have no clue what you are talking about," Ansh replied.

"Will I have to wear a sari and *bindi* and bangles and all of that in your house?" Avni asked waving her hands dramatically.

"Huh? Like after we are married, I guess so, why?" Ansh asked causally.

"Will I? Oh God, I can't even walk straight in a sari! Every day?" Avni asked looking at him hopefully.

"Haha, see, Avni. Just after we get married it would be nice if you could wear a sari for a few days. After a while I am sure you can wear anything you want to," Ansh said going back to his laptop.

"No, stop that," Avni said taking his laptop away. "My mom said I will have to be dressed like those TV serial *bahus* and act or be in a certain way. I don't have a problem with wearing traditional clothes, but not everyday. Also, how do I change who I am?" Avni asked.

"Avni, my mother is very cool about these things. She herself doesn't wear saris everyday so I am sure she won't expect you to," he said, "Besides we will fly to Norway soon and nobody will tell you to be or act differently, so just chill," Ansh said.

"Really, I don't have to! Oh, such a relief. My mom just stresses me out," Avni said smiling at him.

"Finally, I see that smile," Ansh said holding her hands, "Avni, stop stressing, my parents are very broad-minded. I know it's going to be very tough for you, to accept my family as your own. It's tough for any woman. Just don't worry, it will be fine," Ansh said.

"Okay," Avni said, she thought for a while and asked again, "Okay. What if I want to start something of my own?"

"Yes, you had mentioned it before. Look you are getting married not getting jailed that we will change you or expect you to be different. You can do whatever you want to, you want to work, do something on your own, and just be at home to take a break, whatever it is. It is your decision," he said looking at her.

"I don't want to sit at home," Avni said.

"Okay, of course. We can enroll you in the language classes at first. It's important to know their local language for you to get a job or do something on your own," Ansh said.

"I understand that. It will be fun learning a new language," Avni said thinking about it.

"Yes, and in the meanwhile, you can think of what you want to do," Ansh said smiling at her.

"Yes, I think that will be a great start," Avni said, "I can learn the language and see how I want to go further. Oh, this marriage makes me so tensed at times, and my mom too," Avni said looking at him.

"You are really funny, Avni, just relax," he said hugging her, "as long as I am here, don't worry. I will make sure everything is just fine for you."

"Yes, I trust you," Avni replied smiling.

Avni was so relaxed after talking to Ansh. Though she knew it wasn't going to be that easy; it's never easy to accept a new family, or for them to accept someone new as their own. She knew there would be many hurdles to cross with her in-laws. Avni closed her eyes and hoped there would be as few as possible.

As she walked into her house thinking of her conversation with Ansh, she saw Kriti's father sitting in front of the hall with her Jiju. She greeted both of them. They all just looked and smiled at Avni. Kriti was just sitting on one side with her face red. Just then the bell rang, as Avni was right beside the door she opened it. It was Arvind.

"Hi," Avni said.

Arvind forced a smile at Avni. Avni could sense he was really tensed and worried.

"It will be fine," Avni mouthed.

"I hope so," he said in a low voice, holding out his crossed fingers as he walked forward.

"I will excuse myself," Avni said pointing herself to the room.

"No, it's okay, you can stay," her father said sternly.

Avni nodded and sat down beside Kriti.

"Where is Roshni?" Avni whispered to Kriti.

"I don't know," Kriti replied looking down playing with her hands.

Avni held her hands. She saw Arvind seated in front of Kriti's father, who had his hands folded and looked intently at Arvind.

"Papa, Arvind. Arvind, Papa," Armaan said.

Arvind smiled and folded his hands.

Kriti's father just nodded and asked, "So since when do you know each other?"

Arvind looked at Kriti.

"Don't look at her, answer me," her father said.

"Yes, unc… I mean, yes, Sir. We know each other from our first year in college," Arvind said.

"What do you do?" her father asked.

"I am a chartered accountant," Arvind replied.

"And since when has all this been going on," he said sounding a little angry.

Arvind just looked down.

"Papa, I am sorry for speaking in between but does it really matter. They really like each other, he is a nice boy," Armaan said.

Kriti's father looked at Armaan and then looked down with his arms folded.

"If you are saying so, he might be a good boy but…" he stopped, took a deep breath and looked down.

"You are asking for something very difficult, Kriti," he said shaking his head.

Kriti looked at her Jiju then at her dad, a tear rolled down her cheeks as she looked down.

"I will never do anything that makes you unhappy, Papa," Kriti said.

"My happiness lies in your happiness, Kriti, it always did. This is quite difficult for me to accept. You are from different cultures, it will be very difficult for you," he said looking at her. "We don't know anything about your culture," he said looking at Arvind this time

"Sir, I understand. We come from a very different culture, but trust me, Sir, neither I nor my parents will not force anything on Kriti. We will make it as comfortable for her as possible," he said.

"Hmmm," her father said as he shook his head again.

"Kriti, you have put me in such a tight place," he said, "I never thought you would have someone like this but," he took a deep breath, "I also know you are sensible enough. After taking to Armaan I really don't know what to do."

"Papa, it's all about her happiness, even if she gets married to someone else tomorrow she won't be happy," Armaan said, "If Arvind wasn't a nice person, I would have never come to you."

Kriti's father just nodded to himself. He gestured Kriti to sit beside him. Kriti got up and sat beside her father still looking down.

"Do you really want this, Kriti?" he asked her. Kriti just nodded as tears rolled down her face.

"Kriti, don't cry. I am just asking you," her father said calmly looking at her.

"Yes, Papa," she said meekly.

"Will you be happy with him?" he asked patting her cheeks.

She nodded. Her father looked at Arvind.

"I would have never agreed to this, but Armaan spoke to me at length about this. She is very precious to me. Her happiness means the world to me," her father stopped as he looked at Armaan, "I trust you, Armaan and so I will have to trust your choice."

He then looked at Arvind and said, "If I ever get to know you are not keeping her happy, you will regret having met me," he said pointing his finger sternly at Arvind.

Arvind just nodded, "Yes… Yes, Sir," he stuttered.

Kriti just hugged her father. He ruffled her hair. Avni too wiped a tear from her face.

"As much as I don't like this, I will agree, Kriti. Because you will be happy with him also because of you, Armaan," her father said looking at Armaan.

"Trust me, Papa, she will be happy," Armaan said.

At that point Arvind got up and touched Kriti's father's feet. He hesitated for a while, then put his hand on Arvind's head. He gave his blessings to both and agreed to meet with Arvind's parents soon. He then hugged Kriti and bid his goodbyes to everyone as he had to go.

Kriti broke down as her father left, out of sheer relief and happiness. Arvind went up and took her in his arms. He too had tears in his eyes.

"Thanks a lot, Armaan. I can't thank you enough," Arvind said holding Kriti.

"Please, call me Jiju now," Armaan said smiling at him, "don't thank me, I know you are a good guy and will keep her happy. So you better do just that else Papa will kill both of us," he joked.

"Yes, I will. You can count on me for that," Arvind replied.

"Kriti," Armaan went up and stood beside her.

She managed to break apart from Arvind with swollen eyes hugged him, "Thanks," she said.

"Please, Kriti you are like my little sister," he said ruffling her hair. "I am glad this worked out. See I told you, nothing is impossible," he said. "Ahana is out on a business trip but I am sure she will be equally delighted when she hears," he said looking at her. He walked to the door and picked up his bag. "Start your wedding preps," he said as he bid them goodbye.

"Eeeee," Avni screamed as she hugged Kriti and Arvind. "Oh God, I can't believe this, you guys are actually getting married!" Avni said. "I will leave you two lovebirds alone," Avni said as she walked out.

"Hi, Ansh. I am crashing at your place today. Oh, I have such good news. No, I am going to tell you once I am there. Bye," Avni kept the phone to catch a cab back to his guest house.

Ansh too was very happy hearing about Arvind and Kriti.

"That is great news, Avni," Ansh said as he held her.

"I know," Avni replied as she rubbed his arms, "thank god, we didn't have to go through all of this," Avni said looking at him.

"Yes, but we did go through our own trials," Ansh said looking at her, "do you remember the first time we met?" Ansh asked.

Avni laughed thinking about it.

"I was so nervous, I actually thought of saying no to you, as I didn't want to get married then," Avni said.

"Really? That was your plan. Then why didn't you?" Ansh asked teasingly.

"You trapped me," Avni said smiling at him, "You got me so confused, I was supposed to say no and then I didn't know how to. My head wanted to but my heart kept stopping me," Avni said as she hugged him.

"Hmm, so you did like me, you just stalled me unnecessarily for so long," Ansh said ruffling her hair.

"I guess I did, but probably I didn't want to accept it just then. There were so many things going through my mind," Avni said, she looked at him again and held his hands, "I wasn't in the space to get married at that point. I wasn't even thinking of it," she paused for a moment. "Also I think my past haunted me a bit, so I was a bit scared getting into a new relationship," Avni said as she looked down.

"I hope you are not scared now?" Ansh asked.

"Not at all. I trust you, Ansh. I trust you enough to not hurt me in any way," Avni said.

"I won't, Avni, I promise," Ansh said as she kissed her forehead.

She hugged him and smiled.

"I think I will go sleep now!" Avni said breaking apart.

"Okay, I have some work pending, so I am going to crash on

the sofa tonight," Ansh said as he looked at the sofa and the laptop.

"Okay," Avni nodded as she walked into the room.

She was suddenly woken up early in the morning by an unfamiliar voice in the hall.

Who could be home at this moment? Avni thought as she walked out. She stopped halfway when she saw Ansh talking to someone on the laptop. *Oh, it's just Ansh talking on Skype with someone,* she thought as she turned around but stopped as she heard a woman's sobbing voice.

"I don't know what to do, Ansh," the woman sobbed.

"Kripa, I am so sorry for whatever happened. Look if you are so unhappy, you should walk out," Ansh said.

"Walk out? And go where, I can't come to you anymore, Ansh," Kripa replied.

Avni froze in her place, *what was she talking about?*

"Kripa, please let's not go there. I know you are upset, but please let someone help you, it's worrying me," Ansh said.

"Ansh, I wish we had spoken about it. I wish I had told you about my feelings. I wish we could have thought of a future together, I wouldn't have been here then. I didn't want to get married to him, and now all he does is drinks all night. I wish I had chosen you, I know you had wanted this too," Kripa sobbed.

"Kripa, you are not thinking straight right now. Please stop crying. Don't do this to yourself," Ansh said.

"You hate seeing me crying. I know you care, you still care, Ansh," Kripa said.

"Kripa, don't go there," Ansh replied firmly.

"Oh yes, I forgot you are engaged now," Kripa added sarcastically.

"Kripa, please talk to your brother about it or your parents. Get out if you are not happy," Ansh said.

Avni couldn't believe her ears! *Why was Kripa talking about having a future with Ansh? Who was she? Ansh wanted it at one time? How come he never spoke about it? Why was he being the shoulder for her to cry on? Why was he not telling her off?*

"I guess I am too late now, Ansh, isn't it. This is what you do to me just because I went off and got married to someone else?" Kripa sobbed.

"Kripa, it's nothing like that. I wanted us to happen at one point, I won't deny that. I am not doing anything to you. I am so sorry for whatever is happening, it's very unfortunate. I hate seeing you this way. It's just that I am just not where I was a few years ago," Ansh said, "I think you need to talk to someone in your family, you shouldn't be so miserable."

The call cut from the other side. Ansh just stared at the laptop for a second, then shook his head and shut the laptop. He held his head for a while and just sat there.

Avni just stared at him in silence. *Why was he upset?* Avni thought. *Why did seeing Kripa cry make him so upset?*

He took a deep breath and looked up, and saw Avni standing right outside the room.

"Avni, what are you doing here? I thought you were sleeping," Ansh said as he got up.

"Yes, why not? Of course, you thought I was sleeping, so you could have all the time to talk to your ex?" Avni said as a rage inside her started to rise.

"Avni, what?" he said looking at her and then at his laptop, "it's nothing like that."

Tears fell from Avni's eyes; she was so hurt and angry at the same time.

"Then what is it like, Ansh? A woman calls you middle of the night and tells you she is not happy in her marriage, and that she still has feelings for you and is somewhere rooting for you to confess to her!" Avni said as she raised her voice.

"Avni, she was upset. I don't think she was in her right mind to realize what she was saying," Ansh said walking towards her.

Avni held her hand up to stop him.

"Okay, no, actually we should have started from somewhere else. I should have first asked you – who the hell is she?" Avni yelled.

Ansh held his head, "Avni, sit down," Ansh said.

"No, why didn't you tell me about her before?" Avni asked.

"Did you tell me about your past?" Ansh retaliated.

"Yes, I did not at first. But when I did, you should have too," Avni screamed.

"Avni, we were not in a relationship, she is not my past," Ansh said looking at her.

"Then what was that?" Avni yelled pointing at the computer.

Ansh took a deep breath, "Okay, we were in college doing our MBA together. I liked her and she liked me too, and we both knew it. It was just unsaid. I just did not pursue it further because once she had indirectly told me her family was very strict; they would have never agreed to us and it would have only gotten her into trouble and I did not want that for her," he finished as he looked at Avni.

"Why was she calling you now, Ansh?" Avni asked.

"I don't know, she was upset," Ansh said.

"And yet after so long, you are first person she thought of?" Avni asked.

Ansh just looked down and kept quiet.

"You took her call, you told her walk out, and you entertained her talk of wanting to get back with you?" Avni cried.

"I did not Avni, I told her I wasn't where she is now," Ansh said looking at her.

"Why did you have to be the shoulder she wanted to cry on?" Avni asked she stopped for a moment and asked again, "You were so upset after you spoke to her, why?" Avni sobbed.

"Avni…" Ansh started.

"She still affects you, doesn't she? And now you are in a fix because after so many years she has come back. And now she wants to be with you and you don't know what to do, because you are getting married to me," Avni sobbed.

"Avni, please no. What are you saying?" Ansh went on as he walked towards her.

"Ansh, clear your head before we get married. Don't do this to me," Avni said sobbing.

"Avni, I am very clear. Please don't think like that," Ansh said as she held her.

She brushed his hands off, "How do I know you don't want to be with her? Even if not now, how do I know if you decide you want to be with her tomorrow?" Avni cried.

"Avni, I am sorry. I did not realize this would hurt you so much. I shouldn't have taken her call. It was my bad. Avni, I don't want you to think this way," Ansh said as he held her again. "I don't care what Kripa wants, not now, not tomorrow. She is gone, Avni. She was gone a long time ago for me," Ansh said as he held her face.

Avni closed her eyes. She shook her head.

"I need to sleep over this one," Avni said as she broke apart from him and walked into her room to get her things.

"Where are you going?" Ansh asked.

"Back to my apartment," Avni said, as she picked up her purse.

"Avni, now?" Ansh asked looking at his watch.

"It's almost five in the morning, I am sure I will find an auto," Avni said as she walked out.

"Avni, what the hell! Why do we have to give her so much importance?" Ansh asked.

"Because you did Ansh, you did," Avni sobbed as she walked out.

Chapter XV

When Avni finally got home she saw Roshni standing in the kitchen giggling with a guy.

"Hey," Avni said walking in the kitchen looking at Roshni and the guy.

"Hi, Avni. Oh my God, I am so thrilled," Roshni said hugging her. "I knew her dad would agree. Kriti was just stressing over nothing," she added.

"Oh ya, you heard?" Avni asked.

"Yes, Kriti called me, she is out now though," Roshni said.

Avni was still looking at the guy who was now smiling at her.

"Oh so sorry, this is Aakash," Roshni said looking at him, "and this is Avni, my roomie."

"Hi, how are you?" Avni said, "uh, you guys in same office?"

Avni asked trying to recall his face.

"Oh no, we are like childhood friends, at least our parents think so, not that we remember too much of us together then," he said looking at Roshni.

"Aah okay," Avni said, "Roshni, I have something to show you, umm... Can you come with me?" she said holding her hand and then looked at Aakash and said, "Could you excuse us for a second?"

"Yeah sure," he said.

"Come," Avni said taking Roshni into the room. "What's happening? Is he same guy you met the other day? I thought you hated him," Avni said as they entered the room.

"Yes, he is. Okay, I didn't like him at first but then I met him at a house party the other day. Turns out one of my office colleagues is his college buddy. We just got talking and I think I was so mad at my father for making me meet him that I didn't find him nice," she said biting her lip. "But you know he is a nice guy," Roshni said.

"Okay, so you like him now?" Avni asked.

"No! I mean he is nice and I don't like him but we are just getting to know each other," Roshni said looking at her.

"Have you told your dad about this?" Avni asked.

"No ways! If I tell my father the next thing I know, I am marrying him. I don't want to rush it nor does he. We just got to know each other, there is something," she shrugged. "But we want to take our time to figure it out," she explained, "So we have decided not to tell our parents till we know what it is between the both of us," she said.

"Hmm yeah, sounds rational. You guys can take your time," Avni said, "but when I said I needed time you guys never heard me out," Avni complained.

"I am sorry, Avni. I get it now, what you were trying to say. But look everything has worked out just fine so it's cool," Roshni said. "Hey, by the way, it's such great news for Kriti. Shall we go out somewhere to celebrate?" Roshni asked.

"Yeah, how about that cafe that opens at midnight on the outskirts," Avni asked.

"Yeah, that's perfect," Roshni said, "Just us girls. It will be great."

"Yes, it will be," Avni said, "anyways, he must be waiting. You should go," Avni said

"Ya, okay call Kriti and Ria and tell them we will go tonight," Roshni said as she walked out.

Just then her phone rang.

"Yes, Mom. I know, I haven't forgotten. Yes, we will come on time. Okay, bye Mom," she said as she kept the phone.

This was the tenth time her mother had called her since morning to remind her of the lunch party her mother had organized for her family with Ansh. Only she didn't want to go with Ansh now. She remembered talking to him about it.

"Do I have to?" Ansh had asked hesitantly, "It's not that I mind, but it's your whole family," Ansh said.

"Yes, you have no choice I guess. I am sorry, I hate these gathering too but we have to go," Avni had said. "Besides I will do that do too once we are married," Avni had reasoned.

"Oh yes, a lot of that," Ansh said, "Okay, we will go," Ansh had said looking at her smiling.

"Hey by the way, I was thinking of booking tickets for our trek in the Himalayas," he had said.

"Yes, okay that would be great. In December I am sure we'll freeze, but next year early summers when we are in India we can do it," Avni had said.

"Yes, I was looking at that and thought it's best to look for accommodation and everything," Ansh said, "I will send you a tentative itinerary. I think we should do this before I head back to Norway," he had said looking into his phone.

"I can't believe you are here for only two more weeks," Avni had said holding him.

"Breaks my heart too, Avni, but what to do? I have to go, but I will be back soon to take you with me forever," he had said holding her hands tight.

"As cheesy as that sounds, I quite like the idea of it," Avni had said smiling.

"So, you ain't scared of it anymore? Going to another country with me?" Ansh had asked.

"No, not anymore," Avni had said laying her head on his shoulders.

A tear rolled down her cheek. She didn't know if Ansh was actually rethinking about them right now. He said he was past it but he seemed clearly upset after talking to Kripa. Avni did not want to think about it anymore, it was making her go crazy so instead she got up to decide what to wear for the lunch. She wasn't sure if Ansh would be there, *I will just make some excuse for him,* Avni thought if he didn't turn up.

After a while, after Avni had showered, had her breakfast and was siting by her bed putting on her bracelet. She heard her doorbell ring. She could hear Roshni greeting someone.

"Avni," Ansh stood by her room door.

Avni looked at him; part of her wanted to hug him and part of her wanted to turn away and not look at him. She chose to turn away.

"Avni, please don't do this. I am miserable without you," he said as he sat down on the bed beside her, "I shouldn't have entertained Kripa, Avni, but please you have to trust me, it was nothing," Ansh said as he held her hands.

She looked at her hands in his and sniffed, "I don't like anything coming between us," Avni said as she looked at him.

"I promise you, nothing and no one ever will," Ansh said as he looked at her and smiled and before Avni knew he was down on his knees.

"What are you doing?" Avni asked looking at him. He raised his hands to shush her, and continued.

"I know, we met as strangers and had to decide in no time if we wanted to get married or not. I know it's not been an easy journey but now at this moment, having your hands in mine, there is nowhere else I want to be. I love you, Avni," he said beaming at her.

Avni just smiled at him, narrowing her eyes.

"I am sorry, I thought of doing this in a grand way but after today, I thought it's best I do it now," Ansh said as he held out a box in his hands.

"Ansh, what?" Avni gasped.

He opened the box. There lay a lovely solitaire, on a white gold band, which gleamed in all its beauty. Avni's eyes blurred looking at it.

"I know I have asked you before but still," he said as he held her hand, "will you marry me?" Ansh asked.

"Oh my God! Of course!" Avni replied as she hugged him.

He took the ring out and put it on her finger. She just kept looking at it.

"It's the most beautiful ring I have ever seen," Avni said as she looked at it.

"Uhhmmm," Roshni cleared her throat from behind.

Avni looked at the door and saw Roshni and Aakash looking at them.

"Congrats," Roshni said as she hugged them both, "I got a small peep at the ring when Ansh walked in." Roshni said as she held Avni's hands to get a closer look, "It's beautiful," she said looking at Ansh.

Ansh mouthed thanks.

Aakash just shook hands with them both.

"Thanks guys," Ansh said.

Avni kept staring at her ring, she then looked at Ansh, "It's just beautiful."

Ansh smiled at her, he then looked at his watch, "Oh shoot, We are going to be late, Avni. I hope we beat the traffic, I think we should leave for the lunch."

"Oh yes, you remembered," Avni said looking at him and then adjusting her ring, "We should go," Avni said.

Avni's lunch with her family was a riot. Ansh was treated like a king. Avni was quite amused by it. Everybody folded their hands and greeted him. Her mother and her cousins ran helter skelter to get him water and some snacks, while her father and uncles all got up to make place for him. He was made to sit between them. He looked at Avni, pleading for help, Avni just shrugged her shoulders and mouthed *enjoy* as she walked towards the kitchen.

"Mom, I am hungry. You put everything out there for him. What about me?" Avni complained.

"Look at her," her mother said talking to her aunt, "always complaining, here have some," she said giving her some snacks on the plate.

"What will your mother-in-law think?" her mother said.

"Mumma, she won't think anything. She is very cool. Ansh tol... I mean he keeps telling me that she is very cool and open," Avni said eating the snacks.

"She might be, but however cool she is you still have to grow up. Look at your *bhabhis*, so responsible they are," her mother said looking at Bhavya, "Teach her something," she said shaking her head.

"Aunty, don't worry, we were also so clueless when we came in, she will learn," Bhavya said smiling at Avni.

"Avni," her mom said staring at Avni, who was busy looking at her ring.

"What's that?" her mother asked as she held her hand.

Just as her mother asked that, everyone in the kitchen looked at Avni's hand.

"Oh, I forgot to show it to you, Ansh gave it to me," Avni said looking at her ring.

"Really?" her mother asked looking at it, "Is this your engagement ring?" her mother asked.

"Yes, Mom, I know we are going to have a ceremony for that later, but that's okay," Avni said smiling at the ring.

"It's beautiful," Bhavya said as she held Avni's hand.

"Thanks," Avni smiled.

"Yes, it is a beautiful ring," Uma said as she looked at Avni and smiled.

Avni went red. As she walked into the hall, she saw Ansh surrounded by her father and uncles. All of them were swarming around him with questions and he took time to answer to each one of them. Once lunch was served, he got up to wash his hands.

"Avni, oh my God. It was worse than a job interview," he said wiping sweat off his forehead.

"Well, you wanted to marry me so bad so deal with it," Avni said handing out the towel to him.

He smiled to himself shaking his head, "What was I thinking?" he joked.

"Hey," Avni said as she lightly punched him on his shoulders.

"Uhmmm," her *bhabhi* came in, "shall we?" she said as she pointed towards the dining table.

They all got up as Ansh walked in. Avni tried her best to hide her laughter. Ansh sat down sheepishly, everyone followed and started to eat.

After lunch, as they were bidding goodbye to everyone, her mother asked, "Ansh, are you free tomorrow? We were going shopping for Avni's *sangeet lehenga.* We thought it would be great if you were there too," she said smiling at him.

"Oh wow. Yes, Aunty. That would be great," he said smiling back at her.

"Your *sangeet lehenga,* wow. You will look so beautiful, Avni," Ansh said as they got into the car.

"I just hope I don't fall dancing in it," Avni said.

"You won't Avni, stop scaring yourself," Ansh said waving his hands to her family who were frantically waving at them.

"My family is quite crazy," Avni said looking out at them waving.

"No, Avni, they just love you a lot and are very excited about your wedding. That's all," he replied looking at her.

They waved them goodbye as they drove off.

Chapter XVI

"Where to?" Ansh asked.

"I will go home, little tired. Will rest for a while, then I will see you in the evening," Avni said half-yawning.

"Ya sure, I will catch up on some work by then, I will see you tonight," he said as he drove her to her house.

"No, actually, I will be going out tonight," Avni replied.

"Okay, where to?" Ansh asked looking at his phone.

"Oh, we wanted to celebrate Kriti's father agreeing to their marriage. So, we thought we will go have coffee at this cafe that opens at midnight on the outskirts of town," Avni said casually.

"Okay, what time do we leave from here to reach there?" he asked.

"Not us, Ansh. Just us girls. Kriti, Ria, Roshni and I," Avni said.

"Just you girls, on the outskirts of Delhi at midnight?" Ansh asked as he parked the car by the side and looked at her.

"Ya," Avni replied causally.

"No," Ansh said sternly.

"No? What do mean by no?" Avni said, "I am not asking, Ansh. I am telling you that we are going."

"No, Avni. You are not going," Ansh said looking at her.

"What? Why?" Avni said getting a little irritated.

"Avni, because it's Delhi. It's not safe, okay," Ansh said.

"Oh, since when do you know about Delhi so much? I have been here my whole life," Avni said raising her voice.

"Avni, I don't need to stay here to know about Delhi. You know it. I know it. Every sane person knows it. Delhi is not safe! You want to go on the outskirts, just you girls. You know how unsafe that is?"

Ansh asked.

"We have gone there before, nothing happens," Avni said.

"Avni, you must have been every lucky, but I can't possibly allow you now," Ansh said raising his voice.

"Allow me? See there you go again," Avni snapped, "I did not ask for your permission."

"Avni, you are not going," Ansh said, looking at her in disbelief, "and don't start this again. I do have some say in your life."

"You seem to be having a say in everything in my life. I can't even go out with my friends now," Avni retorted.

"Avni don't take this somewhere else. You know why I am saying no," Ansh said getting angry now.

"What is this, Ansh? We have all decided and I will go," Avni said.

"Okay, Avni if you really want to go then just go somewhere in the city where it's crowded enough, why there?" he reasoned.

"Ansh, because that cafe is really nice. We've been thinking about going there for a while and now we have a good reason."

"No, Avni. It is not safe at all," Ansh said.

"I hate this; you can't do this to me. We are perfectly capable of taking care of ourselves," Avni replied.

"Avni, please be a little mature about this," Ansh said.

"I am being very mature. I am actually seeing where my life is going and it is completely changing," Avni screamed.

"Of course, it is, you are getting married for God's sake," Ansh yelled, "things will change, not a lot but a little. We will have to adjust accordingly."

"Ansh, I can't take this. I know it's not safe, but we know how to be careful," Avni said.

"Oh really, how?" Ansh asked.

"We know, Ansh. We will come back safe."

He shook his head.

"This is really crazy, you can't dictate terms to me, Ansh," Avni said getting angry again.

"You think this is dictating. Have you lost your mind?" Ansh said yelling again.

"No, I haven't, Ansh. I live this way and I will. You have to learn deal with this, else we just need some time off."

"It's so easy for you to say this every time. Is this some kind of joke to you? We are not in a casual relationship, Avni," Ansh snapped.

"I know we are not and it's not easy for me to say this. We can't be fighting like this after marriage," Avni said.

"If you get worked up on every little thing I say," Ansh said, "What can I do?"

"If you stop controlling my life like this I will stop getting worked up," Avni replied.

"Avni, you are impossible," he said holding his head.

"Yes, I am and that's why we should take some time off for a while," Avni said as she walked out.

Avni was so angry she just stormed out of the car without even looking back.

* * *

She stormed into her house and said, "Let's go, guys."

"Huh?" Roshni said watching TV.

"To the cafe. Shall we leave?" Avni said looking at them in disbelief, as they were sitting in their pajamas.

"Oh that. Ya, well I don't think we are going," Roshni said looking at Kriti.

"Ya, Arvind strictly said no," Kriti explained shaking her head and turning back to the TV.

"He said no? What is with these guys?" Avni said sitting down, "I don't understand why we can't go?"

"It's not safe," Kriti said.

"Yes, I know, but we have been there before. We can be careful, right?" Avni asked.

"Avni, I think Arvind is right, it's really not a smart thing for us to go on the highway now. It's actually not safe anymore," Roshni said eating the chips kept beside her.

"Oh come on, it would have been so much fun," Avni said.

"It would have, but not so much if we got into trouble," Kriti said, "at first even I got a little angry, but then I understood what he was saying was right."

"Why are you so upset?" Roshni asked looking at Avni.

"Oh it's just," Avni said as she sat down, "I fought with Ansh."

"Why?" Kriti asked.

"He said I couldn't go tonight as it's not safe," Avni said looking at them.

"Okay," Roshni said, "then?"

"That's what we fought about, okay. He kept saying I won't let you go, I won't allow you," Avni started.

"And you thought he is curbing your so-called freedom again," Roshni finished.

Avni just frowned.

"Avni, he cares about you, that's why he didn't want you to go," Kriti said.

"I know," Avni, said looking down, "I realize I overreacted," Avni said thinking about their fight.

Avni had an opinion about so many things in Ansh's life but she hated it when he interfered in the slightest manner. She just looked down, she was being unfair to him. If he had given her the right to speak in his life, then she should too, she thought.

"You are being unfair, aren't you?" Roshni said.

"Ya, a little," Avni said, "Okay, I know I shouldn't react like this every time. It's just that a lot of things will change after marriage. My home, my priorities and I won't be able to do a lot of things so freely. I will have to weigh a lot of things. When Ansh tells me something I just panic and..." Avni said holding her head.

"Avni, see our lives are not going to be how they are now, but I am sure it will be wonderful being with whom we love. We will have to take care of their feelings and so will they. It has to be a give and take relationship," Kriti said putting her hands on Avni's shoulders.

Avni took a deep breath, "I understand all that, I just get so immature at times."

"It's okay, Avni, we all are. None of us are a pro at this, but we will get there," Kriti said.

Avni looked at her phone as it buzzed. It was an alarm that reminded her that she had to go shopping for her *sangeet lehenga* the next day. Ansh was to come too. She didn't know what to talk to him or how to talk to him. It was too late to go to him, and if she called him she would be too tongue-tied, so she messaged him instead.

"Ansh, I am sorry. I shouldn't have reacted so badly. Turns out you were right. I realize it is not safe for us girls to be out in the middle of nowhere so late. I know you were only concerned about my safety. I was immature and impulsive and I lashed out at you. Please forgive me. I hope you're not angry anymore."

Avni read and we read the message a several times. She imagined him reading every line. She paused, read it for one last time and sent it. Way past midnight she checked her phone half in her sleep, there was no reply. She realized he was probably angry and went to sleep. She tossed about in her sleep and told herself she would handle it tomorrow. First thing in the morning she checked her phone again. There was a reply.

"Okay."

She scrolled down, went back and opened it again – okay, that was it.

What kind of a reply was that? She apologized for last night and all he said was okay. She shook her head and got up to get ready. As she got out of the shower she saw five missed calls from her mother. She dialled her mom.

"Yes, Mom," Avni said, "I know, I remember. Yes, I had put an alarm. Yes, he will be there. Mom, I was in the shower, where do you think I will disappear?" Avni asked. "Yes, if you keep the phone will I be able to get ready and come. Okay bye."

"My mom! She still thinks I am a five-year-old," Avni said looking at Kriti who was now smiling at her.

"Yes, I understand. My mother cried so much when she learnt about Arvind. She liked him by the way when she met him, but she kept worrying so much about me going to his family. 'Oh they are Telugu, what do they do? What are their customs? Kriti, how will you adjust? I am so worried. They all seem so serious," Kriti said imitating her mom.

"Didn't you tell her he is from South and not Gujarat where people start doing *garba* at the slightest opportunity they get," Avni joked.

"Oh please, Avni we don't. But yes, we do seem like a livelier lot than them. I am sure his family will be overwhelmed seeing our side at the wedding," Kriti said.

"Yes. I can't wait to attend your wedding. It will be so different," Avni said putting on her *kaajal.*

"So, things sorted out between the both of you?" Kriti asked.

"Yes, I guess," Avni said.

"You guess?" Kriti asked.

"Oh, I will know when I meet him," Avni said smiling at her as she got up to take her purse and went out, "bye."

Avni kept hoping everything was fine, and that her mother shouldn't catch the awkwardness between them. She would kill Avni if she knew she fought with him.

As Avni reached the shop her eyes stopped at this beautiful blood red *lehenga* in the window. *Wow,* Avni thought as she looked at it. It was so lovely she couldn't take her eyes off it.

"You like it?" said a voice from behind.

"Huh?" Avni said as she turned around and saw Ansh. "Hi," she said sheepishly.

He just looked at her.

"Ansh, about last night..."

"Avni, Ansh, oh so nice to see you," her mother emerged from the crowd on the street.

"Namaste, Aunty," Ansh said as he folded his hands.

"Bless you, *beta,*" her mother said.

"Hi, Ma," Avni said looking at Ansh.

"Come, let's go," her aunt said pulling her away and gesturing Ansh to come in.

They struggled to make their way through the rush inside. There so much chaos and the shopkeepers were talking loudly to each other. The customers were all busy looking at the different apparel. Some of them were walking up to the mirror to see how they were looking.

"Mom, how will we shop? It's so crowded," Avni asked making her way through.

"Don't worry, your father knows this owner, we are going up. There we can sit at ease and select a *lehenga* for you, okay."

"Oh, thank God," Avni said finally seeing the staircase.

It was such a relief going upstairs. It was a small section with nice benches at the side and a changing room in the corner.

"I love you, Dad," Avni said as she sat by the bench.

"Shall we, Ma'am?" he said as he started taking out the boxes.

"Can you show us that red *lehenga* in the window downstairs?" Ansh asked.

"*Beta*, which one, tell us?" her mother asked.

"That is from the new collection, it's a beautiful wedding *lehenga,*" the shopkeeper said as he called out to someone to get it.

"Beta, we are looking for her *sangeet,*" her mother said.

"I know, Aunty. But her wedding *lehenga* will come from us and my mother told me that since we are looking for Avni's *sangeet lehenga*, I might as well get her wedding one. If she likes something, I can buy it for her," Ansh said smiling at her.

She whispered into Avni's ears, "Avni, don't like something very expensive, please look at the tag before you say anything."

"Yes, Mom," Avni nodded. She thought for a while and then asked, "How much is too expensive?"

"Avni!" her mother stared at her.

By then a shopkeeper had brought up the blood red *lehenga* Avni was eyeing at the door.

"Oh my God, this seems very lovely," Avni's mother said, "and very expensive," she finished.

"Aunty, please don't see the money. I want and in fact my parents also want that Avni wears something she really likes and cherishes for the rest of her life," Ansh said.

"I just thought it is okay. Ansh, we can see something else?" Avni said.

"Avni, I saw you staring at it. Just try it, if you don't like it, it's up to you," Ansh said.

Avni heart jumped at the thought of wearing the *lehenga*. It was beautiful beyond words. She took it inside the changing room and checked the tag it was Rs. 1, 95, 000.

Oh my God! Avni thought, *That is expensive. What shall I do? I will just wear it and say no.*

As she wore the *lehenga* she fell more and more in love with it. Over the blood red base it had gold work with big gold flowers at the bottom. If you held the *lehenga* upside down it seemed like the flowers were falling, so the flowers became smaller as they went up, down to every petal which was put at the *lehenga's* waist. The blouse had a broad gold border and a golden stem-like design all over it. The *dupatta* was simple yet elegant, blood red with a subtle gold design all over. She saw herself in the mirror with the *lehenga* on and almost died.

I've never looked so beautiful, Avni thought as tears rolled down her cheeks. *As much as I love you, I can't have you,* Avni sobbed talking to the *lehenga. Why do you have to be so beautiful, yet so expensive?* Avni thought looking up at the mirror.

"Avni, come out, *beta.* Are you done?" her mother called from outside.

"Yes, Mom, I am coming out," Avni said.

As she walked out, Ansh almost stumbled on the *chai* kept beside him. She blushed like a bride, she turned her gaze to her mother. Her mother opened her mouth then closed it. She saw her mother eyes moisten.

She held Avni's hands, "Oh Avni, it's lovely!" She then whispered, "how much?"

"Two," Avni mouthed.

"Oh," her mother said.

"It's lovely," Ansh said finally after looking at her for a good ten minutes.

"Yes, but it's so heavy," Avni said looking down.

"Is it, Avni? It looks so beautiful," he said.

"Yes, *beta,* but it's very heavy. She won't be able to walk in it properly. We will see something else."

"Are you sure?" Ansh asked.

Avni's heart sank, "Yes," she said as she walked back into the changing room. Tears rolled down her cheeks as she took it off. It was love at first sight. She walked out with a long face and sat down.

"Show us some more, both for the *sangeet* and wedding," her mom said.

Avni half-heartedly went through the rest of shopping.

"Is this nice?" Avni asked looking at Ansh as her mother and aunt were looking at other *lehengas.*

"Avni, whatever you like," he said.

"Say something, help me. Do you like this? Okay, should I take this or that one?"

He just shrugged.

"Ansh!" Avni said.

"Avni, I am sorry. I don't know if giving my opinion on anything is good because I don't know when you will react again. Rather you give me a list of things I can give my opinion on," he said looking at her.

"Ansh, I am so sorry. I unnecessarily overreacted," Avni said.

"Avni, it's really not fair when every time you say you need some time off," Ansh replied.

"I know, I won't say that again," Avni said shaking her head.

"Yeah, I hope so, Avni," he said looking at her, as he shrugged.

"Ansh, can we move past yesterday, please," Avni asked as she held his hand.

"Ya, I guess," he said looking at her.

Ansh kept quiet for a while and then asked, "By the way you liked that *lehenga*, didn't you?"

"No, I don't, I mean. It's beautiful, but it's heavy and I didn't..." Avni rambled.

"I got it, you like it. When you start rambling like that, Miss Avni, I know you are lying," he smiled at her.

"No, Ansh, please it's too expensive," Avni blurted.

"What! Is that why you said no?" Ansh asked.

"Oh... I..."

"Avni, please don't look at the money. It's your day. It's our day. You looked gorgeous in it. I couldn't take my eyes off you," Ansh said.

"I know. But, Ansh, we will see something else," Avni said.

"No. I know you love that one so we are picking that," Ansh said, "and I love it."

"Ansh no, my mom would kill me," Avni pleaded.

"Don't worry. I will tell her I bought it because I loved it," Ansh said.

"Ansh it's too much, it's not worth it," Avni said.

"You love it, Avni. Then it's worth every penny," Ansh said holding her hands.

She blushed, "Oh I don't know what to say."

"You just have to say it, Avni. I will get it for you... always," Ansh said whispering to her.

Avni just blushed even more.

"Avni. Why don't you look at these," her mother said as she picked up a couple of *lehengas.*

"Oh, this one is so beautiful," Avni said taking one of them from her mother's hands.

"Yes, that is pretty," Her aunt said sitting beside them.

"I love how the colour is blending in," Avni said standing up in front of the mirror and putting the *lehenga* in front of her.

"I think this should be perfect for your *sangeet,* "her mother said.

"What do you think, *beta?*"

"Yes, Aunty, I think it's perfect," Ansh said, "You should try it on, Avni."

"Yes, go Avni, try this one," Her mother said.

Avni tried it on and everybody loved the *lehenga*. It was a cream and wine *lehenga* and looked very elegant on her. It was cream at the top and blended into wine at the bottom with gold thread work all over.

"It isn't very heavy, so I am sure I won't have a problem dancing in it," Avni said circling around.

"Yes, anyway. Avni, go change, till we find something for your wedding," her mother said.

Avni looked at Ansh who just smiled at her reassuringly.

Avni looked at the red *lehenga* lying at the side. She couldn't believe he had agreed to buy it for her. Her heart filled with joy and guilt and the same time for liking it so much. She justified herself for picking such an expensive one thinking even if she refused a million times now Ansh would buy it for her no matter what. She smiled to herself and walked in to get changed.

"Mom, can we call it a day?" Avni said.

"Already? Your wedding shopping has just begun," her mother said.

"One day at a time, Mom," Avni said sitting down.

"But your wedding *lehenga*?" her mother asked.

"Aunty, I think we should pick that one," Ansh said looking at the red *lehenga*.

"Oh no, Ansh, it's too heavy," her mother said.

"I know but it's so lovely. I sent a picture of Avni in it to my mother and she loved it. She insisted I buy this for her," Ansh said looking at Avni's mother.

"Oh, she did? Well, *beta*, if she told you to buy it then okay, but it's so expensive," Avni's mother finally said.

"Aunty, please don't worry. This is for her wedding and we really want the best for her," Ansh said getting up.

"Oh, I don't know what to say, it's too much," her mother said.

"Aunty, please. I really like it too and would love it if she wore this on our wedding," he said.

"Okay, *beta*, if you are insisting so much," her mother said.

"Shall we get them billed then?" Ansh asked.

"Yes, not this. This one we will get," she said pointing at her *sangeet lehenga*. "Just that one," indicating the wedding *lehenga*.

Ansh nodded and went down. Avni literally jumped like a little girl walking down the steps.

"Avni, you told him you liked it, nah," her mother said as she held Avni's hands.

"No, Mom. I did not say anything. He himself liked it so much and now my mother-in-law likes it too," Avni said smiling at her mother.

Uma just smiled and she shook her head as she walked down. Avni looked at Ansh standing down, waiting for her.

"I love you," Avni mouthed to him.

He smiled back and Avni saw him turning red. They bid goodbye to her mother and aunt and drove back to his guest house.

"Are you happy?" Ansh asked as they walked in.

Avni just hugged him, "Thanks!"

"Don't thank me, Avni. My heart almost stopped when I saw you in it," he said looking at her.

Avni smiled.

"Don't ever tell me you want to leave me or think about this, or you want time off. I know I want to marry you, and only you, Avni. It's really hurtful everytime you say that," Ansh said.

"Ansh, I won't. I promise," Avni said.

"I am serious. I won't let you go anywhere," he said holding her.

Avni held his hands and put it behind her back, "I won't, Ansh. I might say of lot things impulsively, but I know I can't do without you anymore," she said as she kissed him.

"Avni, I am leaving in a few days and I don't want any of this between us anymore," Ansh said looking at her.

"I can't believe you are leaving already," Avni said resting her head in his arms.

"Let me take you out for dinner," Ansh said as they broke apart, "I know this lovely place," he said.

"Oh really, you know about Delhi now?" Avni asked.

"Yes, not so much though. A colleague told me about this place," he said smiling at her.

"Okay, pick me up at 8 then," Avni said.

"Okay, Ma'am, I will see you at 8," Ansh said as he hugged her goodbye.

Avni smiled and walked out.

Chapter XVII

Avni was getting ready for her dinner at her apartment. Roshni walked in to her room.

"How did your *lehenga* shopping go today?" Roshni said as she sat on the bed.

"Very well, I have to show you the *lehengas* I bought for my wedding and *sangeet*," Avni said as she sat on the bed and showed Roshni the pictures on the phone.

"Oh wow! This *lehenga*," Roshni said as her eyes widened.

"Isn't it, oh it's so amazing," Avni said looking at the picture again.

"You look lovely, Avni. I can't wait for your wedding now," she said hugging her.

"Yes, now even I can't," Avni said, "I can't believe he is leaving in a few days. I have got so used to him being around, it's funny."

"He'll be back soon to take you far away from all of us," Roshni said still holding Avni.

"Oh I know, and I will miss you so much," Avni said.

Just then her phone rang with Ansh's name on it.

"You should go," Roshni said breaking apart.

Avni nodded and walked out. They drove towards north Delhi. Ansh was right. It was a lovely place.

It was an open restaurant, which had a pool on one side and a bar on the other. It had a beach-like ambience with sand and palm trees everywhere. It had low-lying seats with candles on every table.

"Wow," Avni said she walked in.

They sat down and she looked around, it looked so lovely. There was light instrumental music being played in the background. She saw a couple of guys sitting by the bar counter but did not take notice of them. Just as she turned her gaze towards Ansh, her heart jumped a beat. She looked back and noticed her college friends there, she thought she saw him too.

Avni, Siddhart is not here. Why are you even thinking about him when you are with Ansh?" she thought closing her eyes.

"Are you alright?" Ansh asked noticing her face.

"Yes," she nodded.

"I will get myself a mocktail, you want anything to drink," he said looking at the bar.

"No, I will just have a mocktail as well," she said as she looked back at the counter. It was so dark she could hardly make out anything. She was probably mistaken.

Ansh walked up to the bar. He noticed a bunch of guys looking at him and talking. He just smiled at them and looked at the bartender.

"Can you make us two mocktails, the best in the house?" he said.

There was a guy sitting beside him sipping his whisky. Ansh felt like he was watching him as he ordered.

"You don't drink?" he asked Ansh.

"No, I don't," Ansh answered.

"And your lady?" he asked.

"Excuse me?" Ansh asked.

"I am sorry, buddy. I was just asking," he said looking at Ansh.

"It's okay. No, we don't," Ansh said.

"Surprising," the guy said taking a sip of his whisky and then looked at Avni.

"What? Do you know her?" Ansh asked.

He just nodded.

"You do?" Ansh asked again.

"We knew each other," he said smiling at Ansh.

"Okay," Ansh said looking at him to say something further.

"We were in the same college," he said.

"Oh okay, why don't you come say hi?" Ansh asked.

"No, dude, she wouldn't like that," he said looking at Avni, "We had a fight and..."

"Okay man. I am sure Avni must have forgotten about it," Ansh said.

"So you are her fiancé. Nice to meet you," he said holding his hands out to Ansh.

Ansh just looked at his hands and then at him. He thought for a moment then shook his hands.

"Nice to meet you too," he said as he asked the bartender for his drinks.

"Sorry sir, two more minutes," he said looking at the rush by the bar. Ansh nodded.

"She can be very stubborn, you know," the guy continued looking at his drink.

"Look, you don't need to tell me how she is. I know her very well," Ansh said looking at him.

"Don't mind, buddy, I'm just saying. She has her own mind, doesn't listen to anybody," he said.

"How do you know her again?" Ansh asked.

"I told you we were in the same college," he said.

Just then Avni walked in.

"Ansh, what's taking so long?" Avni said as she held his arms.

"The rush," Ansh said looking at the people at the bar counter.

"Hey! Can you make it fast for them?" the guy called out as he sipped on his whisky.

Avni froze as she heard his voice. She felt like she was transported back to a time she had regretted for so long. She turned around and looked at him, it was him, Sidharth, her ex. All this while she thought she had forgotten everything but a stream of memories came flashing in front of her eyes. She just stood there.

"Hey, Avni, do you know him. He says you were in the same college," Ansh asked casually.

Avni stammered "I... no. Actually, yes. I..."

"You still ramble like that, Avni," Sidharth said looking at Avni.

Avni held on to Ansh tighter.

"We should go," Avni said.

"Oh, come on, Avni, the party has just started. Why can't you introduce me to your fiancé," he said.

"Avni, what is it?" Ansh asked looking at him and Avni.

"You don't deserve to be introduced to him, so just stop this," Avni said.

"Oh, Avni. See, she is very short-tempered. Loses her fuse at the slightest of things," Sidharth said looking at Ansh.

"Look, dude. I don't know who you are but you are crossing the line now," Ansh said raising his voice.

"Okay, let me tell you who I am," Sidharth said finally getting up. "You see I made a small goof-up once, a really small one, which could have been easily forgiven," he said looking at Avni.

Avni just looked away disgusted.

"If not for that goof-up, I would have been standing where you are, buddy," he said finally looking at Avni holding Ansh's arms.

"Oh, so you are that ex. Well I am glad she walked out when she did," Ansh said getting angry.

"You should thank me," he said.

"Ansh, let's go," Avni said as she felt Ansh taking a step forward. "He is just trying to push your buttons. You don't want to get into a fight," Avni said.

"Avni, you don't drink anymore. It's almost unbelievable. Care for a smoke or have you stopped that too?" he asked.

"Sidharth, will you shut up!" Avni screamed.

"Dude, come sit," Sidharth said gesturing Ansh to sit, "I can give you some great tips on how to handle her. She is a difficult one," Sidharth said smiling at her.

Ansh looked at him. He knew Sidharth was just pushing him, so he took a deep breath and said, "I prefer to learn rather than taking tips from you. There is a good reason I don't want to take any tips from you."

Ansh looked at Avni, who looked at him in disbelief at how calm he sounded suddenly.

He turned back, "And yes, I should thank you. Thanks, man, because of you she is with me today."

"Let's go, Avni," Ansh said as he pulled her away.

She looked back and saw his college friends holding him back. She gave the most wicked grin to Sidharth as she held on to Ansh. She still remembered crying into her pillow all night when she had learnt about him. Nidhi and Ria had told her that karma will take care of everything one day, and today Avni realized it did.

Ansh walked towards the car and sat inside. Avni went around to the other side and sat inside quickly. She saw him holding his head.

"He was talking to me the whole time I was at the bar, and I did not even know," he said hitting his hands on the steering wheel.

"Ansh, I am sorry about all this," Avni said.

"How could you date a jerk like him?" he asked looking at Avni.

"Ansh, there is a reason why I left him," Avni said.

"Thank God for that," Ansh said, "picturing you with him makes me so mad," he said getting angry, "that's why I did not want to know anything about him," he said.

"You held your temper there," Avni said looking at him, "I am so glad."

"You were right, Avni, he was just pushing me to fight him. I did not want to lose my cool else I would have given him what he wanted."

Avni held her head.

Ansh looked at her, "Are you alright?"

"I could kill him right now, hasn't changed a bit, the shameless git," Avni said.

"Avni, I am sorry I was just thinking about myself and..." he just stopped, "you okay?"

"Yes, of course. I am way past it," Avni said looking at him.

"By the way, you used to smoke?" he asked.

Avni looked down and shook her head.

"I didn't tell you because I quit long back," Avni said looking at him.

"Avni, it's okay," he said holding her hands.

She just smiled.

"I am sorry, our date got ruined," Avni said.

"Avni, please. It wasn't your fault at all. I was the one who brought you here," Ansh said.

"We will go somewhere else," Ansh said.

"Where! It's a weekend. All the good places will be booked," Avni said.

"Okay, then what?" Ansh asked.

"You know what. I would actually love to have some Maggi," Avni said grinning at him.

"Maggi. Okay, Maggi it is then," he said as he started the car.

As they were driving towards the city, Avni got a call.

"Hi, Roshni. Ooh okay, that's great. We would love to meet him though I have met him once before but not properly. Okay. No, actually we will be there in fifteen. I tell you later why we didn't have dinner there but we are coming home. Is there Maggi at home? Like lots of it, for all of us. Okay then, that's great. You start making some and we will be there soon," Avni cut her phone and looked at Ansh to say something.

"I know, we are going to your place, and we have Maggi for everyone. So, everyone's home," Ansh asked looking at Avni.

"Yes, Arvind and Roshni are there too," Avni said, "and this new guy, Aakash, that Roshni met," Avni continued.

"Oh ya, you told me about him," he replied smiling at him.

"We are here," Avni said as she walked in.

"Wow, you guys are all dressed up," Kriti said looking at Avni and Ansh.

They were in their pyjamas.

"What is this, a pyjama party?" Avni said as she kept her clutch by the table and removed her heels.

"You can say that," Arvind replied smiling at her.

"Hi, Ansh, come sit," Arvind said looking at Ansh.

"Thanks man, how have you been? Congratulations to the both

of you. Such great news," Ansh said looking at both Arvind and Kriti.

They both just smiled.

"Hi guys," Ria said walking out of the bedroom.

"Hey, Ria, are you here for the night?" Avni asked.

"No, I just came here to take this book," Ria said as she held out the book, "I finished the first part of the series. I kept it on your bookshelf."

"Okay but, Ria, please just stay," Avni insisted.

"I can't. I will some other time," Ria said. "Anyways it seems like a couple's night tonight," Ria said.

"Oh, come on, Ria," Kriti said as she got up.

"I was just kidding, guys. Anyways I will take your leave. Bye," Ria said as she hugged Avni and walked out.

"You think she still feels bad?" Kriti asked looking at Avni.

"Bad? No. I think she is over it. She told us the other day remember, I am sure it does bother her at times but she is over it," Avni said as she sat on the couch.

"Am I missing something here?" Arvind asked. Kriti just looked at him. "Should I not be asking? Okay," Arvind said.

"No, come on. It's okay," Avni said.

"She was engaged to someone a while ago," Avni started.

"She was engaged?" Ansh asked.

"Yes, it was an arranged one. That guy looked like such a dream," Avni said.

"Oh, I remember, we were so jealous of her. He was so good looking and charming," Kriti added.

"Then what?" Arvind asked.

"Well he was just that and nothing more. Ria was on the top of the world being with him, but she soon realized he was a complete MCP," Avni said.

"I am sorry, what?" Ansh asked.

"A male chauvinist pig," Kriti replied.

"Oh, okay," Arvind said looking at Ansh, who just shrugged at him.

"He was very controlling. He wanted to know where Ria was going. Who she was meeting every minute. Every time she would come here, he would check if there is anybody else apart from us. He wouldn't let her drink in his absence. She stopped talking to all her guy friends," Avni went on.

"Oh, that's bad," Arvind said.

"Yeah, it was. He had a problem with the clothes she wore, with the way she spoke around his friends. It was too much. He was trying to change Ria into someone he wanted to be with," Kriti added.

"Yes, exactly. Remember he did not want her to work after marriage. He was from a business family, so he said that they were earning enough and Ria did not have to work," Avni said.

"Yeah, I remember that. I mean Ria is a gold medallist – Eco Honours from Shri Ram College," Kriti said.

"Oh wow," Arvind exclaimed.

"Exactly, she is such a brilliant mind. How can you expect her to sit at home?" Avni asked.

"Yes, that would have been very unfair," Ansh said.

"His parents were no less. Everybody wanted to just control her. She tried talking to her parents but they did not understand," Avni said.

"Then how did she get out of it?" Arvind asked.

"Her elder brother, he helped her. I think he could see through her fiancé. He got her out of the engagement," Kriti said.

"Things like these make you realize looks aren't everything," Kriti added.

Avni nodded. "Yes, he was so charming and handsome and everything but I think all of it had gone to his head," Avni said.

"Well, that's really bad. But in a way it's good she got out of it before it was too late," Ansh said.

"Yes, we were really glad when it was over for her," Avni replied.

"Yes, I am sure she can do so much better," Kriti said.

"Yeah, I know. Anyways where is Roshni?" Avni asked looking

around.

"Oh, she is in the kitchen with Aakash making Maggi," Kriti said.

"Maggi needs two people to make now," Avni asked sarcastically looking towards the kitchen.

"Well, they don't want to keep their eyes off each other. I just hope they make the Maggi," Kriti jeered.

"And they want to take it slow," Avni said as she sat down.

"Oh no, really slow," Kriti added.

They both giggled.

"Are they both commitment-phobic?" Arvind asked.

"Beats me," Avni replied.

"In my case Avni was. She still sometimes gets into that phase," Ansh said smiling at Avni.

"Oh please, I am not commitment-phobic," she replied looking at Ansh.

"Oh really. Do they know what happened when we went bowling right after our *roka*?" Ansh said.

"Haha, yes we heard about that."

Avni just smiled.

"Anyways," Ansh said looking at Arvind and Kriti, "I am again very happy for you, guys. So was it tough convincing your parents," Ansh asked looking at Kriti and Arvind.

"No, actually, it wasn't," Kriti said sounding surprised.

"I had told this to her so many times. You just have to try," Arvind said.

"I know, but I was so scared. My family is very strict about these things, trust me," Kriti said.

"We trust you, Kriti. I was a little surprised at how easily your father agreed. Especially after you sister's reaction the other day at lunch," Avni said.

"Yes exactly. First I was so scared, then my sister threw me off for a bit. I thought there is no way, but I have to give full credit to Armaan Jiju for talking to my father," Kriti said.

"Yes, seriously. Arman Jiju really helped us," Arvind said.

"See, sometimes all it takes is to take the first step and talk," Ansh said.

"Yes, and sometimes that first step is the most difficult one to take," Kriti replied.

"I know it is. If I were in your place I too would have hesitated. Most of us do and so many of us don't find the courage to talk to our parents about it," Ansh said, "but sometimes all it takes is just to tell our parents where our happiness lies."

"Yes, all she had to do was talk and see here we are finalizing our wedding dates now," Arvind replied.

"Are they out?" Avni asked.

"We got a couple of options, so trying to figure out which one is the best," Arvind said.

"On Arvind's side weddings happen early in the morning. Ours start in the evening go on the whole night," Kriti explained, "Arvind's mom was so shocked to hear that *pheras* sometimes happen after midnight also."

"That's because we have fun at our weddings," Kriti replied.

"Yes, you do, Kriti, the livelier lot," Arvind said grinning at Kriti, "but I know weddings our side are a little dull compared to the North, so we are trying to figure out a way to do it," Arvind said.

"Yes, it's funny to see their faces as they realize the cultural difference. My father wants it a certain way and Amma wants it a certain way according to their customs," Kriti explained. "So, we might have the wedding in the morning and *pheras* in the evening. Reception in the night or next day something like that," Kriti said looking at Arvind.

"Yes, something. I just hope they find a way out soon," Arvind replied shaking his head and smiling.

"This is going to be one hell of a wedding," Avni replied.

"Yes, it will be, oh the chaos," Kriti replied. "My mom was so surprised." She asked, "You have to wear a sari and Arvind a *dhoti* at the wedding?"

"It's a lot lighter and easier to manage than the *sherwani* and *lehenga* you guys wear on your weddings," Arvind replied, "no offence but it looks so difficult to manage."

"That's the fun isn't it, getting blinged up," Kriti said.

"That's another major problem, these guys are all about bling," Arvind said gesturing at Kriti, "and we are a complete opposite of bling."

"Hahaha, yes, that is there," Kriti said, "It's is going to be a riot. But who cares I am getting married to you," Kriti said holding Arvind's arms.

"Me too, I can get married to you in these pajamas," Arvind replied holding her hands,

"And my father will definitely kill you for that," Kriti replied looking at him.

"Hey, Maggi time," Roshni said as she walked out of the kitchen with Aakash.

They placed a huge bowl by the table and looked all four of them.

"Come," Roshni gestured.

"Maggi took unusually long," Arvind said as he got up.

"Yes, actually, Roshni," Avni said as they walked towards the table.

"Oh, come on guys, this much Maggi takes time," Roshni said.

Aakash just smiled sheepishly.

"Hey," Ansh said standing up, "we haven't been introduced, I am Ansh, Avni's fiancé," he said putting his arm around Avni.

"Hi, nice to meet you," Aakash said.

"Shall we?" Roshni said.

"Yes," Kriti said as she picked up the bowl.

"Where are you taking it?" Roshni asked.

"Nowhere, just here," Kriti said as she sat on the floor with it.

"What are you doing?" Roshni asked.

"Oh, Roshni, what's the fun in eating Maggi at the table?" Kriti exclaimed.

"I will get some mats," Avni said as she got up, "You go get some newspapers," she said looking at Roshni.

"What?" Roshni said looking at Avni and then at Aakash.

"Aakash, haven't you lived in a hostel?" Kriti asked looking at Aakash.

"Yes, I have," Aakash said looking a little confused, "why do you ask?"

"Nothing, the way Roshni is looking at me, I am just trying to make a point. Since you have, you won't have a problem eating Maggi this way," Kriti said holding the bowl.

"Oh. Haha, yes of course. I love eating this way. Roshni, come on, I don't have a problem with this," Aakash said.

"Here," Avni said holding out a bunch of mats for everyone to sit.

They laid the newspapers in between and they all sat down in a circle.

"Some beer would help," Aakash said.

"Oh, ya sure, anybody for beer?" Roshni asked getting up.

Everybody raised his or her hands except for Avni and Ansh. Avni just looked at Ansh.

"Avni, it's okay. Go ahead. You don't have to ask me," Ansh said and then called out to Roshni, "one for Avni."

Avni just smiled at him.

"So," Kriti started, "what can be most irritating thing for you to find out when you start living with someone?"

Roshni was busy gobbling on her Maggi. Kriti looked at Avni.

"Umm. I don't know, snoring," Avni said shrugging her shoulders.

"Really, do you know you snore?" Ansh said looking at Avni as she took the bowl from Kriti.

"No, I don't," Avni retorted as she took a bite from her fork.

"Avni, you do," Roshni said winking at Ansh, "not too much but a little."

"Huh, no," Avni said.

"Anyways for me. I need to walk into a clean washroom," Ansh said.

"Oh yes," Roshni said, "More than that I need complete darkness when I sleep."

"And I need a little light," Aakash blurted.

"Really?" Roshni said looking at him.

"Yes, a little," Aakash said.

"No, not even a little light for me," Roshni said.

"That's why she sleeps in the other room," Avni said looking at Aakash.

"Hmm," Aakash said looking at Roshni.

"How does it matter? You guys are taking it slow right. It's not like you will start living together soon," Kriti joked looking at both of them.

"Ya. Ya exactly, how does it matter?" Roshni said shrugging her shoulders as she took the bowl from Kriti.

"Hey," Kriti yelled.

"You had your share, now my turn," Roshni said twirling her fork in the bowl.

"I am sitting between you guys," Avni said looking at both of them.

"Sorry, Avni, you missed your chance," Roshni said taking her bite.

Avni rolled her eyes, and turned towards Arvind.

"Arvind, what about you?" Avni asked.

"Nobody should touch my cupboard," Arvind said.

"What?" Ansh asked.

"Oh you have no idea. His cupboard is so organized. Everything is colour coordinated and everything has a place. I thought I would clean his wardrobe one day, oh that was our worst fight ever," Kriti explained.

"Really, dude?" Aakash asked.

"Yes, I have this weird OCD," Arvind replied turning red.

"We are definitely not sharing a cupboard," Arvind said looking at Kriti.

"You bet we are not," Kriti replied.

"I hate it when the dining table becomes a dumping ground," Roshni said.

Aakash just stared at her.

"Oh yes, she likes it clean," Kriti said looking at Aakash.

"You will have to clean a lot then," Aakash mumbled.

"Huh?" Roshni said looking at him.

"Oh I meant if…" Aakash added.

"Hope you guys aren't spilling all your beans too soon," Avni said looking at both of them.

"No, this is great, we get to know each other better," Aakash replied.

"So tempted to send this moment to your father, Roshni," Avni grinned taking the bowl from Ansh.

"Avni, you dare do that!" Roshni said.

"Just kidding," Avni replied, "Kriti, what about you?"

"Washing your hands before cooking," Kriti said, "Personal hygiene, you know."

"Yes, personal hygiene is very important," Ansh added.

"Oh it's very important. He can't live without his sanitizer," Avni said. "You won't die of germs," Avni said looking at Ansh.

"You can, you know," Ansh replied.

"You are obsessed with it," Avni said.

Ansh just shrugged.

"Is it over?" Roshni asked as she took the bowl and looked inside.

Aakash too looked into it and said, "Yes, we are done."

"I am full," Arvind said.

"Same here," Kriti said. Everyone agreed.

"Ansh, Aakash, I must tell you," Avni started, "Ow Roshni," Avni screamed as Roshni twisted her hand.

"I think we have had enough for today. No more," Roshni said.

"Okay, leave me," Avni said.

Avni rubbed her hands, as she looked at Roshni. Roshni mouthed sorry to her and turned around to increase the volume of the music, which was playing on her laptop, it was playing songs in the background, only it was so low they couldn't make out much of it.

They were up almost all night discussing about everything under the sun from politics to philosophy to films. They laughed and talked and yelled till one by one they all went off to sleep.

* * *

Avni's phone rang.

"Hello," Avni answered.

"Avni, where are you?" her mom asked.

"Huh?" Avni asked.

"Avni, oh my God, this girl. Are you still sleeping? *Beta*, we have to go to get your wedding card finalized," her mother said.

"Oh, today? What date is it?" Avni mumbled.

"Avni, first get up and get ready and tell Ansh also. I can't get through to him," her mother said.

"Ansh, okay, I will tell him right away. He is just here," Avni said.

"He is there?" her mother asked.

"No, I meant," Avni straightened up. "I meant I will call him, sorry I was in my sleep," Avni said hitting her head.

"Okay, get ready and come fast," her mother said.

"Okay, Mom," Avni said holding her head.

Avni walked to the other room to wake Ansh up.

"Get up," Avni said tapping his shoulders. "We have to go, Mom called," Avni said.

"Huh?" he said from under the blanket.

"Get up, we don't want Mom coming here," she said looking over at Aakash and Arvind, "I don't want to shock her."

"Your mom's here?" Ansh said getting up suddenly.

"She will be if we don't get ready and go," Avni said walking away.

He frowned and got up.

"Twenty minutes and we leave," Avni said as she walked out.

Ansh nodded and started to get ready.

Avni got ready and rushed to the kitchen. Kriti was standing in front of the stove, making coffee. "Anything for breakfast?" Avni asked Kriti.

"Bread butter," Kriti mumbled half in her sleep.

"Kriti, wake up," Avni said shaking her.

"Huh?" Kriti said looking at Avni.

"Your coffee," Avni said as she simmered the gas.

"Oh, yeah sorry," Kriti said, looking at her coffee on the stove, "Where are you off to so early in the morning?"

"It's eleven, Kriti," Avni said looking at her phone, "We have to finalize our wedding card today."

"Oh wow, that's great," Kriti replied yawning.

"Hey, good morning," Ansh said walking in.

Avni just smiled at him, "See, you look so good in shirts," she said as she walked towards him.

"Hmm, so that's why I couldn't find a spare T-shirt of mine here," he replied.

"Yes, and I love this shirt so much," Avni said holding his arms.

"Just this shirt?" Ansh asked looking at Avni.

"Uhhmm, I am right here guys. Just reminding you both before you go any further," Kriti interrupted.

"Whatever, Kriti, pass me the bread," Avni said.

"Here," Kriti said as she handed the bread and walked out with her coffee.

"Uhhmm," Ansh cleared his throat.

Avni just looked at him.

"You look beautiful," he whispered as he put her hair behind her ears.

Avni just blushed. She continued applying the butter on the bread, Just then Ansh's phone rang.

"It's your mom," he panicked.

"I think we should just go," Avni said giving one slice to him and taking another in her hand, "before she comes knocking at my door."

Avni and Ansh sat in the car, ate their bread slices in a hurry and headed towards Chawri Bazaar; the one-stop shop for wedding cards in Delhi. It was very difficult to drive in Old Delhi, so they decided to park their car a little outside and walk.

"Oh God, where will I find Mom now?" Avni said looking around walking towards the bazaar.

"Avni, call her," Ansh said looking around, at the crowd.

Old Delhi had its own charm; it was very different from the main city. The air had a different vibe to it, every street was different, every corner had something new to say.

"It's so different here," Ansh said as he looked around.

"Yes, it is. I quite like it here. You should taste the food here, it's out of the world. I will take you to the *paranthe wali gali* if we get off early," Avni said walking ahead as she dialled her mom.

"Mom, where are you? Yes, I am standing in front of the shoe shop we came to last time," Avni said looking to her left.

"Okay, right and straight, what is the shop's name, okay," Avni said, as she put her phone in her purse, she then looked at Ansh, "Follow me, Ansh," she said holding his hand and pushing through the crowd.

"Avni, finally you are here," her mother sighed as she saw Avni and Ansh.

Avni was sure her mother would have fired her if Ansh wasn't there.

"So sorry, I had an important call to attend to," he said looking down sheepishly.

Avni stared at him in shock, telling her mom such a white lie.

Avni was just smiling at Ansh when her mother clicked her fingers, "What about you, Avni?" her mother asked.

"Uh. I was sleeping, Mom. I forgot, I am sorry. But see I got ready and came," Avni replied.

"Anyways, we have kept him waiting for long enough, come," her mother said.

They walked into the shop; it was small with a low ceiling, heaps on cards lying on one side of the floor and various card designs stuck on one side of their wall.

At one end lay a long table with a sofa on the other side. They sat on a sofa in front of a table piled high with designs for wedding cards.

"Hi, Ma'am," an elderly man came and sat down opposite them, "Please sit, and take your time, here are all the samples I have," he said showing them the designs kept on the table.

Avni picked a few of the designs. Of course, she did realize she was getting married, but holding the cards in her hands made her all jittery. *You are getting married soon,* a voice echoed in her head. She looked at Ansh who was talking to her mother. He looked at her, smiled and went back to talking to her mother. She didn't even realize when and how she had fallen in love.

"One day, Avni, someone will walk into your life and make you fall in love with the word wedding. You won't be able to wait to get married to him," Kriti had said once dreamily.

"Kriti, you are so funny. We are not living in a fairy tale. I am not some princess who is waiting for her Prince Charming," Avni had laughed.

"I am telling you, Avni, someone will come one day," Kriti had looked at her smiling.

"Kriti, you are so silly," Avni had laughed, "no one is going to come. I will just eventually have to say yes to someone and get married that's it."

Who knew, Avni thought, remembering Kriti's words. Ansh had done it. He made her fall in love with a word she resented. Now she couldn't even wait to be wed to him. The wedding excitement was finally getting to her.

"Avni, you like something?" her mother asked.

"I am still looking," Avni said going through the designs.

"Madam, what are the bride's and groom's names?" the guy behind the table asked.

"I can write it down for you," Ansh said taking the pen.

He wrote down.

Avni weds Ansh.

He looked at Avni.

"Sounds perfect, doesn't it," he said smiling at her.

Avni just smiled going red, "More than perfect."

They spent the next few hours deciding on the designs. There were so many different types; one with a card holder which held a card for each event, one opened like a scrap book like reading a scripture, one was like a proper book, hard bound, another was like a scroll. Then they were so many different designs for the card covers as well, there was Radha Krishna, an animated *doli* with people singing and dancing, then there was one with Ganesh.

They both took hours in deciding which one they want. Avni liked the one with Ganesha on it, and the scroll concept, "I think I love the Ganesha design on the card," Avni said flipping a card over.

"Yes, I think it's nice, I like this red one with a gold Ganesha on it," Ansh said picking a card up.

"Yes, even the blue one is nice," Avni said.

"Avni, this is dark green," Uma pointed out.

"Oh, we've been looking at these cards for so long, all my eyes are seeing is blue," Avni said rubbing her eyes.

"Avni, we are left with just four now," Ansh said.

"You decide, Ansh," Avni replied.

"Hmm, okay I like this one," Ansh said picking the red one.

"Are you sure?" Avni said picking the green one.

"Avni, it's your call, take this," Ansh said looking at her.

"Avni Weds Ansh," Avni said looking at the green one imagining their name on it.

"Hmm," she said as she picked the red one up, "You are right, Ansh, this is a lovely one," Avni said smiling at Ansh. "Hmmm," Avni thought and finally said, "Okay, this one," she said giving the red design card to the elderly man behind the table.

"Here is the count, below this are the event details and all the names. Please, it should be in this order only, and I will need it by this date, latest," Uma said handing out a note to the man.

"Okay, Ma'am," he said, as he wrote Uma's name on the top, with the chosen card's number and put it his drawer.

"Finally, the design is final, now one more thing off the list," her mother sighed as she took out a black book and ticked an item off the list.

"Mom, what's this?" Avni asked as she looked at the never-ending list.

"This is a list of your wedding shopping," her mother said smiling as she put the pen away.

"So much?" Avni asked looking at her.

"Yes," Avni mother said as she put her hands on her face, "there is so much to do, your shopping has only just begun, Avni."

"Wow," Avni said.

"Ansh, *beta,* I can take you to the sweet shop now. Avni was telling me you wanted to pick up something for your friends back in Norway," Avni's mother said as she got up.

"Mom, do we have time for *paranthe wali gali*?" Avni asked looking at her phone to check the time.

"Yes, I think we do, Oh, you shouldn't miss that one, Ansh," Uma said looking at Ansh, "After that I will take you to a sweet shop," Uma said as they got up.

"Yes, thanks! That would be great," Ansh said getting up too. Her mother walked out of the shop.

Avni held Ansh's arms, "I can't believe you are leaving."

Ansh pressed her hands on his arms, "It's difficult for me too, Avni. But I have to go, I will be back soon."

Avni just nodded, "I know."

"Shall we?" Ansh asked.

"Yes," Avni said walking out with him.

They had a sumptuous meal at the *paranthe wali gali.*

"I can't believe, they have so many types of *paranthes.* I would have never thought of it," Ansh said looking at Uma and Avni.

"Oh yes, it's one of the best places in world to eat, old Delhi is very famous for that," Uma said smiling at Ansh.

They walked towards the sweet shop.

As their sweets were getting packed, "Aunty, I did not order for these," Ansh said looking at the boxes.

"I know but these are from us," her mother said smiling at him.

"Aunty, there was no need," Ansh replied.

"Yes, there is and you won't say no," her mother said holding his hands.

"Aunty, but... okay thanks," Ansh said taking them.

"Mom, my *badam* biscuits," Avni squealed.

"Yes, I know, I have bought them," her mother said pointing to one of the packets.

Once they were done, they bid her mother goodbye.

"Oh my God, how will I pack all of this?" Ansh asked as he sat in the car putting the boxes in the back seat.

"You have a weight limit, don't you?" Avni asked.

"Yes," Ansh said starting the car.

"Don't worry. I will help you pack or you will have to book extra luggage," Avni said looking back.

Ansh just nodded.

"Packing, just leave it to me, Avni," Ansh said.

"Why?" Avni asked.

"I will do it, don't worry," he insisted.

"But I want to help you," Avni said.

"Avni, trust me I will do my packing," Ansh said.

"No, let me help you," Avni asserted.

She couldn't understand what the fuss was all about. Though she soon understood why Ansh insisted on doing his own packing. He was so particular about it. Everything went in different bags and everything had a particular place. All the T-shirts were rolled up, the shirts put straight at the bottom, the socks were put in a separate bag.

"Why are you being so particular? Just put everything in," Avni said tired of making different sections for everything.

"Avni, I told you I will do this on my own but you insisted. No, they can't just go in. They have to go in properly," Ansh said looking at her.

"What's the big deal? They just have to get there," Avni said.

"Yes, but again in a proper way so I don't get confused," Ansh replied packing his watch.

"You are too particular," Avni said looking at him.

"And you are too casual," Ansh said.

"Not too casual, but a little at ease," Avni replied, sitting down. "Do you keep your house this way too?" Avni asked looking at him.

"Not really but, Avni, it will be our house soon," Ansh said.

"I am not going to be so particular about it," Avni said.

"Hmmm. It can be a little like you and a little like me," he said, smiling at her.

"Umm, but my room will be…" Avni started.

"Avni, we will have one room, remember," Ansh cut in reminding her.

Avni stopped for a moment and then said, "Oh yes, we will work it out then, won't we?" she asked looking at Ansh.

He came and sat beside her, "Of course, Avni," he said holding her hands.

"I still can't believe you are going," Avni said looking around at the packing.

"I can't either, but I am so glad I came here," Ansh said.

"Me too, Ansh. It made all the difference in the world," Avni said as she moved towards him, "I was so unsure at first, I know I was being silly then when I doubted us. I am just a little stupid at times. I know I should grow up, also I am..."

Ansh put his finger on her lips, "You are perfect to me, Avni, just the way you are, I don't want you to change. Ever."

Avni went red.

"I love you just as you are," he said he kissed her.

"I love you too," Avni said as she laid her head on his chest.

She stayed there for two minutes.

"Shall we continue packing? A minute more in your arms and I won't be able to let you go," Avni said.

He nodded and got up to pack the rest of the things. After about two hours, "Are we done? Please tell me we are," Avni said as she sat down.

"Yes almost," Ansh said wrapping his slippers.

"If you ever go on a trip again, do your own packing," Avni said looking exhausted.

"Told you I will do it on my own," Ansh said looking at her, "you did not listen."

"If I knew your packing will take hours, mine would have been over long time ago," Avni said as she got up.

When they finally finished, "Phew, I need to sleep," Avni said.

"I think you need some coffee," Ansh said.

"Yeah, that could work too," Avni said looking at him.

"I will make some," he said going out to the kitchen.

"When is your flight?" Avni asked sitting out by the hall.

"Late, 2:30 am," Ansh replied from the kitchen.

"It's 7 now," Avni said looking at her phone, "You don't have much time now. We will have to leave at least three hours before. Crazy traffic besides you have to report an hour and half earlier I guess."

"So, it's best we leave by 9:30-10:00 p.m.," Ansh asked.

"Yes, something like that," Avni replied taking her coffee.

"Mom and Dad will also come to see you off," Avni said sipping on her coffee.

"Avni, they don't have to. It's so late in the night," Ansh said as he sat down with his coffee.

"Ansh, I know, but they won't listen. They will come see you off," Avni replied. "They will pick me up from my house and then come pick you up. So you will have to drop me to my house," Avni smiled looking at him.

"Okay, Ma'am, once we finish our coffee I will take you home. I will say my goodbyes to Kriti and Roshni too," Ansh said sipping on his coffee.

Ansh drove Avni to her house. Avni had called Kriti and Roshni to check if they were home. They were and were waiting for them.

As they entered they saw Roshni and Kriti sitting by the dining table.

"Hey," Roshni said getting up, "All packed and ready."

"Oh yes, finally," Avni said rolling her eyes.

"Huh?" Roshni asked.

"She wanted me to dump everything in, but unlike her I decided to pack," Ansh replied jokingly.

"Hahaha, Avni doesn't have the patience for all these things," Roshni replied.

"Whatever," Avni replied.

"Anyways, Ansh, lots of luck to you. I am so glad you could come here. Avni has got herself so sorted now and it's so nice to see her excited for this wedding now," Kriti said as she hugged him.

"Thanks a lot, Kriti. I'm glad I could do this trip. It was great meeting you guys," Ansh replied hugging Kriti.

"Bye, Ansh, can't wait to see you again at the wedding," Roshni said as she hugged him goodbye.

"Bye, Roshni. Yes, I will see you guys at our wedding," Ansh said bidding his goodbye.

Avni sniffed.

"Hey Avni, it's only a few months," Ansh said looking at her as he held her hands.

Avni nodded.

"Yes, only a few months, then you will be with him forever," Kriti said putting her hands on Avni's shoulder.

"How cliché!" Avni replied.

"Ya, but that's the truth," Roshni replied.

"Hey by the way, these are for you. I hope they fit in your luggage," Roshni said handing out a small box to Ansh.

"What's this? You guys did not have to," Ansh said looking at it.

"Oh, it's nothing. Just *ladoos*. We made them for we knew you won't get them in Norway," Roshni said smiling at him.

"Oh wow, this is really sweet. Thanks," Ansh said taking the box.

"You will love them, they make awesome *ladoos,"* Avni said looking towards the kitchen.

"We do have extra," Kriti replied looking at Avni.

"Great," Avni said smiling.

"Anyways, Ansh I think you should go back to the guest house. Mom and Dad will come here soon," Avni said looking at Ansh.

"Okay, great, see you guys, bye," Ansh said as he walked out.

"Are you okay, Avni?" Kriti said as she walked towards Avni.

"Yes, it's only a few months right," Avni replied as she took a deep breath.

"Yes, he will be back soon," Kriti said as she lay her head on Avni's shoulders.

Avni nodded.

On the drive to the airport with her parents and Ansh, Avni just looked out of the window. She couldn't bear to look at Ansh or even talk to him.

He was mostly talking to her father. Her father always had these questions about life in Norway, the weather, the food they get there.

"Oh really, wow that must be so nice," her father squealed like a small kid.

"Yes, it is, they really believe a lot in work-family balance," Ansh said.

"That is so nice, Avni, did you hear that. You can come back early every day," her father said looking at her.

"Yes, Papa, it is," Avni replied looking out of the window again.

"Will she get a job there soon?" her father asked.

"Yes. She just has to learn the language, do a basic course. I don't think it should be that tough. We spoke about it so we will get her enrolled once she is there," Ansh said looking at her father.

"That's great. We are almost here," her father said as they approached the airport.

Avni's heart sank. Something felt so heavy inside her. She couldn't move.

"Let's go, come on, Avni," her mother said as she got out of the car.

"Yes, Mom," Avni said as she choked on the tears she was trying really hard to stop.

Her mother looked at her face, then turned towards Arun. "I think we should give these kids some time," she said holding her husband's hands.

He looked at his daughter and nodded, "Avni, we are waiting by the gate, you guys just... umm... say your goodbyes, okay," he said as he walked towards the gate with Uma.

Avni just nodded, sitting in the car but couldn't get herself to get out. The moment she lost sight of her parents, tears rolled down her cheeks. Ansh looked at her and sat in the car.

"Avni please don't cry," he said holding her in his arms.

"This is not fair, I did not know it will be this tough," Avni said crying in his arms.

"I know, this is tough. I hate leaving you here. I wish I could take you with me," he said kissing her head.

"Then take me," Avni said.

"I wish I could but I will be back soon," Ansh said as he held her face. She could see Ansh's eyes moisten.

"Three months, Ansh!" Avni exclaimed.

"You will get busy with our wedding shopping, trust me," Ansh said, "it will pass by."

Avni just nodded and hugged him again.

"Hey, I had got something for you," Avni said as she reached in her purse and took out a wrapped box.

"Really, for me?" Ansh said as he took it.

"Yes, now open it," Avni said as she gave it to him.

He opened it, and a smile spread over his face, Bose headphones, "Oh my God, Avni."

"I knew you wanted them," Avni said excitedly as she looked at him.

"Yeah, I did, thank you so much," he said as he hugged her.

"I love you," Ansh said.

"I love you too," Avni replied.

"I think we should go. Your mom and dad must be waiting," he said.

"Yes, okay," Avni replied as she got out of the car with him.

They walked up to the gate. Avni held on to Ansh's hands.

"Bye, *beta.* It was really nice you could come here," her mother said as he took her blessings, "God bless you."

"Bye, Ansh, God bless you," Avni's father said as he hugged him.

He looked at Avni. Held her hands, "Bye, Avni, take care."

She pressed his hands, "Bye, you too take care. Have a safe flight and please call when you reach."

He nodded and smiled at her. She just looked at him till she lost sight of him in the crowd.

"Shall we go, Avni?" her mother said putting her hands on her shoulders.

"Yes, Mom," Avni said as she walked towards the car and sat down with a heavy heart.

"Avni, I know you are upset," her mother said as she sat in the car.

"No, Ma, I am not upset," Avni said as she looked out.

"Avni, it's okay for you to be upset. I am so glad now that you are happy with him," her mother said.

"I am finally getting married, willingly, all your prayers are answered, nah, Mom," Avni said smiling at her mother.

"Yes, they are," her mother said pulling her cheeks.

"Ow, Mom," Avni said rubbing them.

"So, since you are free from tomorrow. Pack your bags, come home. I have taken off till your wedding," her mother said.

"Really?" Avni asked looking at her father.

"It's not paid leave," her mother reminded.

"Oh, but still that's a lot," Avni said.

"Yes, I did not push you much since Ansh was there, but we have a lot to do," her mother said.

"Yes, Mom, let's go shopping," Avni said.

Chapter XVIII

The best way to keep her mind off Ansh not being around, Avni decided, was to get busy with wedding preparations. She realized it was time for her to start packing her belongings from her apartment to move home.

"Avni, do you have to?" Kriti said as she watched her friend stuff her things in a box.

"Aww, I really wish I didn't have to leave, but I want to spend some time with Mom and Dad before I leave," Avni said as she folded her *kurtis*.

"This sucks you know, getting married," Kriti said looking down.

"Really, why?" Avni asked.

"My parents have been telling me to leave my job and go stay with them as well," Kriti said looking at Avni, "I think I should."

"Yes, you should," Avni said.

"Okay, getting married really sucks," Roshni said who was standing by the door listening to their conversation.

"Okay, now why according to you?" Kriti asked.

"Don't you realize it? I will be all alone when you guys leave. Avni is leaving now, you will leave a while later," Roshni complained.

"Aww… Roshni, we never thought of that," Kriti said looking at her.

"Yeah. I will have to find new roommates. I cannot pay for the whole flat," Roshni said sitting down, "and of course, I won't be able to find roomies like you guys."

"I am so sorry for all this, Roshni, we never realized this," Avni said as she got up and sat beside Roshni.

"Yeah, don't fret. I will be fine," Roshni said patting Avni.

"Hey, why don't you do one thing," Kriti said looking at Roshni.

"What?" Roshni asked.

"Why don't you ask Aakash to move in with you," Kriti said smiling at Roshni.

"What? Are you crazy? Aakash, move in. No ways," Roshni exclaimed.

"Why? Roshni, you guys like each other and don't shake your head like that. It won't help, we all know," Kriti said pointing her finger at Roshni.

"Since you don't want to get married now, don't you think this is the best way to find out if you guys are compatible at all?" Kriti asked.

"Moving in will be too fast and it's too soon," Roshni said, "probably we will after a while, when we feel we are ready," she added.

"Hmmm, I still think it's a good idea. Anyways, whatever suits you," Kriti shrugged, and then continued, "You will have to start searching for roommates then," Kriti said.

"Yeah, I don't even know where to start. I will think of something," Roshni said looking at them.

Avni hadn't realized how hard this would be, leaving the office was one thing, but leaving her friends would not be easy. She tried to focus on all that she needed to do before the wedding. She had put on some weight since she quit and wanted to work on losing it.

"Empty mind is a devil's workshop," Ansh had said when she cried about how fat she was getting.

"No, empty mind is a hungry body, a really hungry body which needs to be fed every freaking hour!" Avni had cried looking down at herself.

"Oh my God, please don't tell me this doesn't fit," Avni said out loud trying on the new jeans she had just bought.

"How can you do this to me?" Avni asked the jeans as she struggled to zip up.

"Avni, you can't get fat, you are getting married," Avni worried looking at herself in the mirror.

"I guess, I will start swimming or something," Avni said looking at her stomach.

She sat on the bed looking at herself in the mirror. She hated her new self.

"No food for you," she said looking at her body. She changed into her pyjamas. "So much more comfortable," she took a deep breath and went out to the kitchen.

Kriti was opening a Maggi packet.

"Hey, want to have some?" Kriti asked.

"No, I am getting fat. No Maggi for me," Avni said looking in the fridge.

"Huh, are you kidding me? You are not fat," Kriti said looking at her. Avni did not reply.

"Avni, please have some, it's our last few days together. It will be so nice if we can have Maggi together," Kriti said hugging her from behind.

"Kriti, I can't," Avni said searching for something healthy to eat in the fridge.

"Oh, come on Avni, one Maggi won't do any harm," Kriti insisted.

"Ughh, you guys hate seeing me thin," Avni remarked.

"Yes, we do. Now I am making some for you, so just have it." Kriti said looking at her.

Avni smiled at her sheepishly as she knew deep inside she wanted to have some.

"Anyways, how is Ansh? Is he coping well without you?" Kriti asked as they sat down with their Maggi.

"Fine, I guess," Avni said taking a bite.

"Okay," Kriti smiled to herself, "So, when is your *lehenga* coming?" Kriti asked.

"In two weeks. I can't wait for it, Kriti, it's the most gorgeous piece," Avni said sounding excited.

"I know and it's beautiful," Kriti said.

"What about you, Kriti?" Avni asked.

"Well, the wedding is definitely next year, probably January or

February. We are not sure about the dates yet," Kriti said.

"Have you decided on what to wear?" Avni asked.

"Well, I will wear a *lehenga* on our reception, a silk sari for the main wedding and I don't know, it gets a little confusing coordinating the functions and things to wear when you are from different cultures," Kriti said looking at her.

"Yes, it does, but isn't that double the fun?" Avni asked.

"Well I really hope it will be at the wedding," Kriti said smiling at Avni.

Avni's phone buzzed.

Her mother had sent her some designs for her wedding stage.

"Oh God, how am I to decide?" Avni said looking at the designs.

"Decide what?" Kriti asked.

"Okay, help me out. Mom sent me design options for the wedding stage," Avni said passing the phone to Kriti.

"Wow, there are so many. Oh my God, this is so pretty, Avni," Kriti said as her eyes widened. "They all look so good. How does one decide?" Kriti asked, as she went through the pics.

"Exactly," Avni said.

"Don't you think you should be showing these pictures to the person you will share the stage with?" Kriti said.

"Yeah, I am sure he will be able to decide," Avni said taking the phone from Kriti and forwarding the pics to Ansh. "I can't believe the d-day is coming," Avni said.

"I know! I can't imagine I am marrying Arvind. I hope I don't end up crying like a baby," Kriti said.

"Awww and I hope I don't trip on the stage with my *lehenga*. It is really heavy, you know," Avni said, "Anyways I think I should leave, my mom must be waiting for me."

"When are you leaving, by the way?" Kriti asked looking at all the boxes lying around.

"I should have left by now, but I am just stalling Mom, telling her there is lots to pack. But I won't be able to stall her much longer," Avni said looking at all the boxes.

"I hate seeing you go. I will too go in some time. It will all change very soon, right," Kriti said looking at Avni.

"Yes, it will, you will go to Hyderabad. I will go to Norway, and Roshni will be here till she decides to do something about her and Aakash," Avni said.

"Yes. Ughh, Hyderabad is so hot but Arvind wants to stay closer to his parents," Kriti shrugged.

"I know, and Norway is super cold. I just hope I survive the winter there," Avni replied.

"Hahaha, we will be living in two extremes," Kriti said.

"Yes, I know. Anyways I will see you later," Avni said as she walked out.

This was her usual routine since Ansh left. She got up in the morning, got ready and headed out for shopping. Shopping was a lot of fun for Avni, but there was just so much to shop for it never seemed to end. She couldn't believe there was so much to shop for a wedding.

"Mom, I am so tired of looking at saris," Avni said as she shuffled around a bunch of them at a shop.

"Avni, don't be so difficult. Just tell me which one will be best for Kitty," her mother said looking through the saris.

"Uma, I think this colour will really suit her," her *chachi* said, who accompanied them through most their wedding shopping.

"I don't know. You guys decide," Avni said.

It was fun while they were shopping for her, but now they started to shop for the whole family, which was a never-ending process.

"Okay, Avni, let's go. We have to go buy your shoes now," Uma said.

"Mom! There is more?" Avni asked.

"Yes, there is. Don't you want nice heels for your wedding functions?" Uma asked.

"Yes, I do, okay."

She must have tried a million shoes before they finally agreed on the one's she would wear with each of her outfits.

"Are you sure?" Uma asked as the helper packer her heels into the boxes.

"Yes, Mom. I am," Avni replied.

After a long day her mother finally uttered the magic words to Avni.

"I think, let's call it a day. We will head home," her mother said.

"Thank God, Mom. I will push off too," Avni said.

"Where to?" Uma asked.

"Home, Mom," Avni said.

"Avni, you have to come back home now. I have been home for a week already," Uma said.

"I know, Mom. I just have a little more packing to do," Avni said.

"Avni, you know what? Tomorrow me and Aunty will come and finish your packing so that you can come here," Uma said.

"No, Mom, that's not necessary. I will try finishing up by tomorrow and will come by the end of the day," Avni said looking at her mom.

It was so hard for her to move out of the flat but she knew she had too. Everything was changing and a lot more would soon. It was difficult for Avni, but she also knew it was inevitable.

"Come with us tonight. We will go have dinner now. It will get quite late for you by then," her mother said as she held Avni's hands.

Avni nodded her head, as she obliged. She got up the next morning and left for her flat.

"Hi," Avni said nonchalantly as she walked into her flat.

"Hey, Avni, how was your shopping?" Roshni asked, she was sitting at the table with her laptop.

"Oh, don't ask, it's driving me crazy," Avni said as she sat down.

"Really, I thought you loved to shop," Roshni said stressing on the love.

"I do, but this is maddening," Avni said.

"Thank God you get married only once then," Roshni said going back to her laptop.

"Yes, thank God to that, and let's hope it's just once," Avni said.

"As far as I know Ansh, he is not going to let you go," Roshni said looking up.

Avni just smiled and sat by the table. "Anyways, I have been stalling Mom, but I can't anymore. I will have to move out by this evening," Avni said looking at Roshni.

"What?" Roshni said as she closed her laptop. "You can't go," Roshni said as she got up.

"Is that an order?" Avni asked looking at her.

"Yes, it bloody well is," Roshni said folding her hands.

"Oh, Roshni. I too hate leaving you guys like this," Avni said as she went over and hugged Roshni.

"You better do," Roshni said.

"Okay, so let's get packing, I am almost done though," Avni said looking at the boxes by the corner. "Just some last bits are left, my mom can't wait to have me home," Avni said.

"You are going home?" Kriti asked as she walked out of the room.

"Where are you off to?" Avni said looking at her dressed up in a lovely sea blue *anakarli* suit.

"I am going to meet Arvind's parents for lunch. I was just trying it on to see if it fits, they have come to the city for a few days. Am I looking okay?" Kriti said looking down at her suit.

"Yes, you are looking so cute, Kriti," Avni said as she walked up to her.

"Anyways where are you going?" Kriti said.

"Back home, Mom has given me an ultimatum to come home by today," Avni said looking at Kriti.

"What? Really, so you will just leave?" Kriti asked.

"Okay, now don't make this any harder for me," Avni said as she held her hands.

"Oh my God, Avni. This is too fast. I will miss you," Kriti said, hugging her.

"I will too, but hey I am not flying off to another city just yet. I am still here in the same city," Avni said looking at them.

"Yes, and we will crash in whenever we miss you," Kriti said holding Avni's hands.

"Yes, please do. Mom will be more than happy," Avni said, "Oh look at how thin these girls are," Avni said imitating her mother, "and then she will feed you with loads of butter and ghee."

"Hahaha, ya actually now that your mom is in town. We are so going to come over every other day. I love your mom's food," Roshni said.

"Yes, you guys better do," Avni replied

"Let's get your packing over with," Roshni said as she walked into Avni's room.

"Yes, I have a little time in my hands, I will help you till then," Kriti said as she too walked into the room with Roshni and Avni.

She bid her roommates goodbye with teary eyes. Once they were done with Avni's packing, her mom came over to pick her up. They all cried, hugged and finally bid her goodbye.

Chapter XIX

"Are you okay?" her mother asked as she put her hands on Avni's shoulders.

"Yes, Mom, I will be," Avni said wiping a tear as she sat in the car.

"I know this is a little tough for you, you've been staying together for a while but Kriti will leave in a while and eventually Roshni will too when she gets married. All of you could not stay this way forever," Uma said.

"I know, Mom," Avni sniffed.

"I have made you your favourite – *palak paneer*," her mother said pressing her hands.

"Thanks, Mom," Avni said looking at her.

"You will not be here much longer. I want to make all your favourite dishes every day. Soon you will get married and go to another country," Uma said.

"Mom, don't make me cry more now," Avni said looking at her mother's moist eyes. "Besides if you feed me all of that, you will make me fat," Avni said.

"No, I won't, Avni. If you feel you are getting fat, you can join me and *chachi* for our morning walks," Uma said.

"Morning walks, Mom, you guys leave at 5:30 in the morning!" Avni said.

"So?" Uma asked.

"That's too early," Avni said, "I want to enjoy this time," Avni said spreading her arms.

"Yes, please do. But promise me you will be more responsible after your wedding," her mother said.

"Yes, Mom. Ugh, I hate growing up," Avni said as she kept her head on her mother's shoulder.

"Everybody does. I hated leaving your Nana Nani too. Going to a new place. Your Dadi was very strict, you know," her mother said.

"Really?" Avni asked.

"Yes," Uma said looking at Avni who was waiting to hear more, "but that topic is for another day."

"How to make your mother-in-law happy?" Avni asked.

"Haha, yes. How to earn lots of brownie points!" her mother said laughing.

"You think my mother-in-law is strict?" Avni asked.

"I don't think so, Avni. You are very lucky, today people are very broad-minded and open. They are not rigid like in our time. She seems very easy-going," Uma said, "but she is your mother-in-law. However open-minded she is, you will have to act like a responsible daughter-in-law," Uma said looking at Avni.

"You think she will be upset if I make any mistake?" Avni asked looking at her mother.

"I hope not. Avni, you have to act like the mature one if she does act up at times," Uma said.

"Like keep quiet if she keeps saying things to me," Avni said.

"Avni, she is not a typical TV serial mother-in-law who will grill you for everything. I am just saying that small things here and there, learn to turn a blind eye. But yes, if something very big happens, then you should speak up for yourself. Though I am sure they are not like that, besides Ansh is there," Uma said pressing Avni's hands.

"It worries me a bit, Mom, I don't know anything of their family, I don't even know if there is a particular way in which I am supposed to act," Avni said looking at her mother.

"Avni, you will learn in time. If ever in doubt, go talk to your mother-in-law," Uma explained.

Avni nodded, "Marriage is a big deal," she said as she looked out.

"Yes, it is. But I know you will do just fine," her mother said.

"I hope so," Avni said as she took a deep breath.

A week passed by. Avni was getting thoroughly pampered at home. Nobody said anything to her even if she got up in the noon.

Her father would say, "It's okay, let her sleep in. God knows if she will be able to once she is married."

She did whatever she wanted to with ease.

The wedding was just two months away, and now it just didn't seem like enough time to do the rest of the arrangements. The wedding planning and preparations never ended. Every day there was something new to discuss about. Weeks later, when Avni was out shopping.

"Why are you giving her a suit? Just give her a sari, nah," Avni said sitting at a boutique.

"Oh, she doesn't like saris much, we all usually give her a suit piece," her *chachi* said.

"Oh, the confusion, now who else is left?" Avni asked scribbling in the black book.

"We have to get some clothes or toys for her kids," Uma said, asking the help to pack the saris and the suits.

"For the kids! Mom, why are you going crazy? Why are you buying for the whole world?" Avni said looking at her mother.

"Because that is how it's done, Avni. Everyone has always given for you and your sister, so I will have to do the same," Uma said looking at her, "so write it down," she pointed at the black diary in Avni's hands.

"Uff. Okay, then there will be something for the uncles too?" Avni asked.

"Yes, suit pieces," Uma said casually.

Avni rolled her eyes and went back to writing in the black book.

"By the way did you try the *lehenga*, is it okay?" Uma said.

"Yes, Mom I did. Sorry, I forgot to tell you, it fits perfectly," Avni said smiling at her mother.

Uma just smiled

Then there were some days when they decided who is staying in which room during the wedding. One such night, as they were all sitting and wrapping the saris.

"Mom, I got mixed up again," Avni said looking at the items kept on the carpet beside her.

"Avni, I gave you a list of things to pack with the sari, how difficult can it be?" Uma said looking at Avni.

They were all sitting in the hall on the carpet with saris and suit pieces, which had to be packed to be gifted during the wedding.

"Yes, you did, Mom. Only I don't know where it is now?" Avni said looking around searching for the list.

"Here it is," Priya, said as she walked in with the coffee, the list was lying next to her feet.

"Oh, how did it reach there," Avni said reaching out for the list. "Hmm, so let's see, bangles, *sindoor*, *bindi*, toe rings, *mehendi*," Avni said pointing at each item as she read through the list.

"Okay," Avni said to herself as she packed all the items with each sari.

"Mom, by the way," Priya started as she sat down with her coffee, "have we decided where and which rooms people will stay in during the wedding?"

"I think we should just let people decide where they want to be," Uma said, as she wrapped the packages made by Avni with ribbons.

"No," Priya, disagreed, "Mom, that will be a total chaos. What if ten people want the same room? How will you manage?" Priya reasoned with her mother.

"Then what should we do?" Uma asked looking at Priya.

"Mom, the best thing is to make a list, put it outside the rooms, so that everyone knows which room they are in," Priya said taking the black book from the table.

"How do we decide that Priya?" her *chachi* asked, as she folded the suit pieces.

"Don't worry, Aunty. I know which people get along. Nobody will have a problem with my list. Mom, you just give me a list of rooms, the number of beds in it, and the list of guests," Priya said smiling at her mother.

"Priya I don't know if this is the right way," her mother said taking her cup of coffee.

"Trust me, Mom, this is the best way. No hassle for you at the last moment," Priya said sipping on her coffee.

And on some days, they went crazy deciding the menu. Weeks later, after they had finally zeroed in on a caterer, they were all sitting in the hall deciding on the menu for the wedding. Each of them had a pamphlet in their hands which displayed an array of dishes they could decide to have for the wedding.

"Baby corn, who likes baby corn? We are cancelling this," Priya said looking at the menu.

"No, we are not cancelling that. A lot of people like baby corn," her father joined in this time.

"Are you only speaking for yourself, Dad?" Priya asked smiling.

"No, I know a lot of people who eat it, just put it on the list," Arun said looking at Priya.

Priya put a tick beside it unwillingly.

"*Moong dal halwa,*" Avni's *bua* said, "everybody loves it at the wedding."

"*Moong dal halwa*, oh my God, Bua," Kitty said, "No ways."

"Oh, it tastes very good," Kitty's mother said, "You are right, Jiji," she then looked at Uma, "we should add that."

"What about you, Avni?" Uma asked looking at Avni.

"Make sure there is *paneer* and ooh… *jalebi* on the menu," Avni said, "How many main dishes are we having by the way?"

"Oh, I don't know four-five *sabzis* at least," Uma said looking at everyone, "and three-four types of *roti* and *naan*."

"Mom, that will be too much," Priya said, "you just made me add noodles and *gobi* manchurian, who will eat that much?"

"Oh, trust me they do," Avni's *bua* said smiling.

"Okay, Bua. Anyways so we have the starters here," Priya said showing them a list, there is going to be a *chaat* corner also in the wedding," Priya said looking at another list. "Mom, after a while we will have to direct people towards the main food, else they will fill themselves up with *chaat.*"

"Okay, *beta,* but we can't force people. We will tell them politely. By the way do we need a *dosa* stand too," Uma asked looking at Arun, "they are from Bangalore."

"Yes, I think we can add that as well," Aru said.

"Okay, but let's not get overboard with it. I will read what we have already ticked and then we go over the desserts," Priya said.

It took them four days to decide the menu. By the end of it Avni was so confused she couldn't figure out what exactly was there. All she knew was there was a *paneer sabzi* and *jalebi* in the list as she kept insisting on it.

Almost a month away from her wedding, she could feel the wedding chaos building up. One day, they sat down, deciding on the *sangeet* songs.

"Okay, the opening song can be yours," Priya said looking at Kitty and Tamanna, Avni's cousins.

"I want a peppy song too, I can't dance on this. It's too slow," Avni whined, looking at the list Priya handed over to everybody to go through.

"Avni, you are the bride, so just dance on this," Priya said swinging her pen at her. "Sana will teach you, won't you, Sana?" Priya said looking at one of her cousins.

Sana just shrugged, "Okay."

Just then Uma walked in, Sana showed her the list, she looked at it for a while and then looked at Priya and asked, "Do we have to do this too? Why can't you kids dance on *sangeet*?"

"Mom!" Priya exclaimed looking at her mother.

"Aunty, please it will be fun. See I will not give a lot of moves. I will keep it very simple. Your piece is just for five minutes," Sana said looking at Aunty.

"Oh, Uma I don't know if we will be able to do this," Kitty's mom said as she too went through the list.

"It's almost like these kids are deciding everything for the wedding," Uma said, she then went and caught Priya's ears, "and this girl thinks she knows everything."

"Oww! Yes I do, it's all about right management, Mom. You will thank me later when you find everything so properly managed," Priya said looking at her mother.

"What about our *dholaks*? When will we sing our songs?" Avni's *bua* asked, who was sitting on the sofa and listening to their commotion.

"Don't worry, Bua, that is also arranged. Actually we will start with your *dholak* songs first, but I can give you only twenty minutes for it," Priya said going back to her diary.

"Just twenty minutes, Priya that is not fair," Uma said sitting down on the sofa.

"It is, Mom, there are a lot of things to be done for the *sangeet*," Priya said looking at her mom.

"But twenty minutes," Uma started but said, "oh, okay do what you want, as long is Avni is happy," Uma said.

"I will be if I am given a faster song," Avni said.

"Avni! Stop whining please," Priya said looking at her.

Avni frowned as she looked at her list again.

It took days before they could decide on anything, which was also subject to change at any moment.

A few days before the wedding, Priya looked around for her mother and shouted, "Mom, did you speak to the *mehndiwala*?"

"Coming, Priya," Uma said as she walked into the room, "Yes, tell me fast. I have to go pack all the sweet boxes."

"Mom, *mehndi*. Did you tell them to come?" Priya asked getting impatient.

"Yes, you had told me day before. I did call them and confirm," her mother snapped, "Can I go now?"

Priya just nodded, "And a special person to do Avni's hands and feet."

"Yes, *baba*. I told them, now let me go, I have a lot of work. The *pandit* will also come in the evening so we can discuss which *pooja* will happen when and I can then decide the list of things needed," Uma said looking at Priya.

"Okay, Mom," Priya said going back to her phone.

The house was turning more into a mad house everyday as the wedding date was approaching. No matter how experienced you were or how managed, they was always some chaos which added to the wedding flavour.

A few days before her wedding, people started pouring in little by little and Avni was soon kicked out her room. They all played dumb charades and *antakshari* every night.

Avni had sung and yelled so much in the last couple of days, she had started to lose her voice. The wedding fever was seeping into everybody, weddings in India are like a festival in itself; one would always wait for a close family or friend's wedding to leave all their baggage and stress and soak up the zest of the wedding.

Wedding planning was a big task; everything was decided months before, and was executed accordingly. But no matter what, something always got missed out.

One such day, when they were going through their final count of guests, box of sweets and gifts to be given out, Avni's father came running into the hall.

"The transport, what happened to the transport?" Arun asked looking at Priya.

"Dad, what transport? You are freaking me out now," Priya said flipping the pages of her diary.

"Priya you told me you will take care of everything," Arun said looking right into Priya's eyes.

"I did, but you never mentioned any transport," Priya said looking at her father.

"Oh, We need some sort of transport in case people have trouble reaching the venue for the functions, especially for Ansh's family," Arun said.

"Okay, Dad, don't get tensed. I will figure a way out," Priya said getting worried by the moment.

"Rajesh Uncle," Priya shouted suddenly as she saw him walk by, "I need transport, please help me. We need some transport."

He looked at her perplexed.

"Okay just hear me out. I know you know someone. You had arranged for those buses and taxis long back for our family picnic. We need something for Avni's wedding too," Priya asked anxiously.

"Yes, *beta,* I do know someone, he is a dear friend of mine. You should have told me before. I am not sure if he is free now," Rajesh Uncle said as he took out his phone.

"Please, Uncle, do something," Priya said.

"Let me talk to him," Arun said looking at Rajesh.

"It's okay, Bhaisaab. I will talk to him," Rajesh said taking out his phone.

After a few minutes, when he kept the call, he looked at Arun and said, "Bhaisaab, don't worry. He says he will arrange something, it's last moment but he will figure a way," he then looked at Priya, "Don't worry, Priya, we will manage this."

"Phew," Priya said looking at Rajesh Uncle, "thanks."

He just patted on her shoulders, "It's okay, I will give you the details once I get them."

Priya nodded, making a note of it in her diary.

"I need a glass of water, Ramu," she shouted at the kitchen, as she sat down.

A tall, thin man came running from the kitchen with a glass of water, "Here, Didi."

"Thanks, Ramu, is it tea time? I think you should make *chai* for everyone now," Priya said looking at the time.

"Yes, Didi. I have already put it on the stove. It will be ready in ten minutes," he said as he walked back to the kitchen. They had hired a cook. Amidst all the chaos, they really needed someone to take care of the food. People kept pouring into Avni's house as the wedding grew closer.

"Hi, Ansh. Yes, I can't hear you. I will just step out," Avni said as she looked around.

"Avni, is that Ansh? Please ask him about the couple dance," Sana shouted from one end.

"Yes, I will," Avni shouted back as she walked out.

"Wow, finally some quiet," Avni said as she took a deep breath, "It's maddening inside, and this wedding work just doesn't seem to end."

"Hahaha, well it's a wedding house, Avni, what did you expect," Ansh said.

"Is it as crazy in your house too?" Avni asked.

"Well, I presume so. My parents don't talk to me for more than five minutes. They are pretty busy too," Ansh said.

"This is a lot of work," Avni said.

"Yes, I know," Ansh replied.

"The amount of money they are spending, if they could just give it us," Avni said jokingly.

"Sometimes I too wish we could just have a simple marriage and use all the money in some kind of an investment, but then what's the fun," Ansh said.

"Yes, and my parents would definitely kill me if I even mention it to them," Avni said, "Hey by the way, what do you think about a couple dance?" Avni asked.

"A couple dance?" Ansh asked, "Oh, you know it will be little weird."

"Oh, Ansh, this is so boring," Avni complained.

"I know, Avni, but to dance in front of your family and mine. It will be a bit too much," Ansh said.

"So, you won't dance with me at our *sangeet?*" Avni asked.

"However you try put it, I won't. I can't, Avni. It's just too embarrassing for me. I can come shake a leg when everyone is on the dance floor," Ansh said.

"I was half-expecting you to say this," Avni replied.

"I am sorry, Avni," Ansh said.

"It's okay. I will be dancing though on a super slow song trying to act all coy and demure," Avni said rolling her eyes.

"Really, can't wait to see you like that," Ansh laughed.

"Yeah whatever," Avni said, "anyways when are you coming?"

"I don't know. Since you don't seem to miss me so much," Ansh said.

"I do. I only don't get time. Everybody is driving everyone crazy inside," Avni said.

"I told you these three months will just pass by and you won't even realize it," Ansh said.

"I know, but seriously you have to come now, when are you coming?" Avni asked again.

"On November 22," Ansh said.

"That's like a week away," she squealed, "but I of course won't get to see you because you will be in Bangalore then, you will only to come Delhi once the functions start," Avni said.

"Yes, my mother has already decided a list of things for me to do from the very day I reach Bangalore," Ansh said.

"Wow, so I will see you at our wedding now," Avni said.

"Yes, I guess," Ansh said.

"Can you believe it, we are getting married!" Avni asked.

"I always did, but do you now? Especially after seeing the chaos in your house," Ansh said.

Avni looked towards her house door. She could hear noises of so many kinds from inside; it was like everybody was speaking at once. Her house was lit up, it stood out in the street.

She smiled, "Yes, now I do. I am actually getting married," Avni replied. "I will go now, I can hear someone call my name," Avni said as she kept the phone.

"Okay, bye take care, love you," Ansh said.

"Avni!" Priya screamed as she came out, "I have been searching for you all over," Priya said as she held her hand, "Come inside now."

"I am, what's the deal?" Avni asked.

"We have to pack your things, in case you have forgotten," Priya asked looking at her.

"Oh God! There is so much to pack, where do I start from?"

Avni asked going inside.

"Well, you will know when you do start. I don't have time for this. You should be doing all this on your own, Avni, you are a big girl now," Priya said impatiently.

"Okay, I will do it. Stop getting so impatient," Avni said.

"Your wedding is a few days away," Priya said looking at her.

"And you have to relax, else you will lose your mind. Who told you to manage everything, see now it's taking a toll on you," Avni said.

"I wanted to look at everything because it's your wedding, Avni. I did not want anything going wrong. I just want everything to be perfect," Priya said holding Avni's hands.

"Aww, Di, I love you for this, but please just relax. I just want you to enjoy my wedding," Avni said holding her hands too.

"I will, trust me," she said smiling at her, "Now come, we have to pack."

"Avni, what with these dark circles?" Kitty asked, as Avni walked into her room, "Isn't the parlour lady coming every day?"

"Yes, she is, I just slept for a few hours yesterday. They will go away, Kitty," Avni said looking at her cupboard.

"Oh I really don't know where to start from," Avni said looking back at Kitty.

"You won't be able to take everything to Norway at once, let's segregate clothes you will take when you first go," Kitty explained.

"You can leave some in Bangalore too. We will have to sort that out first," Sana added.

"Yeah, okay let's get started," Avni said looking around at her room.

She couldn't believe she was leaving it all. This was her cupboard, it had been for ages, even when she shifted to her flat, this was never empty. Her heart broke at the thought of emptying it now.

Amidst all the chaos, merriness, she quite forgot that she would be leaving her house soon, tears began to well up inside her, she took a deep breath and stopped, she couldn't let this spoil the mood around her.

She looked back at her cupboard and asked, "Okay, I will start segregating the clothes and you guys can help me fold them."

All her cousins nodded in agreement. The next day, Avni was woken up by Ria's call.

"Ria, what happened?" Avni spoke half in her sleep.

"Avni, I am so confused. Can you run the functions by me again?" Ria said, "I can't quite decide what to wear."

"It's written in the card," Avni said.

"I don't know where I kept it. Don't worry, it's safe somewhere, only now it's kept somewhere way too safely and I can't remember," Ria replied.

"Hmmm. Okay, listen up," Avni said thinking hard.

"There is Ganesh *pujan* on the 9th in the morning, followed by the *haldaat* and then there is *tel baan* on 10th and the *mehndi sangeet* in the evening. Then there is *chaak bhaat* on the 11th and engagement in the evening. Finally, there is another *haldi* on 12th morning and the wedding in the evening," Avni said in one breath, "Phew, I hope I got that right."

"Wow, that's a lot of functions, what is *haldaat* and this *tel baan* and *chaak bhaat* now," Ria said.

"Well, this is what my mom told me, so *haldaat* is the first time they put *haldi* from my feet to face, *tel baan* is when they put *haldi* with oil," shuddering at the thought, *the things you have to go through to get wed,* she thought and continued, "*Haldi* is the final time they put *haldi* on me from face to feet and *chaak*, they do some *pooja* with the mud pots, I don't quite know why," Avni finished.

"Oh my god, Avni. I can't believe you are going through all this. So this is what happens in a Rajasthani weddding," Ria said smirking.

"Yeah, pretty much," Avni said shifting her bangles.

"Okay, loads to outfits to decide now, will call you later," Ria said as she kept the phone.

"Yeah, bye Ria," Avni said as she turned around.

She could still hear a lot of noise from the house, not of the chaos anymore, but of laughter and joy of her family.

Kitty came out to the balcony, "Avni, come in. Everybody is looking for you. It's dumb charades time."

Her functions were starting from tomorrow and there were butterflies going crazy in her stomach.

It starts tomorrow, there is no looking back now, she thought looking around, *you are getting married now.*

Chapter XX

"Wake up, Avni," Priya said as she tried waking Avni up.

"Huh?" Avni mumbled from under the blanket.

"I can't hear a word you are saying, Avni, get up. We have to go for the Ganesh *pujan*," Priya said.

"Di, it's just 4:30 in the morning," Avni said taking her blanket off her face.

"Yes, and the *pooja* starts at 6. You have to get ready," Priya said shaking her, "Avni, I can't keep waiting for you all day. Get up and get ready."

"Okay, okay give me a second, who keeps a *pooja* this early," Avni said as she slid out of her bed, "by the way what am I wearing?" Avni asked rubbing her eyes.

"I have kept the sari on the table there," Priya said pointing at the table in the room.

"Di, but I don't know how to wear one," Avni said looking at her.

"Avni. Mom will be here in a while, go take a shower now," Priya said, "I am going now, lots of work to do. You, please don't sleep again."

"I won't, I am going." Avni whined as she got up and went in the bathroom.

Struggling to keep herself awake. Avni somehow managed to get ready. She walked till the *pooja* room downstairs half asleep.

"Sorry, *panditji,* we are a few minutes late," Uma said as she walked in with Avni.

"It's okay. Is she the bride?" The *panditji* asked to which Uma nodded, "okay let's start then."

Avni couldn't stop yawning, even as she sat in front of the *panditji*.

"Sorry," Avni said as she yawned at him.

He just smiled and started assembling the *pooja* items together.

The functions continued in full swing, the day just passed by without notice. The next day after her *tel baan*, Avni took a shower as she was soaking in *haldi* and *tel*.

Oh my god, Avni thought as she went in for a bath, *never again.*

Once she was done, she went out on to the balcony. They had booked a guest house by the garden itself, it had rooms all around it with a courtyard in the middle and a lovely balcony on the first floor. Tea was being served to everyone with *pakoras*.

"Thanks," Avni said as she sat down with her family.

"Uma, all the gifts are packed and ready, I hope you named them right," Arun said as took some *pakoras* in his plate.

"Yes, everything is ready and kept in that room," Uma said as she pointed out to a room in front of them.

"Hmm, when will the ladies come to put *mehendi?"* Arun asked as he sat down with his tea.

"Dad," Priya interrupted this time, "everything is ready, they will be here in half an hour, and everyone, whoever wants to put *mehendi*, please be free by then," she finished looking at everyone sitting by the balcony.

* * *

"Avni, how has your *mehendi* come out?" Ansh asked as he called her.

"I am not going to tell you that," Avni said as she looked at the *mehendi* on her hands. They were all the way up till her elbows; there was a beautiful design of a *baraat* along her wrist on one hand, and a procession with the *doli* on the other.

"How is it going there?" Ansh asked.

Avni looked around. Everybody was busy getting ready in the room, some were doing their hair. Some were pinning their *dupattas*.

"Mom, no not like this," Kitty screamed, "I want it this way."

"Who puts it this way?" Kitty's mother asked.

"I do, please, Mom just pin it here," Kitty said.

"Sana, my earrings?" Drishti asked in the other corner.

"I don't know. I just kept it on the bed," Sana replied as she put on her bangles.

"I can't find them, are you sure you put it here?" she asked looking for it frantically.

"Yes. I am sure I put it there, Dhrishti," Sana said as she joined in to look for her earrings.

On another corner Priya was going through a list with her mother and her aunt.

"Okay so we start with your songs. I have three *dholaks*. You all can sing to your heart's content, let Bua be happy. Then Sana and Drishti will come in. After that I want Avni's dance. In between the performances, we can call everybody on the stage to dance. So, I will give this list to the DJ, so he knows what to play when," Priya said as she held out a duplicate list.

"Yes, I think we can go by this. Priya, I want everybody down in twenty minutes," Uma said. "The guests will start pouring in," she said looking at her watch.

"Okay," Priya nodded.

"It's still chaos, but there's so much fun in this chaos," Avni told Ansh, smiling at all of them.

"I know, it's the same here," Ansh said, I haven't attended a wedding in my family for ages and now that I am here, I can see how crazy this all gets."

Avni looked at her *mehendi* again.

"Do you know you will have to search for your name in the *mehendi*?" Avni said smiling.

"Hahaha, really?" Ansh said.

"Yeah, she has apparently put it somewhere," Avni said trying to tilt her hands to find it.

"Ma'am, can you please close your eyes?" her make-up artist said.

"Oh, okay sure," Avni replied as she closed her eyes, and said, "Ansh, I will call you back," Avni said, "Bye."

"I can't wait to see you, Avni, bye," he said.

Even though Avni's eyes were closed she could feel her face burning up. When she finally got ready, she turned around and saw, her mother, her sister and her cousins sitting in front of her.

"My God, Avni. You look so beautiful," Sana exclaimed looking at her.

"Yes, and the *lehenga* is so lovely," Kitty said.

"Oh wow," Roshni exclaimed as she left her earrings she was trying to put on.

Uma walked up to her with moist eyes, "Never looked so beautiful."

"Thanks, Mom," Avni said and hugged her.

"Okay, Mom you will spoil her make-up," Priya said tearing up.

"Yeah okay, I won't," her mom said putting her hands on Avni's cheeks.

Avni walked out to the balcony of her wedding garden. The *sangeet* was arranged in a garden adjacent to the wedding one. It looked fabulous. Avni could not believe it looked so pretty in such less time.

There was a beautiful stage set with fuchsia and orange glitter drapes, which fell on the sides from the centre, which had a lovely chandelier hanging from the top with lovely pink and orange roses at the centre of the backdrop. A small dance floor was made just beside the stage, and next to it was the DJ console. There were sofas placed in the front, and chairs behind, which were draped in cream with fuchsia ribbons. She could see waiters getting the drinks and snacks ready at one end, they too were dressed in white shirts with fuchsia waistbands.

She could see her father looking around to see if everything was in place. Everything was and it was picture perfect.

"Avni, walk slow," Priya said from behind.

"Yes, I am trying," Avni said as she walked towards the *sangeet* garden.

Everyone got up one by one as walked Avni walked past them. She was so embarrassed as she walked forward, she looked down to make sure she didn't trip. As she neared the stage, she saw Ansh's mom. She bent down to seek her blessings.

She saw his sister, who hugged Avni, "You look gorgeous, Avni."

Avni then shifted her gaze towards Ansh. He was wearing a maroon *kurta* with cream pajamas. As he stood there looking at Avni, she felt herself going numb little by little. He just smiled at her, she blushed and looked down. Avni was gestured to sit beside Ansh. Everybody teased and giggled at them, which made it even more difficult for Avni to sit beside him.

"Wow," Ansh whispered. Avni just smiled.

They just sat there as the *sangeet* started. Even after two performances Avni hardly looked up. She very funnily was acting like a coy and demure bride who couldn't stop blushing,

The surrounding is making me do this, Avni thought to herself.

After two performances, her sister got on the stage, "Okay guys, we will all take a break, so everyone on the dance floor."

Avni looked around, her cousins gestured her to get up, and she did. As she walked up to the stage, she turned around and looked at Ansh, he was just standing there smiling at her.

She mouthed, "Come."

He gestured her to go ahead. She turned around and walked up the stage. Her father was waiting for Avni.

"Shall we?" he asked holding his hands out to Avni.

"Is this a father-daughter dance?" Avni asked taking her father's hands.

"Yes, you can call it that," he said as he danced with Avni. "You remember how you used to step on my toes and dance?" he asked.

"Yes, Dad, how can I forget our birdie dance?" she said looking at him.

"I can't believe you have grown up so much," he said as a tear trickled down his cheek.

"Dad, please don't make me cry," Avni said looking at him.

"Yeah, okay," he said as he wiped away the tear.

"By the way, you are looking nice, Dad," Avni said as they danced.

"Well, see I did wear the green *kurta* and this jacket, I actually quite like it," her father said looking at his outfit.

"I told you it will look good on you, and Mom looks so beautiful," Avni said looking at her mother dancing with her sisters.

"Yes, she does," he said, "but you look beautiful too, Avni."

"Thanks," Avni smiled.

"Uncle," Kitty cut in, "I am sorry for cutting in between but I think it's his turn now," Kitty said as she got Ansh to the stage who was reluctantly standing beside her.

"Oh no, you please dance," Ansh said.

"No, *beta,* it is your turn now, I have danced enough with her," Arun said as he handed Avni's hands to Ansh.

Something hurt Avni very badly inside as she saw her father walking away, and a tear trickled down her eyes.

"Avni, are you okay?" Ansh asked.

She turned towards him and realized her hand was in his hands now, she looked at his hands. They had held her tight. She held his hands too and put one hand on his shoulder and smiled at him.

As she danced with him she looked at him and realized that her life was changing, she was going to be his wife soon. From now on, she was going to share every waking moment of her life with him.

"So, are you sure you want to sit in the *mandap* with me?" Ansh asked looking at her.

"Are you kidding me?" Avni asked.

"Just double checking," he said smiling at her.

Avni just smiled back and shook her head. Ansh left soon after dinner was served, but Avni and her cousins danced till the wee hours of the morning.

Avni was half-dazed when she got up the next morning.

"Oh, my head hurts," Avni thought as she held her head.

"Avni, good morning! Oh my God! It's your wedding day," Kriti chirped as she hugged her.

"Wow," Avni said as Kriti crashed into her.

"It's all getting very real for me," Avni said looking around.

"Yes, and you will have to get ready soon. Priya told me the *haldi* is going to start soon."

Roshni said, "You have wear the yellow suit in your cupboard."

"Oh not again, how many times will they put *haldi* on me," Avni said as she got out of her bed, "Yes, I know. Di told me about it last night," Avni yawned and continued, "God, I don't like this *rasam*. I don't want to be smeared with *haldi* so many times."

"Oh we so love doing that, Avni," Roshni grinned.

"Ughh," Avni frowned as she got up.

The *haldi* was like a nightmare for Avni. It was all going well while everybody was applying it little by little according to the customs, but suddenly all hell broke loose. Everybody attacked Avni with their hands full of *haldi*. She tried pushing everybody away but it was in vain.

After she took a shower a third time, she let out a scream looking at herself in the mirror.

"What happened?" Bhavya came running in.

"I am all yellow. Look at me," Avni said looking at her face.

"Oh dear, you are actually a bit too yellow," Bhavya said looking at her.

"What do we do now, Bhabhi? The wedding is today, see you guys put too much *haldi* on me these few days," Avni said.

"Wait, I will call Uma Aunty," Bhavya said as she walked out.

Avni just sat there in despair till her mother came in running.

"Oh," she said looking at Avni.

"This is too yellow, Ma," Avni said.

"Don't worry, Avni. We will apply some curd on your face," Uma said gesturing Bhavya to go get some curd.

"No, Mom. We are not applying anything on my face now," Avni said.

"Avni, but this will help you," Uma said.

"Mom, what if something else happens? We can't afford it right now," Avni replied.

"Avni it's just curd. It will do no harm and will take the *haldi* colour off your face," Uma paused and looked at her daughter, "Do you want to look this way in the evening?"

"No," Avni said.

"Then just trust me," Uma said patting her.

So Avni sat around all day with curd on her face.

"This is my wedding day, can you believe it," Avni exclaimed as Sana walked up to her.

Sana just laughed at Avni,

After she stopped laughing, she said, "Oh by the way, Uma Aunty told me to tell you that you can wash your face now."

"Finally," Avni said as she got up to go, "This smell was getting to me."

Avni washed her face and looked at the mirror.

"Oh thank God, the colour is gone," Avni said looking at her face.

Avni walked into her room, relieved, as she was sitting down, her sister came in, "Avni, please eat something," Priya said as she walked in with *samosas* and *kachoris*. "You will have to start getting ready soon, so eat something before that," Priya said as she kept the plate by the table.

"Ooh, yummy," Avni said looking at the plate.

She sat down to eat. The nervousness was making her really hungry.

"Here it is," Uma chirped as Avni was eating her *samosa*.

"Your *lehenga* is so beautiful," Kitty said as she walked in with Avni's wedding *lehenga*.

Avni looked at it, it gleamed in all its beauty.

I can't believe it's time to wear you finally, Avni thought looking at the *lehenga*.

"Whenever you are done, Avni, let's get you ready for your wedding," Priya said as she smiled at Avni.

Avni took a deep breath, this was it. All her functions were done. She was now getting married and going away. Her hands started to shiver little, a mix of feelings engulfed her. As she closed her eyes, she pictured Ansh. As she saw him, she knew she wanted to do this.

"Okay," she said getting up to get ready to be a bride.

So many thoughts kept zooming past her mind, so many feeling kept bursting inside her. Avni did not quite realize where the time flew. She could feel everyone's running around, chirping, yelling as the time got nearer.

"The *baraat* will be here in fifteen minutes," Arun said as he walked in.

"We know, Arun. Don't keep coming here and telling us this every ten minutes," Uma snapped.

"I am just telling you, Uma. We have to welcome them at the gate," Arun said with his hands behind his back.

"Okay, we will be down in ten minutes," Uma said as she pinned her sari.

"Dad, don't worry. I will get everybody down soon," Priya said as she put on her *dupatta*.

"Okay, I don't want to come back in here again," Arun said as he walked out.

"How much is left?" Priya asked the make-up artist who was dressing up Avni.

"Twenty minutes, at least," she replied.

"That is okay, we won't need Avni right after the *baraat* is arrived, but we will have to go," Priya said.

"Roshni, Kriti, Ria," Priya called out.

"Yes, Di?" they all said in unison.

"We will all be going down as the *baraat* will be here any moment," Priya said, "You three please stay here with Avni."

They nodded and got back to getting dressed. After ten minutes.

"Okay, everyone please let's go. I really don't want Dad coming back," Priya said.

"Yes, okay we are all done," Sana said looking at all of them.

"Okay, then you come with me," Priya said holding Sana's hands, "We have to go get the *thaali* ready."

Avni looked around as she was almost done. Everybody had gone. Only Kriti, Roshni, and Ria were sitting. They were busy discussing their outfits. Her hands shivered, she put them together and took a deep breath.

She was getting married to Ansh, he was just someone she was supposed to say no to. She still remembered how he looked at her when she met him first. *What if she had said no after that breakfast the next day?* She couldn't believe she had panicked so much at the lunch right after their *roka,* how confused she was about him. She was so glad now that she held on to him, as all the thoughts kept squirming through her head, she smiled as she remembered the moments she spent with him.

"Okay. You are done. Just get up and look properly. If there is anything you feel is missing, I will fix it," the make-up artist said.

Avni took a deep breath and got up. The *lehenga* made her look like a million bucks. She almost didn't recognize herself in it.

Make-up can really do wonders, Avni thought, as she looked at herself closely, *I almost can't recognize myself.*

"Guys, how do I look?" Avni asked as she turned around which was quite a task in the heavy *lehenga.*

"Oh my God, Avni, is that you?" Roshni asked.

"Haha, I asked myself the same question," Avni said as she looked down at the *lehenga.*

"You are looking beautiful," Ria said she walked up to Avni, "I can't believe it's actually happening."

"Yeah," Avni replied standing amidst the eerie silence.

"Anyways," Avni said as she looked at the make-up artist, "thanks a lot, you did an amazing job."

"Okay, is there anything else you want me to do?" she asked.

"Can you take this *dupatta* off? It's so heavy," Avni said holding her head.

"Well, I am afraid I can't do that," the make-up artist said, "That will have to stay."

"Oh my God, this is going to be tough," she said looking at her.

"Don't worry, once you will go down, you will forget all about it," the make-up artist said.

Suddenly a loud noise broke the silence that had ensued for a while.

"The *baraat* is here," Kriti squealed as she ran out.

Avni could hear the band *baaja* in full swing. She too stepped out, but in the darkness she could hardly see anything. Avni sat there for the next fifteen minutes after the *baraat* arrived.

Just then her *mami* walked in.

"Let's go, Avni, it's time," she said.

"Okay," Avni nodded as she got up.

It was like walking into a dream as Avni walked up to the stage. It was just as she wanted it; the stage backdrop was that of a palace, it was done up in gold of different shades, there were red roses placed on the top of the backdrop, a majestic royal sofa sat in the middle of the stage. She looked around, everything was in shades of gold and red, the drapes, the canopies, the chairs, the waiters today were in white shirts with red waistbands, they were walking around with trays of drinks in hand.

She walked under a blanket of flowers, which was held by her brothers and friends. It was a little embarrassing and exciting for Avni at the same time as everybody looked at her walking up to the stage.

She saw Ansh standing on the stage waiting for her. Right at that moment she felt like she walked into a Bollywood movie. He held her hands as she walked up the stage.

"Your hands are shaking," Ansh said as he held them.

"Yes, I know," Avni replied as she sat beside him.

She looked down at the crowd and the lights.

This is the real deal, Avni thought.

Throughout the photos and the welcoming of guests, keeping a constant smile on her face with the camera and stage lights on her face, Avni could not take one good look at Ansh. They were so busy attending the guests, they had no time to sit or even talk to each other. Once they were done with the *varmala,* which was a ritual as they were both lifted up, and it seemed like a task to put the garland on each other; once a zillion more photos were taken, they proceeded to eat.

"Avni, eat well, you have a long night ahead, " Priya said putting her hands on Avni's shoulders. Avni nodded.

"Are you okay?" Ansh asked looking at her.

"Yes, I am. But this *dupatta* on my head is giving me a hard time," Avni said adjusting the *dupatta* a little.

"Oh, it is very heavy, isn't it?" Ansh asked.

Avni just smiled at him.

"I think I need a shawl," Avni said as she got up.

"Yes, I will get one for you," Uma said looking at Avni.

"Avni," Ansh said.

"Yeah," she replied looking at him as she shivered.

"I know it's really cold. You need a hug?" he asked smiling at her.

"Yes, please," Avni replied smiling back.

He moved forward.

"Hey," Avni said stepping back, "were you serious?" she asked looking around at both their families.

"Yes," he said looking at her.

Avni looked around and shook her head.

"You should go inside before you freeze," Ansh said gesturing her to go.

Avni nodded and walked inside. It was almost 12:15 in the night and the *pheras* were to start at 1:00 a.m.

Her mother got her a shawl as she sat inside the room.

"You rest here, I will come in sometime," her mother said, "You need something, Avni, *beta?*" her mother asked.

Avni shook her head. She was so tired already, the *lehenga* was really heavy, and she couldn't seem to carry herself in it anymore. How would she sit through the *pheras* now? She yawned as she put her *tika* straight. She had half-slept when her sister called her.

"Avni, are you sleeping?" Priya asked looking at her.

"Huh? Oh, I am so sorry. I am so tired," Avni said yawning, "What time is it?"

"It's almost 1:00," Priya said looking at her.

"Yeah, okay. Let's go. No, wait help me stand up. I can't seem to get up," Avni said looking at her sister.

Priya rolled her eyes and walked up to help Avni. It was even colder as Avni walked out.

"Oh my God," Avni said as she held her shawl really tight.

"Yes, it is exceptionally cold today, but you will feel better near the fire," Priya said as she walked her towards the *mandap*.

Avni nodded. Priya stopped her midway.

"What happened?" Avni asked.

"Avni, remember I told you that only and only if you are ready will I make you sit in the *mandap*. I know you are but I want to hear it from you. You will get married now and there is no going back once you sit there. Are you happy with him? Do you want to marry him?" Priya asked as her voice broke down.

"Di," Avni said as she held her sister's hands, "Yes, I do remember you telling me that. Thanks for always standing by me, however silly I sounded or acted. Yes, he does keep me really happy. I know that if there is anyone in the world who I want to be with it's him."

"Really?" Priya asked.

Avni pressed her hands and nodded.

"Then let's go," Priya smiled as she took Avni to the *mandap*.

It looked so serene. It was decorated with red and gold drapes in a circular fashion lifted up till the centre to make a canopy with another piece of lovely chandelier with crystals hanging at the top.

There were mattresses on the side on which everyone was sitting tucked in their blankets. Her parents were sitting in one corner. She could see her mother sniffing. Avni got goose bumps as she sat in the *mandap*. It seemed so surreal as she looked around at the pious fire, the *panditji* and Ansh who was sitting beside her.

"Shall we?" Ansh asked as she sat down beside him.

"Yes, let's do this," Avni replied smiling at him.

Epilogue: Eight Years Later

Avni sat by the porch in front of the garden. She was knitting a mitten. She had learnt knitting from one of her neighbours' mothers; she would, however, always forget the pattern.

"What was it? One, one and three," Avni said to herself as she kept looking at the needles. She frowned.

"What happened?" Ansh asked as he came up to her.

"I forgot how I was making it," Avni said looking at him.

"Pregnancy brain catching up again. It's one, one and three. I remember you telling me," he said as he walked towards the garden.

"I knew it," Avni thought, "Thanks!" Avni called out to him.

She looked at her feet, they were starting to swell up. She moved her ankles in a circular motion, the left one still hurt her a little after all these years. Avni still remembered the dreadful day right after the wedding when she fell.

"Avni, please be really careful, you can't take this ice lightly," he had reminded her as she walked on the snowy roads of Norway.

"I will be, stop worrying so much," Avni had said excitedly as she walked forward.

Only she wasn't careful at all, she was so excited to walk on a road full of snow. Her leg slipped on the ice beneath the snow, as she was busy looking at the barren trees laden with snow. The pain was so excruciating she couldn't even seem to scream when she fell.

She just sat there numb. She still remembered Ansh running to her holding her and taking her to the hospital.

All through the ride Avni kept crying. She refused to let the doctor examine her as her ankle was paining so much.

"Please do something," Avni had screamed.

"She has had a bad ligament tear," the doctor explained, "If she doesn't take proper rest, we might have to operate."

"So bed rest 8-12 weeks," the doctor said looking at her.

Only it wasn't 8-12 weeks, it was almost a year before it healed completely. The winter slowed her healing time, the muscles got stiffer and more painful making it impossible for Avni to walk or even stand for five minutes.

"I am so sorry," Avni had cried, "I can't believe we are cancelling our Himalayan trek trip."

"Avni, please your health is my priority now," Ansh had said looking at her.

"We will not be able to trek for a long, long time. I don't know if I will ever be able to walk again," Avni had sobbed looking at her foot.

"Avni, are you kidding me? Of course, you will be able to walk. This is temporary, it will go away," Ansh had said holding her hands.

"It's been months, Ansh. I am just sitting on this couch. I am so frustrated," Avni had said crying.

"Avni, please don't be. I know this is very unfortunate. We will get through this together. I love you," he had said holding her.

"How can you? I am all sloppy, and horrible looking. I am so fat, just sitting around all day. I can't go for walks with you. Can't cook dinner with you. I can't go to parties with you. I can't do anything we thought we would. I just sit here nagging and crying all day and you still love me?" Avni had asked sobbing.

"Of course, Avni. I love you and that's why I married you. How does it matter how you look right now? You still look beautiful to me," Ansh had said.

Avni had looked up with her swollen eyes asking how.

"Avni, we are in this together. No matter what. I could have been where you are," Ansh had said, "Don't think about it. It will pass," he had said hugging her.

As Avni pondered over her memories, looking back she realized the true meaning of being in love. That one year had made her grow up so quickly. She became less whiny for starters. She started to appreciate the little things in life she had always taken for granted. Looking at Ansh take care of her tirelessly all day made her realize what being married was all about.

It was not about going out and having a good time. It wasn't about going on lovely vacations and splurging money on each other. It was so much deeper than that. She realized it with every day when he held her, cooked food for them, helped her with her physiotherapy. It dawned on her that marriage was about being there for each other no matter what.

Right after her recovery, he encouraged her to get a job. She tried a lot but in vain. He then pushed her to pursue her dream. Something Avni always liked but took only as a hobby. She never thought of making it a profession... writing. She was today an author, a blog writer and a freelance editor, and not a bad one at that.

She looked up at him. He was playing ball with their four-year-old son. Just then it started to drizzle.

"Ansh, it's starting to rain. Both of you get inside," Avni said as she got up.

"Mommy," her son called out as he ran up to her.

"Yes," Avni replied ruffling his hair.

"How is my sister doing?" he asked.

"You just asked me that an hour ago," Avni replied.

"Tell me, nah, Mommy, is she sleeping?" he asked.

"No, she is kicking away to glory," Avni replied putting her hands on her belly.

"You think she wants to play with me?" he asked.

"Oh, she can't wait to play with her brother," Avni replied holding his hands and taking him in.

Ansh too came in and held his son's hand, "Let's go inside before it starts to pour."

Together the four of them walked into their happy abode.

--END--